La Frontera

SAM HAWKEN

BETIMES BOOKS

First published in the English language worldwide in 2013
by Betimes Books

www.betimesbooks.com

Copyright © Sam Hawken 2013

Sam Hawken has asserted her right under the Universal Copyright
Convention to be identified as the author of this work

ISBN 978-0-9926552-2-8

La Frontera is a work of fiction. Names, characters, places, and incidents
are either the product of the author's imagination or are used fictitious-
ly. Any resemblance to actual persons, living or dead, events, or locales
is entirely coincidental.

Cover design by JT Lindroos

For the migrants

Hoy cruzo la frontera
Bajo el cielo
Bajo el cielo
Es el viento que me manda
Bajo el cielo de acero
Soy el punto negro que anda
A las orillas de la suerte

— "La Frontera," Lhasa De Sela

PART ONE
ANA

1

A na Torres could not be sure of the time, though it had to be close to noon. The sun was an unblinking white disk overhead, blanching rocks and dirt alike and cutting through her clothing like a heated blade. She was glad she was not on foot, though the sorrel gelding she rode had to be suffering, too. Soon they would stop and share water, though they would not have the luxury of shade.

This was ranch land, but of the poorest quality. There were grasses cattle could eat, but mostly there was cactus and yucca and the occasional cluster of mesquite trees. Ana saw one of these trees off to the southwest, standing sentinel on a finger of exposed white rock that could have been the bone of a giant. She clicked her tongue and urged Rico toward it.

She wore a Stetson and wraparound sunglasses, but the glare was still intense. There was something about that black, twisted mesquite, and it was a few more yards before she realized what it was: a pink cloth caught in the branches.

"Come on, lazy," Ana said to Rico. The animal picked a careful path among loose stones and patches of dirt. A person could easily twist an ankle on the uneven ground and Rico was not a foolish animal.

Closer, she saw that there were more bits of cloth in the branches, some yellow and some white. Ana already knew what she was looking at, but she hoped it was not. The nearer they came, the more likely it was, and her heart sank with every step.

Finally they were beside the tree. Like all mesquites it was ugly, and at this time of day it cast no shadow. A breeze cut across the scrub flat, but it was a hot breath, not a relief. The cloths fluttered in the air current, but they were not cloths; they were panties.

Ana dismounted. There were tracks all around the tree and she didn't want to spoil them any more than she already had. The tree was so stunted that it wasn't much taller than Ana herself. She counted six pairs of panties in total. Some were new, others were worn. One pair had a pattern of little lambs running across it.

She opened the saddlebag and rummaged around in it until she came up with a digital camera. "Don't wander off," she told Rico and the horse remained obligingly still.

And then she took photographs: of the tree front and back and of the panties collectively and individually. She scrolled back through them to make sure the images were good before putting the camera away.

Across the back of her saddle lay a heavy pack of water, like an inflatable toy. Ana poured water into her cupped hands and offered some to Rico, who took it. Then she had some of her own, swishing it around her dry mouth before swallowing. She was not drinking enough for the terrain or the weather, but she did not plan to be out here that much longer.

The tracks were a few days old at least, their outlines softened. Ana spent some time crouched over them, picking out tread marks and sizes until she could estimate that about a dozen came through here. They lingered awhile and milled around, and the panties in the tree told why.

A glint of gold caught her eye and she went to get a closer look. A .45-caliber shell casing was half-buried in the dirt. A quick check around and she spotted four more. The spread indicated that they had been fired in quick succession.

As for the rest, they had been carrying heavy packs. That much she could still tell, and they had struck out northeast. All except for a trio that headed northwest and traveled lighter.

Ana took Rico's reins and turned him around. They went northwest.

The earth wrinkled a little here and at first she didn't see the body. It was in a depression in the ground, lightly dusted by blown sand. A man's body, Ana saw, wearing a dark blue windbreaker, jeans and sneakers. He lay on his face. When Ana came close, she saw he had heavily salted black hair.

She dismounted and stood over the corpse. Even in a landscape where nothing seemed to change, a dead body was even more immobile. The breeze didn't even clip the edges of the dead man's windbreaker.

There were three dark patches on the dead man's back. Bullet entry wounds. The greedy earth had soaked up any blood that spilled from the exits, because there was no trail of dried red. Without the marks, it might have seemed as though the man had tripped and fallen onto his face, never to rise. Death by natural causes.

Ana looked north and south, as if she might catch sight of the others still toiling across the broken ground, but there was no one and nothing. Ana took off her hat and dried her forehead on her arm. She took a palm-sized GPS from a clip on her belt and marked her position. The glare was almost so much that she couldn't read the screen.

She wouldn't touch the body. That would have to wait.

Back on Rico, she followed the trail another dozen yards or so until they crossed another spur of bare rock and vanished. Whoever the dead man had run with had vanished. She watched their ghosts disappear.

Another pass on horseback cut the other trail. She tracked the larger party until she could be sure of where they were headed: the cutoff that led to FM 170. These, too, would vanish at the blacktop.

Ana called out on the radio.

2

While she waited, she took pictures of the corpse. The little screen on the back of her camera was almost completely washed out by the sun, so she shielded it with her hand. When she felt she had documented enough, she put the camera away.

Ana looked south. Here the land rolled in gentle swells, just enough to bring the horizon closer and make judging distance that much harder. She was miles away from the border, but closer than appearances would belie. In the dark, this would all look the same. In the full glare of the sun, it was a moonscape.

She did not know how long she would have to wait and she paced out the minutes back and forth. Rico was still, watching her. Ana already had her sleeves rolled up and the first buttons of her shirt undone to reveal the white t-shirt underneath, but she was sweating. More than anything she wanted to be in a nice, air-conditioned place well away from the tree and the body. She would be happy with filling out reports, printing her pictures — all the little, boring things — in exchange for some respite.

After an hour had passed, the thin sound of an engine carried across the dry land. Ana turned toward it and caught a spark of light on metal. The truck drew closer, dipping out of sight here and there, then crawling up again with the same, careful progression of a working animal. The men inside would be bounced around, rattled in their seat belts. Ana preferred Rico.

The truck pulled up a few yards from Ana and the engine silenced. Up close she could see the light bar on top and the green Border Patrol markings on the doors. The doors kicked open and disgorged three men. Ana knew them all by name.

"Could you pick a harder place to get to?" Darren Sabado asked her. He wore sunglasses, but shaded his eyes from the sun before he put on a cap. The other officers were Julio Stender and Tyrone Trumble. Trumble wore a Stetson like Ana's.

Ana shrugged. "You made it."

"Barely. The truck almost bottomed out in some of those gullies."

"Where's the body?" Stender asked.

"Over there," Ana replied.

The four of them moved to stand over the corpse. Ana noticed that her shadow was just a little bit longer than it had been earlier. The sun still seemed to be right overhead, but it was moving.

"I haven't touched it," Ana said.

"We'll need to take pictures," Stender said.

"I took some."

"You know we need to take our own."

"Be my guest."

Trumble brought a camera from the truck, and Ana waited while he circled the body with it, documenting everything. Soon they would touch the dead man, but until all the forms were observed, it was almost an object of reverence, or maybe of fear. Holy things were untouchable, and evil things, too. Ana did not know if this man had been evil.

"How long do you think he's been out here?" Darren asked.

"Tough to say. His hands don't look too dried out. No sign of animal activity. A night or two. We'll know better when we see his face."

When Trumble was done he said, "Okay."

Ana checked the dead man's back pockets, hoping for a wallet, but they were empty. She looked to Darren. "Turn him over?"

Darren took the shoulders and Ana the legs. They eased the body over onto its back. The hidden blood was exposed, gathered and coagulated under the corpse. Two of the bullets had exited the front, the third was still inside.

The dead man's face was a blank. He was clean-shaven, his features dusted with sandy earth. He had broken his nose when he pitched forward onto the ground, and there was blood on his upper lip.

Ana fished through the pockets of the windbreaker. These, too, were empty. And then she searched the pockets of his jeans. From the beginning she had half-expected to find nothing, but she had hoped for more. The dead man's t-shirt was soaked in red. One of the bullets had emerged right over his heart. He was probably dead before he crashed to earth. Ana was glad for him, because this was no place to die slowly.

"Another one without a name," Darren said.

"Maybe his fingerprints will turn something up," said Trumble.

"Maybe," Ana replied. She was looking at the dead man's face: the bent nose, the bloody discharge. Some people said the dead looked like they were sleeping, but Ana knew this wasn't true. The dead looked *dead*. There was not even the slightest bit of animation about the corpse. She made herself look away.

"Body bag's in the truck," Darren said.

"Shell casings are back there," Ana said. "Pick them up?"

"Sure. Let's just get the body squared away."

Stender went back to the truck and opened up the back. He came back a few moments later with a rubberized canvas bag folded up into a neat square. He unfurled it on the ground beside the dead man, undid the zipper and spread out the flaps like a maw.

Again, Ana took the legs and Darren took the shoulders. They lifted the body clear of the ground and swung it onto the opened bag. For one so slight, the dead man was heavy.

They tucked in the corpse's feet and arms and pulled the body bag closed. The zipper closed over the dead man and his face vanished from view.

"I'll help get him into the truck," Stender said. He and Darren took hold of the carrying straps and hoisted the bag. They carried it to the back of the truck and struggled a minute before they managed to get it in.

Stender closed up the truck. Darren ambled back to the empty space where the body had been. He toed a pebble into the bloody patch with his boot. "We passed your truck on the way in," he told Ana. "You need anything? Extra water?"

"We'll make it back all right."

"Somebody will have to tell the Bowders what you turned up out here."

"I'll take care of it," Ana said.

"You sure?"

"I'm sure. Evidence bags? I need about ten."

"We have some in the truck," Trumble answered and went to get them.

"Ten? How many shots he get off?"

"Four."

What else you got?" Darren asked.

Ana pointed back toward lone sentinel mesquite. "Rape tree," she said.

"Goddamn it," Darren said, and he kicked the earth again.

Ana said nothing.

"You figure this guy was one of them?"

"Tough to say. He was running, got shot. More likely he wasn't."

"Still...."

"I know."

Trumble came back with a fistful of clear plastic bags. "I think there's ten there."

"It'll do."

Stender and Trumble went back to the truck. Darren lingered.

"I've got this," Ana told him.

"Okay. See you back there."

"See you."

Ana waited until the truck made the turnaround and began heading back the way it came before she took Rico by the reins. The horse followed obediently, full of patience.

First, she collected the shell casings one at a time, careful not to touch them with her bare fingers. Cases had been made and lost on evidence from shell casings. She did not forget.

At the tree, Ana used the blunt edge of her pocket knife to lift the panties from where they tangled in the branches. She put each one in its own bag and then put the evidence into Rico's saddlebag. "There," she said to herself.

She saddled up and pointed Rico northward.

3

Ana and Rico followed a ragged line back to the truck
and trailer. At cattle guards Ana threw pieces of waiting particle board across the pipes to allow the horse to cross,
then put the boards away against the fence. The boards were
eaten up by the elements and would have to be replaced soon.

Eventually she reached a flat pan of dried earth and stones
where hardy patches of grass still managed to grow. The truck
gleamed white, a horse trailer hooked up behind it. No one
else was visible for miles around.

She guided Rico into the trailer, gave him more water and
shut him in. Behind the wheel of the truck, she put her hat
on the seat beside her and started up the air conditioning. At
first nothing but blazing-hot air circulated around the cabin.
Finally a trickle of cool came through and dried the sweat on
her face.

It was a mile back to a gravel road. Ana drove ten minutes until she reached asphalt and right-handed the truck onto
the blacktop. A short hop, and she saw a low, white-painted
house set two hundred yards back from the barbed wire fencing that enclosed everything.

The sun beat down on her again when she got out to
open the gate, but by now the truck's cabin was comfortably
cool. She came up the long drive, stopped a ways short of

the house and killed the engine. She took up her hat and put it on.

There was a neat yard of yellowing grass, just a square of lawn, and a concrete path to a screened-in front porch. "Hello the house!" Ana called as she came closer. She heard the front door open somewhere in the shadow of the porch, and a figure materialized out of the air within.

"Ranger Torres?" asked Claude Bowder.

He was an older man, in his sixties, but still built solidly. A white beard scrubbed his cheeks. He wore a work shirt and jeans, like he had just come in from the day's efforts, and maybe he had.

"Mr. Bowder," Ana said. She approached the porch and faced Bowder through the screen door. "Just finished looking over your back forty."

"Oh, yeah?" Bowder asked. "Find any wetbacks?"

Ana didn't wince. "I found a dead man," she said.

"What?"

"A dead man, shot three times in the back."

"You better come in."

Bowder unlatched the screen door and held it open for Ana. She came in and took her hat off. It was good to be in the shade, though the air was still and warm.

"I got iced tea if you want any."

"That would be fine."

They went into the house. It was a simple home. Not spartan, but functional. A few pictures hung here and there, mostly of grandchildren. There was an upright piano in the corner of the living room and where the space bled into the dining room there was a long table for family gatherings.

Bowder led Ana into the kitchen. He poured out a measure of iced tea into a big glass and added lemon. Immediately the glass began to sweat and it was wet in Ana's hand.

"Bad enough those wetbacks are crossing my land, now they're killing each other," Bowder said. "Sure he was shot?"

"I'm sure," Ana replied. She tasted the tea. It was sweet.

"Damned wetbacks," Bowder said, as if that was the end of the discussion. Then he said, "Am I going to have to pay some kind of fee on account that you cleaned up his corpse?"

"No fee," Ana said, "but we're going to have to keep a lookout on the area. If we have crossers using it once, they'll use it again."

"Whereabouts was it?"

Ana told him. She drank more of the tea.

"At least they're not coming through where my herd likes to graze. That's the last thing I need. You know one of them open-border groups tried to put a water station on my property without asking? They came right through the gates and put a whole bunch of water jugs under a tree on prime grazing ground. I run 'em off. Told them I'd have the sheriff on them for trespassing, they came around again."

"Like I said, we're going to have to keep a close eye on your property for a while," Ana said. "That means more Border Patrol presence, and I'll come through once a week just to see if they missed anything."

"That's fine by me. Whatever you have to do."

"Okay, good."

"But what about this dead Mexican? That going to be a problem for me?"

Ana tried to take Bowder's measure, but he seemed guileless enough. The dead man had been a long way from anywhere, on ground that Bowder didn't use for much anyway.

She regretted not checking the surrounding area for tire marks, but it was too late in the afternoon to go back now. Rico needed rest.

"I don't know," Ana said finally. "Depends on what we find out."

"How do you mean?"

"Well, a medical examiner's going to have to look at the body for starters."

"I thought you said he was shot."

"Still have to do it. Procedure."

"Shit," Bowder said. "Goddamned wetbacks. Cause trouble even when they're dead."

Ana finished her glass and put it on the counter. "I wouldn't worry about it for now, all right? We'll take care of things."

"All right," Bowder said reluctantly. "Let me show you the door."

He escorted Ana all the way out into the sun, where she put on her hat against the glare, then closed himself up behind the screen door again. "As soon as I know more, I'll let you know," Ana told him.

"I'll be here."

"See you, Mr. Bowder."

She went back to the truck and was happy to get the air conditioner running. Ana made a careful turn to bring the trailer around and headed out the front gate. Once she glanced in the rear view mirror and saw Bowder watching her. When she looked again, he was gone.

4

The offices of United States Customs and Border Protection were housed in a flat, dun-colored building in Presidio, Texas. It was not along a main thoroughfare and was remarkable only for the large flagpole out front that flew both US and Texas flags. A man in uniform was present every morning and evening to handle the colors.

Ana had unhitched the trailer. Rico was back at a stable where Border Patrol housed their own animals. There were plenty of shade trees, ample food and water, and softer ground to traverse. All of these things must have seemed like paradise after the rocky terrain of Claude Bowder's ranch.

She parked around back of the building. There were only a few trucks and a pair of cars. The total CBP presence consisted of less than a hundred officers, minus support personnel. Presidio was not a large town.

Presidio sat on the border two hundred forty miles southeast of El Paso. It was not all desert and rocks, though it took only a few minutes to reach no man's land. There were fewer than five thousand residents, and the port of entry from Ojinaga in Mexico was small. Ana had never even heard of Presidio before she was sent here. A sign at the city limits said, "Welcome to the Real Frontier." When the weather was hot and dry and the streets deserted of people, that seemed very true.

The back entrance to the building was protected by a card lock and a watchful video camera. Inside it was chill, almost cold, and despite herself Ana shivered.

She would not have been here if it hadn't been for the governor's initiative. He had pledged Texas Rangers to ports of entry all along the Texas/Mexico border. They were called "Ranger recon teams," but sometimes there was only one Ranger to do the job of two or three. Presidio did not merit more attention than it got.

The Border Patrol had graciously offered her an office of her own, but she took one of the cubicles near the front of the building where agents took calls and filled out the endless parade of paperwork generated by the border. The undersized building had a holding and processing area for illegal crossers, and space was at a premium for everything that needed to be done. Ana wanted to be as little trouble as possible.

She put her hat on a rack and found her place. Around her telephones were ringing constantly. Residents called in tips. Someone at the port of entry had an urgent records request. Something always needed attention and needed it *now*.

Ana had not decorated her cubicle; it was as plain as the day she'd taken over the spot. There was just the old, beige computer terminal and a chair. She did not even have a coffee cup.

The dead body called for at least three reports. One would detail why she had been on the Bowder property in the first place, one would discuss the disposition of the corpse when it had been found and what transpired from that, and the last would outline the next steps in the process. First would come examination by the country medical examiner's office to confirm cause of death, followed by attempts to identify the body. The dead man's fingerprints would be taken and run through the database. If they were lucky, they would know who the man was within a day or two.

And then there was the rape tree. That deserved a mention all on its own. Ana realized she'd left the fistful of evidence bags out in the truck. She would get them later, check them in with an agent at the property room. Nothing would come of it, she knew. Rape trees were a tragedy, but they were just punctuation marks in the tale of the border.

Ana had seen her first rape tree a week after arriving in Presidio. She hadn't know what it was then, but she'd taken pictures of it anyway and collected the panties there. Some of the Border Patrol agents filled her in on the details, and she had been sick at the sight of the trees ever since. She had seen four. Today made five.

She put the rape tree out of her mind and turned her attention to her reports. The language had to be clinical, detached, regardless of the content. A dead body was remarkable only in that it had to be examined and catalogued and added to the statistics that ruled border protection. It did not matter that once there had been a living man and he had been murdered. That was beside the point. It was not as though they would ever catch the murderer.

It took an hour and a half to finish, and by the time she was done, she felt strain in her shoulders from hunching over the keyboard, pecking out words with two fingers. She leaned back to stretch and saw Darren Sabado across the room. He raised his hand to her and then came over.

"How you doing?" he asked.

"All right. Just sending things up the pipe."

"We got the body to the medical examiner with no problem. He says to give him a couple of days and then he'll have something to share."

Ana nodded. She did not expect a speedy turnaround. Presidio was not like that.

"How did it go with Bowder?"

"Fine. He's worried he might get a fine or something."

"Figures he would."

"He says those activists from Free Borders have been trespassing again. Will you call the sheriff's office, let them know?"

"Sure. What did they do this time?"

"Same as before: put out some water."

"As long as that's all they do, I don't mind."

"Bowder thinks they're trying to turn his land into a highway for crossers."

"You tell him otherwise?"

"What's the point?"

Ana got up. In her boots she was almost as tall as Darren. He was not a large man. "I need to catch some lunch, and then I have to stop off at the consulate to let them know what we found. Did you eat?"

"A while ago. Doesn't mean I couldn't drink a soda."

"Okay. Let me get my hat."

5

Lunch was a cheeseburger and a pile of fries, washed down with Coke. Darren kept her company, trading on office gossip. When Ana was done, they parted ways. Darren vanished in his truck and left Ana on the sun-washed street.

The Mexican consulate did not have its own building. It was the third floor of a four-story structure that also held a bank and a doctor's office. Ana parked out front and signed herself in at the front desk. A boy and his mother were leaving the doctor.

Upstairs it was quiet and cool. The carpet was deep red and the consulate itself looked like just another office, except for the Mexican state seal on the front door. A lone receptionist sat waiting for visitors who rarely came, surfing the internet on her computer. She took Ana's name and called it back.

Jorge Vargas appeared after just a few minutes. He was short and kept his hair pomaded. He offered Ana a hug and ghost kiss on the cheek. Ana allowed it. She liked Vargas.

"*Ana, ¿cómo estás?*" he asked.

"Just fine," Ana said. "How are you? It's been a while."

"Three months at least," Vargas said. "Why don't you ever visit?"

"Busy, busy," Ana said.

"Everybody's always busy. Even I'm busy."

"You could always visit me."

"I'm allergic to police stations. It's an old habit."

Vargas showed Ana to a back office where there was furniture made of dark wood and comfortable chairs. He offered her a spot and took one for himself. When he crossed his legs, she saw his polished loafers. He always dressed well, though no one would have noticed if he took off his jacket and rolled up his sleeves once in a while.

"Tell me everything," Vargas said.

"I was out patrolling one of the local ranchers' property this morning," Ana said. "I came across a dead Mexican."

"Oh, no."

"He didn't have any ID on him. He was shot in the back."

"This is terrible news."

"I figured you'd rather hear it from me directly instead of in a letter."

"And you have no idea who it could be?"

"When the medical examiner's done with the body, we'll run his prints."

"If you send copies, we will do the same."

"All right," Ana said.

Vargas' face was dark. For a moment he chewed at his knuckle, then stopped as if he had just realized what he was doing. "You think he could be a *narcotraficante*?" he asked at last.

"Could be. There were signs that the group he was with were carrying heavy packs. That could mean narcotics."

"You'd think we were far enough away from the major crossings for all of that," Vargas said. "But it's everywhere now. I can't tell you how sorry I am."

"You don't need to apologize to me. It's one of your people that got shot."

"It makes us all look bad," Vargas said.

Ana changed the subject: "The medical examiner says it'll be a couple of days before he can rule officially on cause of death. I figure another day or two to see if the prints hit in the system. After that we can make arrangements for the body to be turned over to the consulate."

"Yes, I thank you. But without a name, he'll only go into limbo."

You ought to be used to it by now, Ana thought, but she didn't say it. On the far side of the border there were bodies piled up by the dozen, some of them missing heads, hands or whole limbs. Namelessness was part of the landscape. "We'll figure out who he is," she said instead.

"Do you have time to make a statement about the discovery?" Vargas asked.

Ana checked her watch. "I can make some time."

"Good."

Vargas brought in the receptionist, who carried a stenographer's pad and a sharp pencil. The woman sat off to the side, just enough to stay at the corner of Ana's vision. And then they talked about the body.

It was easy to go over the details again. She had just written them down in her report. The receptionist scratched on her pad while Ana talked, and Vargas only interrupted to clarify some point or the other. When they were done, the receptionist left without being asked to go.

"I appreciate that. I'll put it in my dispatch this afternoon."

"I'm sorry," Ana said. "I never like finding bodies."

"No need to apologize. In fact, it is we who should apologize to you for bringing this kind of violence to your country."

"It can't be helped."

Vargas considered. "Maybe it can't," he said. "But it's distressing all the same. We should keep our problems on our side of the border."

Ana stayed silent. They regarded each other quietly for a while. Finally Ana said, "I should go."

"Of course. You're busy, busy."

"Always."

They walked back to the reception area. The woman was no longer surfing the web, but typing up the notes she'd taken. She barely looked up from her work.

"You should come by more often, not just when there's bad news," Vargas said.

"I'll see what I can do."

Vargas fanned a kiss on Ana's cheek and saw her to the door. "Good-bye, Ana."

"Jorge."

She left the building. It was closing in on four o'clock. Behind the wheel of her truck, she made a u-turn in the middle of the street and pointed herself south. She hadn't lied; she was always busy, busy.

6

The Presidio Port of Entry was not large. It was only two lanes, a third for close inspections and fourth for heading back into Mexico. There was a plain-looking building to one side that held offices, a fingerprinting station and a cell big enough for two. Ana parked behind the building and made her way around to the front.

Traffic into the United States via Presidio was not as heavy as it was in places like Laredo or McAllen or El Paso, but there were still a good number of cars and trucks steaming in the hot sun, waiting their turn at the gates. Both lanes were open, each one staffed with three agents. A seventh agent moved back and forth between then, leading a German Shepherd on a leash. He spotted Ana and waved. She waved back.

The agents at the nearest lane were examining a pick up truck with its bed piled high with junk. One agent interviewed the driver in Spanish while a second walked around the perimeter of the vehicle with a mirror on the end of a long metal stick. A third paced a little behind the second, knocking on sections of the truck and listening to the sound his knuckles made on the metal.

The German Shepherd was motioned over. His handler skirted the truck with the dog, pointing into the wheel beds and under the frame. The dog did what he was directed to do, but did not hit. The truck was allowed to go on. Ever so slowly, the column of vehicles inched forward.

"Howdy, Ranger," said the interviewer. He was already taking the next driver's identification for inspection. "Bored?"

"No, Sandy, I'm just making the rounds."

"Well, if you're looking for something to do, you can spell me a while in line," Sandy said.

"I'll pass."

The dog and handler approached. Ana knelt down so she could pet the animal. "Hello, Frankie. Who's a good boy?"

Frankie's handler was named Pollen. He offered his hand for Ana to shake. "No hits today," he said. "We've been working on and off all day."

"I'd say that's good news."

The same procedures were repeated on the car. The mirror was deployed, an agent tapped at the vehicle's body and then the dog was called over. Ana watched all this idly, because she had seen it a thousand times before. Teams would repeat this series of steps all day long and into the night. The port of entry never closed. Only the faces of the agents changed.

Sandy waved the car through. On to the next.

Pollen came back again. He stood so that he and the dog were always shaded by the covered gates, but Frankie panted hard in the heat. "I heard you found something interesting today."

"You heard that all the way over here?"

"People talk."

"People ought to talk a little less."

"What'd you find?"

Ana paused, then shook her head. "Nothing to worry about. Dead body."

"Exposure?"

"Gunshot."

Pollen whistled low. "A real mystery."

"Probably just a *narco* who stepped wrong once he got on our side of the border."

"Still...." An alarm went off on Pollen's watch. He silenced it and turned back to Sandy. "Time, man. See you in an hour."

"I show you *this* in an hour."

"Buy you a free cup of coffee?" Pollen asked Ana.

"Sure."

They went to the building. There was no air conditioning here, only windows opened to catch the weak breeze. Fans blew in every corner of every room in the little place. A soda machine stood beside a coffeemaker and a spill of cups and creamer packets.

Pollen and Frankie worked one hour on, one hour off. Only he knew the schedule to keep it random for the people passing through the port of entry from Mexico. Every *narco* feared dogs.

Frankie got a bowl of water, which he lapped eagerly. Pollen let the dog loose and Frankie went to his corner, where a dog bed with chewed edges lay.

"How do you want it?" Pollen asked Ana.

"Actually I'll pass."

"Suit yourself. Coffee's actually fresh today."

"It's too hot for coffee."

"You know, the hotter the day, the hotter the coffee. Makes you sweat."

"I'm sweating plenty." Ana picked a spot in front of one of the fans and let it blow over her.

Pollen fixed himself a cup and stood for a while watching the incoming lanes. Sandy and the others passed vehicles through steadily. Ana followed some of them with her eyes as they drove away, idly wondering where they were going and what they would do when they got there. She had no way to know.

"It's hypnotizing," Pollen said.

Ana nodded.

"Tell me about your dead guy."

"Not much to tell. Mexican. Back-shot. Left facedown in the dirt for the buzzards to pick up. Found him by accident when I was out patrolling Claude Bowder's place."

"Bowder, huh? Couldn't have picked a better spot to die."

"Anyway, it's all been taken care of. We'll dot the i's and cross the t's and ship the body home before the end of the week."

"Mmm," Pollen said. "Hey, Karen was asking about you the other day. She wants to know when you're going to come by and eat some brisket again."

Presidio was a small town. The agents stuck together. Barbecues and parties were common. Sometimes Ana went to these and sat to one side, close but not too close. She was not one of them, though she wore a badge, but Pollen's wife made her feel welcome, and that was a good thing.

"Soon," Ana promised.

"She's going to hold you to that."

"I know."

7

The house was right at the town limits up a gravel road and perched atop a low hill spotted with stubborn green. Ana hadn't chosen it for its isolation, but rather because it was cheap and available, though the quiet appealed to her, too. The driveway was long and winding, and her closest neighbors were half a mile away.

She let herself in and was assaulted by the stifling air inside the house. She twisted the knobs on an old air conditioner mounted in the living room window and cold air started flowing. In a little while it would be habitable in here.

Her hat went on a hook by the door and her boots came off right away. Ana undid the leather thong holding her hair back and shook it out, then she walked in her sockfeet into the bedroom to strip out of her work clothes.

Texas Rangers wore no uniform, but they were held to certain styles. Sometimes Ana felt too duded up in her western wear. She was more comfortable now in shorts and a t-shirt, her bootless feet on the wood floor. The temperature dropped steadily in the living room.

The television provided a distraction. Ana put herself on the couch and flipped through satellite channels until she found a cooking show that seemed innocuous enough. She watched it for half an hour and then kept watching well into the next program. It hardly mattered what was on, just so long as it was pleasant and undemanding.

When it was dinner time, she made her way to the kitchen and prepared for herself a pork chop she'd put out in the morning. She forced herself to have some salad with it, along with some beans. She ate in front of the television set, leaving it on the cooking channel and just letting the recipes and techniques roll over her.

The house was plain inside, with blank walls. The furniture had already been in the place, and Ana had not decorated when she arrived in Presidio, expecting only to be there six months or less. Six months had turned into a year and then eighteen months, and now she was sliding into her second year in Presidio County. She tried not to let the thought depress her. As night fell outside, the light from the TV flickered across those empty walls and made weird shadows.

Eventually she grew tired, and the parade of kitchenbound ladies began to irritate her. Ana switched off the television and sat in the dark. The only sound was the blowing of the air conditioner, because outside it was utterly still.

She took her plate to the kitchen and washed it in the sink. It looked lonely on the rack by itself, but it had been a long time since she'd had guests for dinner. She looked in the refrigerator for beer, realized she hadn't bought any, and closed the door annoyed.

In the bedroom her bed was made. It was her habit to make it every morning. She turned back the sheets and went into the bathroom for a shower and brushing teeth. By the time she was finished, she had begun to drag, and she barely made it beneath the covers before she fell asleep.

8

She awoke and didn't know what time it was. The room was still dark. She looked at the clock by the bed. It was just past one in the morning. She'd been asleep three hours.

Ana lay in the bed listening. The air conditioner was still blowing away in the next room and tendrils of cool had crept into the bedroom. She wasn't sure what had awakened her.

Headlights flashed across the front windows of the house and Ana heard the sound of a truck engine. She got out of bed.

She met Darren Sabado at the front door before he could use his key. "Hey," she said.

"Hey. Sorry I'm late. I only got a break just now."

"How long have you got?"

"About an hour."

They stripped in the bedroom and went to bed. Darren was urgent with her, and Ana realized it had been almost two weeks. Their lovemaking did not last long. When Darren was spent, he rolled to one side and held Ana in the crook of his arm while the perspiration evaporated from their bodies.

"Now we have to figure out what to do for the next forty-five minutes," Ana teased.

"Shut up! It was longer than that."

Ana put her hand on Darren's stomach. They were both lean, whittled down from long hours outdoors and constant exertion. Darren could walk eight hours in the blazing sun and not complain. Ana could do the same.

"Where's Jeannie tonight?" Ana asked.

"At home with the kids, like always."

"Does she ever wait up for you?"

"Not when I'm pulling a double. I don't blame her; I'd want my sleep, too."

Jeannie Sabado was not like her husband. She was small and soft and looked like she had come to Presidio by accident. Ana had met her a few times at the Pollens' barbecues. They had little to talk about.

"Anybody see you head out this way?"

"Nobody. I told dispatch I was going to take a nap in my truck for an hour."

"When does your shift end?"

"Why?"

"I thought maybe we could get breakfast together."

Darren shook his head in the dark. "Too risky," he said.

Of course, she knew he would say that. They had already taken lunch together. Presidio was a small town, and people would notice if they were seen together too often. It would not take long for Jeannie to make the connections she needed to.

They had kept it secret for a year and a few weeks now. So long that the mechanics of remaining under the radar had become almost second nature. Darren came to her when he had the time — usually late at night or early in the morning — and Ana was all right with this. He was not very demanding of her, and she did the same favor for him. They were not in love. No one was going to run off with anyone else.

"How did things go with Vargas?" Darren asked.

"Fine. He's not going to raise a stink about it."

"I didn't think so. He's all right. Besides, he ought to be used to it by now. I remember a couple of years back we were picking up bodies by the road every other day, it seemed like."

"They're weren't shot," Ana said.

"That does make a difference. You got any beer?"

"Nope. Next time you bring some."

"I could really use a beer."

Ana sat up in the dark. Darren traced his hand down the line of her spine. Then she got out of bed and picked up her pajama shorts from the bedroom floor.

"What's wrong?" Darren asked.

"Nothing. I just feel like moving around."

"We can move around over here."

"Think you're up to two rounds tonight, cowboy?"

"I'm willing to try."

Ana put her top on. "Not tonight."

She went to the kitchen and poured herself a glass of water from the tap. After a while Darren followed her, dressed only in his underpants. He tugged at her waist. "Come on," he said. "There's time."

"I said *not tonight.*"

"All right," Darren said, but in a way that suggested it was not. Ana finished her water. She put the glass in the sink.

"Dead guy bothering you that much?"

"Not the dead guy."

Darren paused, thinking, and then he said, "The tree."

Ana nodded, though it was dark.

"You tell Vargas about that?"

"What difference would it make?"

"I don't know. It's worth bringing up."

"He couldn't do anything about it. No sense muddying the waters."

Ana leaned against the counter. The rape tree was in her mind's eye now, and clearly, where before it had been pushed to the side, eclipsed by the question of the dead man. Darren stood silently, not offering words.

"I guess it bothers me more than I thought," Ana said at last.

"It's understandable."

"Is it?"

"Sure, because—"

"Because I'm a woman?"

Darren looked guilty in the shadows. "That's not all I was going to say. Hey, it bothers me, too. But there's nothing we can do about it. The dead one, we can see that through, but the tree... that's too complicated."

"I wish it wasn't."

"You and me both."

They didn't talk for a long time after that, until the alarm on Darren's cell phone began to chirp in the next room. He abandoned her to fetch his uniform and dress without turning the lights on. Ana watched him from the bedroom door.

"I'm sorry," she said.

"Don't be. Everybody has feelings."

"Texas Rangers are supposed to be tougher than that."

"Well," Darren said, and he came close to kiss her, "I'm glad this Texas Ranger isn't. Then she wouldn't be human."

"When do you think we can...?" Ana asked.

"I'm not scheduled for another overnight until next week."

"Think you can last that long?"

"I can if you can," Darren said.

Ana followed him to the front door and stood watching him from the window as he turned his truck around and headed down the long drive to the road. After a few minutes it was if he had never been there at all. Even his taillights were swallowed up by the night.

Sleep did not come quickly for her. Ana lay on top of the sheets, staring at the dark ceiling, but now that she had thought of it, spoken of it, the rape tree was the only thing her mind could engage. She saw herself plucking the panties from the thorny branches of the mesquite tree and carrying them back to where the body lay.

"Go to sleep," she said out loud, but her body refused to obey.

Ana tried rolling onto one side and then the other, forcing her eyes closed, concentrating on her breathing... anything that would still her thoughts. They drifted back to the tree again and again, only now they were mixed up with the memory of Darren's hands on her, of him inside of her, his weight pressing her into the mattress.

What if it had been rocky ground?

Two hours passed. Ana got up. She fled to the television and turned it back to the cooking channel, only now they were showing infomercials instead of how-to programs. She watched anyway, soaking up the blue light of the screen and putting everything else far away from her.

Eventually it was daylight outside, or the beginnings of daylight, and her eyes felt as though they had been scoured with sand. She was unrested, and when she unwound herself from the couch, her legs were achy.

She prepared breakfast of eggs and bacon with toast and ate all of it mechanically. With the sunlight came new freedom to think of different things, and she was able to turn her thoughts to what the day would bring. Eye drops took away the itching and the redness. Strong coffee dispelled her fatigue.

Ana dressed in a fresh shirt and jeans and clipped her gun to her belt. She put on her boots and stepped out into a surprisingly cool morning. There was dew on the windshield of her truck that the wipers whisked away.

9

No matter how early she came to the stables, the workers were already out of bed and doing their jobs. They lived in a long house on the property, just a half-dozen Mexicans who spoke Spanish to one other all day long and stayed out of everyone's way. Ana did not know any of their names, or anything about them.

The horses were out in the yard, idly nuzzling fresh piles of hay or just staring off into space the way horses did. Ana saw Rico by the far corner, chewing away. He could be a greedy horse when the mood struck him.

Ana's trailer was parked alongside a few others on one side of the horse barn. She took some time hooking it up, then brought the truck around to the corral.

The air was still cool. It was always cold in the desert at night. Ana saw one of the Mexicans cutting the wires on a bale of hay and raking it out into a ragged heap for the horses. She raised her hand when he looked up. He raised a hand in return.

She walked along the fence until she was parallel to the man. "*¿Cómo estás esta mañana?*" she asked.

"*Estoy bien,*" the Mexican replied. Then he looked down at what he was doing as if it was physically painful for him to maintain eye contact for more than a second or two. This was the way Ana always saw them: scuttling around the property, always keeping busy, but with nary a second for anyone outside their circle.

"Going to be a hot one," Ana said in Spanish.

"*Sí*."

For a moment Ana had a flash of herself asking to see the Mexican's papers. It was only an instant, but she saw it clearly. The desire was involuntary, reflexive, and of course the Mexican would do what he was told. And of course his papers would be in order. The Border Patrol and the Sheriff's Department kept their animals here. There would be no illegals doing work for them.

"Have a good day, then," Ana told the man.

"*Gracias, señora. Buenos días.*"

Ana went into the barn. The air was thick with the smell of hay and manure. She spotted another Mexican bringing a shovel to muck out the first of ten stalls. This time she did not try to engage the man in conversation; it would only go the same.

She found her saddle and tack by Rico's stall and hauled it onto her shoulder. When she came out of the barn again, she saw a new truck pulling up alongside hers, marked with the Sheriff's Department logo. The man behind the wheel was Clayton Sellner.

Sheriff Sellner walked up to the split-rail fence that closed in the horse corral and put his boot up. "Morning, Ana," he called.

"Sheriff. What brings you out here? Going to ride?"

"Not today. Got a minute?"

"Sure."

Ana came to the man and mounted her saddle on the fence's top rail. Sheriff Sellner took off his hat to show his white hair, studied the brim for a moment or two and then put it back on. He was facing the sun as it rose, and the morning light flushed his face rose and orange.

"Heard you found a dead Mexican out on Claude Bowder's property yesterday," Sheriff Sellner said finally.

"That's right."

"I heard it from Courtney Passey when CBP brought the body in for autopsy."

"Oh."

"Yeah, that's right. Nobody thought to call the sheriff about a killing in the county."

Ana shook her head. "I'm sorry, Sheriff. It slipped my mind. Maybe I thought CBP would let you know. Everybody else heard the news."

"Not me. And I haven't gotten copies of the reports like I'm supposed to."

"Those went into the system yesterday. You should have been emailed copies."

"Not yet this morning."

"I really am sorry about that."

A gray mare passed close to them, as if eavesdropping. Sheriff Sellner gently waved his hat at it, and the animal turned away. Ana glanced over to Rico. He hadn't even acknowledged she was in the corral.

"The Rangers are getting awfully cozy with the Border Patrol," Sellner said.

"That's part of the job. The governor wants us working with the CBP."

"But not at the expense of the county!"

"You're right about that. I'm sorry."

"Stop saying you're sorry. More times you say 'I'm sorry,' the less it feels like the genuine article."

"Okay, then."

Sheriff Sellner was older, but he was still sharp. His eyes were clear. He fixed Ana with his gaze. "I want to know *first* the next time you come across something like a dead body. If it's bundles of weed or that kind of thing, I'm happy to play second fiddle to Border Patrol, but some things have to come through the Sheriff's office."

"I'll do that."

Sheriff Sellner looked at her a while longer, until finally his expression softened and his eyes wandered away to survey the corral. "I do appreciate you doing those patrols out on ranch land," he said. "Even when you don't turn up something. It makes the people around here feel safer, knowing they have a Texas Ranger looking into things."

"I do what I can."

"Surely. It's just the personal touch. CBP can run their trucks and horses all up and down the river, but that's just business as usual. Background noise. People get used to it."

Ana nodded and said nothing. She wanted to get Rico saddled up and in the trailer. The early morning was the best time to hit the ridges and runs of the back country, before temperatures rose to a boil. She felt the minutes slipping away, but Sheriff Sellner was in no hurry.

"How did the Mexican die?"

"Back-shot."

"That's no good. Vargas over at the consulate going to raise a stink?"

"I don't think so."

Sellner put his boot down. "Well, all right," he said. "I guess I've said my peace."

"Anytime, Sheriff."

"Whose place you going to hit today?"

"The Hudnalls."

"Rough out there."

"I'll make do."

"I'm sure you will. Just remember: come to me first thing."

"All right."

Sheriff Sellner tipped his hat to Ana and ambled back to his truck. He waved from behind the wheel and Ana waved back. Then he was gone. She hoisted her saddle once again.

10

There were twenty ranches of varying size in the land immediately surrounding Presidio. Ana concentrated her attention on those south of Farm-to-Market 170, figuring that any crossers who managed to reach the roadway would meet a truck and head off to parts unknown. None would pass that strip of asphalt and venture off into deeper, more treacherous territory. For one thing, there was nothing out there.

Sheriff Sellner called the Hudnalls' land rough country, but the truth was that all this country was hard. Some folks raised a hardy breed of cattle that could subsist on lousy grass and little water, but most put out great flocks of sheep or goats. Sheep and goats could find a way to survive in the most hardscrabble of conditions, eating things at which cattle would turn up their noses.

Of the twenty ranches, Ana had free access to ten, all in her favored area of operation. These ranchers also let in the Border Patrol, but it was Ana who laid the groundwork, going from household to household securing permission to cross without notice. It was for their own benefit, but sometimes it took some persuading.

Ana took the hardtop as far as it would go and then turned off onto a two-rut roadway that cut across a rugged stretch of ground. There were high fences on both sides, the borders of two properties. The barbed wire shuttled Ana and her trailer down a narrow chute that ended in a chained and padlocked gate.

She had the key on a chain and let herself through, careful to secure the gate behind her. That was the first rule of crossing ranch land: anything you open, be sure to close again. Whole herds had gone wandering because someone forgot such a simple thing.

Now she was on the Hudnalls' land. Mesquite trees were thick here, but they rapidly petered out for more of the same rocky expanse that she found on the Bowders' property. She reached a spot where the ground was cleared for a turnaround and parked.

It was silent out here. The open space swallowed up sound and reflected nothing. Even a gunshot would make the noise of a snapping twig and just disappear. Shout at the heavens, and the sky would only glare empty blue.

She let Rico out of the trailer and walked him around a little bit to stretch his legs. When she saddled up, she marked the spot on her GPS and put it in her hip pocket. She set out over open ground.

Today she would venture closer to the border than she had the day before. At the southernmost point of her course, she would be near enough to see the banks of the river before looping around and coming back to where she started. She would cover maybe a quarter of the Hudnalls' lands, maybe less, but Sheriff Sellner was right when he said it made the ranchers feel better.

At least it was early enough still that it made spotting sign a little easier. With the shadows long, she could spot an impression without having to lean over heavily in the saddle, squinting at the ground. By the time it was midday, the whole of the range would be washed out by the sun, and she would be on the lookout for big things like abandoned bundles or rest stops. Or bodies.

Ana had read somewhere once that human beings had a tendency to walk in circles unless they had something concrete to follow: a line of fence, a major landmark or the stars. Compared to some spots along the border, freedom wasn't all that far away, but crossers still sometimes got lost once they made it across the river.

This wasn't so much when they had a *coyote* leading them. *Coyotes* knew where they were going because they had been that way a dozen times before, or a hundred. The most sophisticated among them used a GPS just like Ana's, so it was impossible to get lost. But if a *coyote* decided to leave his crossers behind, everything changed.

Over the years Ana had occasion to meet a *coyote* or two, usually when they were locked up at the Border Patrol's station. They were hard men to pin down and they never confessed that they were *coyotes*. There was just something about them that gave them away. Perhaps it was the stink that came from disregarding human lives.

The worst thing a border crosser had to fear was not the elements or Border Patrol or even the Texas Rangers. The *coyotes* were the biggest threat. At the first sign of trouble, they would leave their charges in the desert to find their way on their own, or they would rob them or, worse, there would be another rape tree to mark their passage.

Without a *coyote*, the crossers were helpless. With a *coyote*, they were marks.

Once Ana had come across a quartet of crossers without a *coyote*, resting in the shade of a mesquite tree in the middle of nowhere. She'd cut their trail three times on her way to them. Like the article Ana read, they had been wandering in circles, always coming back to the same stand of trees. They had been at it two days without water or food, and the temperatures during the day were over a hundred degrees. They treated Ana like an angel, even when they had to march for two hours over rocky ground to her truck just to meet with Border Patrol and be arrested.

Chances were good they tried to cross again.

11

Ana rode a few miles until she saw a dense thicket of mesquite trees appear ahead of her. She'd passed a few cactus here and there and hardy bushes that grew low to the ground, but this was the only real life in sight.

The distance was deceiving and she was forced to ride a while longer before the trees finally drew nearer. When she was close, she guided Rico through the trees to a depression in the earth surrounded with real mud.

She didn't know what source fed the tank, but it was partially shaded by the leeching trees, which kept the water from evaporating away. The surface was impenetrable with suspended earth, so it was impossible to know how deep the water lay.

Ana dismounted and led Rico to the water. She let the horse alone to drink. He would not wander.

There were cattle tracks here, some new and some old. The Hudnalls let their animals roam this whole expanse of open ground, grazing where they may, and this was a regular stop. What animals came and went weren't her concern.

She found sneaker prints on the far side of the tank, sunk deep into the damp earth. Up the bank and under the branches of the mesquite trees, she found a cache of snack food wrappers and an empty, plastic gallon jug.

The crossers had come across this water by luck or by planning and taken a rest in the shade. The water wasn't fit for a human being to drink, but when a body cries out for moisture, any source will do. Among the footprints Ana found markings where crossers had gone down on their knees to fetch water to their mouths.

Ana checked her GPS to see how far from the border she was. It was a long hike from the river to this point. They would have come across at night and maybe taken shelter here when daybreak came. Maybe they lasted out the hottest part of the day, drinking filthy water meant for animals and eating energy bars and chips. She tried to imagine them and found the image came easily.

There were six, she figured. When she'd had enough of reading their sign by the waterside, she mounted up and made a slow circle around the ring of guardian trees and the tank. She found where their prints came in, and in a few minutes she singled out their passage north.

She rode slowly alongside their trail, glancing down now and again to be sure she was still on the right track. They seemed to be going straight north, directly toward the distant promise of FM 170. They did not wander left or right. They had a *coyote* with them.

Eventually the prints began to fade. She was on rockier ground now, turned to gravel, and there was not so much loose dirt. Once she lost the trail and had to cast about for it again. When she lost it a second time, she was not able to cut the trail. She checked her GPS: she'd tracked them two and a half miles.

She turned back south without disappointment. These six had been through a while back, and she would not find them waiting by the roadside for their ride. They were long gone. Time and again, this was what she found, if she found anything at all: the washed out remains of a trail that had long since gone cold. Only once in a while did she come across something like the body of the dead Mexican.

Ana spent the rest of the morning picking her way slowly to within a mile of the border. She passed out of the dirt and gravel and into a richer band of land with rugged greenery. The river lay flat somewhere beyond the trees, more of a presence than anything else. If Ana did not have her GPS, she wouldn't have known it was there.

From time to time she considered making her patrols at night, when the crossers were more likely to be active, but she disposed of the notion whenever it occurred to her. She was alone out here, and even with a gun she was exposed. The four Mexicans she'd found that time were too worn out to be a threat, but at night with a *coyote* they could have been dangerous.

Finally, she completed the far end of her loop and led Rico back along the trees toward the north. The sun was high overhead now and she was feeling the heat. She helped herself to some water, swished it around her mouth before swallowed, and kept on. *And miles to go before I sleep*, she thought.

Once she thought she spotted something unusual in the distance, off among the rocks, but it turned out to be a collection of odd-shaped chunks of earth and shortening shadows. A deep sense of boredom descended upon her, the product of too much of the same thing seen over and over again. Eventually she would grow so tired of the scenery that an odd collection of cactuses would cause her to take notice.

She saw dust raised to the northeast. Someone was driving out there, probably one of the Hudnalls. She knew they had a herd out here somewhere but, except for the occasional sign, she had seen no animals. They might not even pass by the tank for days, seeking water and shade elsewhere.

Eventually the haze of dust settled, and even that novelty was gone. Ana rode with her eyes half-lidded, just letting Rico pick his way along with minimal guidance from her. It was a full-bore noontime by now, and she would find nothing of interest unless she literally stumbled across it.

She kept on.

When she'd had enough of ambling across the broken ground with only the vaguest of directions in mind, she found a stand of mesquite and dismounted. There was a little shade and the faintest breath of a southerly breeze, and it was almost pleasant to sit on the stones and unpack her lunch.

She had a sandwich and an apple, and she took her time eating them. All the time she watched the horizon, but nothing appeared. Ana did not know what else she expected.

Water from her CamelBak was tepid, but it was water. Ana tried to imagine taking big handfuls of that stagnant, earthy tank water and shook her head at the thought of it. Desperate and thirsty was no way to be out here.

Ana could not last in this country even if she tried to. The human body needed more liquid than she could carry on horseback without weighing Rico down, and she needed more than a scant meal in her stomach to get by. And Rico needed food and water, too. The tank could provide the latter, but the scrubby grasses available made for poor grazing. Ana wasn't sure how the cattle managed to get by, though they always seemed skinny to her.

In and out, that was all Ana could do. She rode until she was in the worst of it, then retreated back to her truck and air conditioning and all the rest of civilization's pleasures. She certainly would not want to be out here trying to cut fences and force-march to the highway. But she was not a crosser, and crossers were a different kind.

When she was done eating, she stretched out on the uncomfortable ground and put her hat over her face. It was good to shield her eyes from the glare that cut right through her sunglasses and assaulted her. She let herself drift a little and she even slept for a while, though she didn't know how long.

Rico waited patiently in the bastard sun for her to be finished and when she had done she mounted up and they continued on their way. She was sweating hard, and the sunlight bore down on her relentlessly. If she stopped sweating, then it would be time to worry: then her body was overheating and she was too far from anywhere to make it safely home.

She passed over the worst of the Hudnalls' land, carefully navigating a split in the earth that formed a natural funnel for heavy rainwaters when they came. Finally she was back among the trees and thought she might have heard the lowing of cows somewhere off to the west.

The GPS led her back to the truck, which stood baking in the heat. Ana loaded Rico and got behind the wheel, headed back out the way she'd come.

There would be no mountain of paper to climb today. Back at the CBP station, she would fill out a report explaining where she had been and why and submit it up the chain of command. She wasn't even sure who was reading them, but no reprimand had come down the line, nor any suggestions as to what she might do instead.

The governor intended for his "Ranger recon teams" to operate like the legendary Rangers of old: making up their own assignments, carrying out the will of the government with a badge and a gun. The only addition was the bookkeeping. Sometimes Ana wished for more guidance, some special assignment that would mean a break from endlessly patrolling back country or serving as a second line of defense when the CBP could not do for themselves.

She thought maybe she would never get out of Presidio.

The town itself was not so bad. She knew the people by now and they knew her. Some gave her wide berth because of the Ranger mystique, but others were just curious. She answered a lot of questions about her work and she was sure that none of her answers were as exciting as the questioners had hoped for. Ana simply did not see herself setting down roots here, and hadn't yet in even a small way.

There was Darren Sabado, but she could say good-bye to him easily if her assignment to the border ended tomorrow. All she had were the contents of her dresser drawers and her closet to pack, and then she could be gone. She didn't wish herself away from Presidio. She didn't think of what she might be doing instead. She just kept on because it was what was expected of her, and Presidio was the place she was expected to do it.

Voices murmured on the radio as she approached the Hudnalls' gate. She had the volume turned down. Mostly, it was idle talk among the CBP agents that watched over this section of the border. Ana rarely listened in; she was detached from it.

She let herself through the gate and locked it securely behind her. She wondered if the crossers whose trail she'd spotted had come this way. The fences here were high and made of barbed wire. Climbing them could be a painful proposition. Maybe they followed the two-rut roadway all the way to FM 170 and a truck picked them up like a car service. In her mind's eye she could see it.

The truck and trailer kicked up dust on the bumpy way out. Ana glanced in the rear view mirror and saw Rico's long face there, still as a Zen mask. If he had complaints, he kept them to himself.

On the highway she opened up the engine and headed for home. *Home.* Home that was Presidio, Texas. Was she thinking of it that way finally? She did not know.

12

Ana heard her name spoken three times on the radio before she realized someone was trying to reach her. She turned up the audio and picked up the mike. "Someone calling for me out there? This is Ranger Torres."

Tyrone Trumble's voice came across the band, scratchy and distorted. "Ranger Torres, this is Trumble. What's your twenty?"

"I'm on FM 170 headed into town. Maybe ten miles from the Hudnall place."

"Think you can make it to the Sheedy property in a hurry?"

"Sure, what's up?"

"We got some bodies set off the sensors coming across the river. We're headed that way now. Figured you might want to be in on it."

Ana was tired of the heat and wanted nothing but to drive and be cooled by the air conditioning, but she thumbed the microphone and said, "I can do that. On my way."

"Ten-four."

She slowed and made a careful u-turn on the asphalt, then throttled the truck back up to speed heading the other way. The entrance to the Sheedys' ranch was about six miles past the two-rut into the Hudnalls'. Ana had patrolled their back property the week before and turned up nothing. Now there was something.

It didn't take long for her to get there. She spotted a CBP truck with a broad green stripe off the side of the road, waiting at the gate. Ana eased onto the shoulder and pulled up short. She left the engine running and got out.

Trumble was there. He tipped his hat to her. "Ranger. That was quick."

"I like to catch bad guys."

"The sensors are deep in the back forty. Thought maybe once we got in close enough, you could take that horse of yours in, and we'll pincer them off. Got an eye in the sky coming, but they're waiting until we have a better idea what we're looking for."

"Lead the way."

Ana followed the Border Patrol truck through the gate and waited while they closed it up behind them. She tailed the truck along a raised gravel road that looked as though it saw more use than the Hudnalls' bare track, and it probably did. They were both kicking up enough dust to be seen from a long way off. Ana hoped they weren't tracking experts.

They moved south six miles and then stopped. Trumble got out of his truck and indicated that they were going off-road. Ana shut her truck down and went around to let Rico out once more.

The horse was reluctant to come back into the heat after a nice, breezy ride, but he settled down quickly. Ana mounted up and came abreast of Trumble in the truck. For the first time she saw Stender, sitting behind the wheel.

"We'll take the long way west and circle around. You come at 'em straight on, try to cut their trail. As soon as you do that, we can guide in the bird."

"Got it."

The CBP truck trundled off the gravel track and onto the uneven ground between clusters of trees. It headed off west. Ana waited until she could not hear the engine anymore and then clicked her tongue to get Rico moving.

It was not an easy task. She had only a general idea of direction and knew nothing about how many she would find when she got to them. Once she picked up their trail, she would know more, but first she had to find it – a dim line in a vast expanse of dry earth.

She kept her radio on, and it crackled from time to time as Trumble counted off the miles. Rico kept up a steady pace, walking in the stifling heat. Ana took off her hat and wiped her brow with her forearm.

The trail turned out to be easier to spot than she expected. The group was maybe six strong and not moving in such a way that might hide their sign. Ana came upon it suddenly, unexpectedly, when she had started to let her attention wander. She radioed Trumble. "Picked them up," she said, and then she read off the coordinates from her GPS.

"Got you," Trumble replied. "We're comin' around."

Ana dismounted to get a closer look at the tracks. The men were heavily laden and in this heat they must be suffering terribly. They hadn't passed this spot that long ago. Ana got herself back in the saddle and followed.

She spotted them after thirty minutes and called Trumble again with new coordinates. "You have that chopper in the air yet?"

"It's on its way. And we're close."

"They haven't seen me yet. I'm going to keep my distance until the chopper makes a pass."

"Roger that."

The men kept walking without looking back, or they would have seen her easily. Ana wondered why they were making the crossing in broad daylight, with the temperatures hovering around a hundred degrees. She had plenty of water and no pack to carry and she wished she could find cover and wait out the sun. They were force-marching all the way to their destination. What desperation were they feeling?

She heard the helicopter before she saw it, a whipping noise carried on the weak breeze. The men heard it, too, and she watched them pick up the pace. They were almost out of the worst of the terrain and into the cover of many trees. Ana gave Rico a nudge and started to close the distance between her and them, not worrying now if they spotted her; they had nowhere to go but straight forward, into the arms of Trumble and Stender.

The helicopter swooped over Ana and made a graceful bank toward the men on the ground. The downdraft buffeted her and kicked up a little dust storm. She saw the men looking back, running at top speed. Surely they knew she was there now; she had cut the space between them by half and was closing faster than they could go by foot.

They made the tree-line and began to break up, each one heading his own way. Ana spotted the white and green of the CBP truck, coming down a short rise. The helicopter hovered over the scene, low, blasting the fleeing men with wind. Ana could hear the pilot talking to Trumble over the radio.

Ana made it to the trees, picked one runner to follow. If there had been more ground cover, they might have tried to hide and wait the Border Patrol out, but here there was nothing. She chased the runner down, shouting to be heard over the din of the rotor blades. "Texas Ranger! Down on the ground!"

The man carried a duct-taped cube two feet on a side with duct-tape straps for his arms. He zigged and zagged trying to lose her, but Rico kept the pace easily.

"Lie down on the ground!" Ana commanded in Spanish.

Finally, the man flopped forward onto his knees and then flat on his stomach. He held his hands out where Ana could see them. The pack jutted up off his back like a silvery snail-shell. Ana slid out of the saddle. She wrestled the pack off him, then put him in handcuffs. The roar of the helicopter was deafening; she could barely hear Trumble and Stender shouting commands at the men they caught.

Ana left the cuffed man where he lay and saddled up. She saw that Trumble and Stender had three of the men, which meant two more were on the loose. Above her, the helicopter slid to one side, pointing its nose toward the fleeing men. Ana followed.

She caught up with them without trouble and herded them like sheep. They gave up without trying to split apart and make the chase more difficult. Ana pushed them back toward the rest. Trumble and Stender had cuffed their men with plastic zip-ties and rounded up her catch, too.

The helicopter lingered a few moments longer and then rose back into the sky, peeling away. Ana could hear herself think again, and the voices of the CBP agents as they spoke to the men under arrest.

"What are you carrying?" Trumble asked them. *"¿Qué llevas?"*

"Marijuana," said one of the men.

"At least he's honest," Stender remarked.

The men were drawn and perspiring heavily where dust had not caked to their skin from the rotor wash. They were all young, and most of them were not dressed for the heat or the sheer, blistering glare of the sun. None of them wore even a pair of sunglasses or a hat.

"Call in another truck, will you?" Trumble asked Stender. "I'll get 'em hydrated. Ranger?"

"I'll help," Ana said.

They went to the back of the Border Patrol truck where there was a case of plastic water bottles along with a massive first aid kit that carried everything from Band-Aids to bags of saline solution.

The men had their hands cuffed in front of them. When they raised the bottles to drink, they looked like they were praying.

Ana, Trumble and Stender gathered up the bundles and stacked them in front of the CBP truck. "Thanks for the assist, Ranger Torres," Trumble asked.

"Not a problem. How much you figure?"

"Just eyeballing it? Hundred and fifty pounds, maybe. Crazy to be carrying that kind of weight in this heat."

Stender cleared out the men's pockets and found only a little Mexican money, and the odd piece of pocket litter. None of them carried a GPS or a map. "Somebody in this group is experienced," he said. "They knew where they were going."

"*¿Quién es el jefe?*" Ana asked the men.

They looked at each other and then at her. "No boss," said one.

"No boss," Trumble repeated. "Right."

Ana kept talking to the men in Spanish: "You'll be taken to the station. Your fingerprints will be taken. We'll know who you are."

"Let them," said another man. "I've never been to America before."

Ana looked at the man who'd spoken. He was no different from the others in the way he was dressed, and he carried a bundle the same as the rest of the group, but he looked her in the eye when he spoke. "*Usted es el jefe,*" she said to him.

"Maybe," the man said in Spanish, and then in English: "Prove it."

13

The men were loaded into two trucks and brought back to the Presidio station. Ana caught up with them after returning Rico to the stable. She watered the horse and brushed him down and then let him get comfortable in his stall before leaving. It was almost three hours before she saw the men again.

All of them had been fingerprinted. Two of them were in the system for illegal entry into the United States. The others were a blank.

"What about the smart aleck?" Ana asked Trumble.

"He said it: he's clean. If he's ever been in the US before, he didn't get caught."

She dropped by the holding cell where the men sat waiting. The man with the mouth saw her coming and smiled a little when she came close. "How are you doing, *chica?*" he asked.

"I'm doing fine, *pendejo*," Ana answered.

"You can call me a dumbass, but I'm smart enough to know you won't keep me here."

"You'll see a judge tomorrow. Carrying drugs into the US is a crime."

"They'll give me a slap on the wrist, send me back to Mexico."

"Maybe."

"You'll see."

Ana looked the man in the eyes. She did not turn away. Finally he blinked. "Yeah, I guess we'll see," Ana said.

She left him and wandered to the back of the station where the secure counting room was located. She knocked on the door and Stender let her in.

The bundles had been cut open, and the separate, smaller packets had been removed. Each one was the size of a brick and wrapped tightly in plastic. Trumble was building a wall of marijuana, packet by packet, on a wide table. When he was done, he would load the packets onto a heavy-duty digital scale and get the final weight.

"I've changed my mind," Trumble told Ana when she entered. "I'll call it at two hundred pounds."

"Good haul."

"Not bad. I've had better."

"Not lately."

"No, not lately."

Ana watched Trumble finish unpacking the last of the bundles. He counted the packets and made note of how many there were. Stender recounted them and confirmed the number. Then they started the weighing process. At the end the entire haul ended up as 210 pounds.

"Almost," Trumble said.

With weighing done, the packets were once again wrapped, this time in blocks of fifty pounds each, in clear plastic. The weight and number of packets was noted in marker on the side. The whole process of accounting for evidence took over an hour.

"Call McClees and tell him we're ready to put it all away," Trumble told Stender.

"I'll do it," Ana said. "I have to make my reports anyway."

"Thanks again. For today."

"Anytime."

Ana found McClees in the evidence room. He rubbed his hands together. "Big load of weed. Gotta love it."

She went to her cubicle and sat down. It was quiet in the station and the reports simple to fill out. She was vaguely aware of Trumble and Stender and McClees transporting their bounty to the evidence room, crowing about it and trading stories. In a port of entry like McAllen, seizures of weed up to a 1,000 pounds were common enough for CBP agents to form "1K Clubs" and celebrate with beer and barbecue. In Presidio, 200 pounds was cause for a weeklong jamboree.

Ana kept a lookout for Darren, but he was not around. She thought about asking after him, then thought better of it. Instead, she finished her reports and pushed back from her terminal with her back protesting. She checked her watch. Dinner time.

She said good-bye to the agent manning the front desk and left the station. She felt like walking a little bit, especially now that the sun was well past its peak and the day was not so oppressive. Kids were out playing and riding bikes.

In the end she settled on a little restaurant that served comfort food. She had a hamburger and a beer and thought through her day. Ana found it was a good thing to make an accounting for herself of what she had done, even when the day seemed totally lackluster. Her job was full of long stretches of inaction and boredom and if she allowed it, she could be overwhelmed by a sense of ennui.

Dessert was offered, but she turned it down. She paid her bill and left.

Her refrigerator was almost empty, so she stopped for two bags of groceries at the mom-and-pop store off Main Street.

By the time she got back to her truck, the sun had dipped low enough that the scattered clouds were blushing pink.

She drove home without the radio on and came into her house to quiet. At times like these she wished she had a dog to greet her, but getting a dog meant treating this place like a permanent address, and she wasn't quite ready to do that yet. Maybe she *had* begun to consider Presidio home, but it was not *home*.

A long shower got the dirt off and cooled her down. She changed into her lounging-around wear, and then she remembered to check her voice mails.

There was an automated message from the Texas Ranger Association Foundation about a fundraiser in faraway Grapevine, Texas. They never held anything closer than El Paso, and even that was a haul for a formal dinner and shaking hands with donors all night long. She had nothing from her higher ups, though every day she hoped for some news, especially if it meant picking up and moving on. And then there was a message from her mother.

Ana, it's your mother. It's been a month since I called last and I was wondering if you could make the time to call me back. There's nothing serious going on. Me and Dad are fine. We just want to hear from you, that's all. Give us a call when you can. Love you! Bye.

She hadn't realized it had been so long. Days in Presidio were starting to blend into one another. Ana resolved to call her mother back... tomorrow. Tonight, she was too tired to make small talk. She just wanted the TV and some alone time.

Ana fell asleep in the middle of one program and woke up in the middle of another. She hadn't realized she was drifting off at all. Finally she shut off the television and went to bed in the dark.

Tomorrow. She would be better tomorrow.

14

Ana awoke thirsty, but she didn't rise from her bed. She lay still in the quiet, listening to the sound of the air conditioner in the next room.

Finally Ana got out of bed and had a glass of water from the sink in the bathroom. It was pre-dawn and she considered trying to sleep again, though she knew it would be useless. She went to the living room where it was cooler and got down on a rug for push-ups. She did a hundred and switched to sit-ups until her midsection ached.

Today she had planned to patrol another rancher's land, but the thought didn't appeal to her any longer. As she dressed, she considered her options for the day. Staying home was out of the question, and besides she could think of nothing in the house that would occupy her for all that time. When she was dressed, she switched off the air conditioning and left the house.

The roads were quiet at this hour. Most of the town wouldn't wake up until business hours, and the ranchers wouldn't come in until they were done with their animals. The ranchers were probably the only ones up, out on their property before the sun shone in earnest and it became too hot to think.

Ana let her hands take the lead, and she drove through the heart of Presidio and out to the port of entry. The lights were still shining there and the lanes were practically empty. She parked by the building.

It was too early for Pollen and Frankie to be on the lanes, but she saw Henry Million and his dog, Paco, at work. She went into the building and found herself a cup of coffee. As she drank it, she watched the CBP agents working. The process did not stop because it was early or late or even in the middle of the night; everyone was subject to the same scrutiny. Ana could not imagine the boredom.

Once she was done, she went into the small office area and took down two large binders from a plastic shelf. She had a notebook with her and flipped it open to a blank page where she wrote the date. Then she sat down and began to examine the contents of the binders.

One binder contained work logs. Mostly it was a record of agents signing in and then signing out with nothing interesting happening between. When there was a hit on contraband, that was noted, with a reference number that referred Ana to the second binder for a more complete report. Whenever someone tried to come through with fake ID or expired ID, or when they had a black mark on the books that kept them out of the United States, this too was recorded. It was these things that interested Ana, and she made note of each take, along with salient details from the full reports.

It was slow going, and not unlike what the CBP did on the lanes all day. There were no great revelations contained in the binders, but Ana was obliged to research them at least once a month and compile the data into a summary that could be sent to Austin.

Ana found the exercise wasteful, because the same information could be had in official reports from the CBP. For some reason the higher ups found it more reliable to receive the identical data from one of their own. Ana suspected the governor had something to do with that; his antipathy toward CBP was well known.

The door to the outside opened and one of the agents came in. Ana thought his name was Plante. They had not spoken much. He went to the coffee pot and poured himself a cup into his own mug.

"Morning, Ranger," he said.

"Morning."

"Checking up on us?"

"Just doing what they ask me to do."

"I understand. Everybody has to have their fingers in. I'm Willie."

"Ana Torres."

They shook hands. Willie Plante lingered by Ana, watching her transcribe the last of the information into her notebook. Her handwriting was cramped and hard to read, she knew, but no one besides her would see it.

"What do you do when you're not taking notes?" Plante asked.

"Whatever needs doing. The Rangers have broad discretion."

"Must be nice. Around here it's just the same old, same old."

Ana found herself wishing the man away. It was difficult to concentrate on copying when he was standing over her. She did not know him to dislike him, but she didn't need the hassle.

"You know—" Plante started and then the radio at his waist squawked.

"*Willie, we need you in secondary.*"

"Something's going on. Excuse me, Ranger."

Willie left his coffee cup beside Ana and hustled back to the lanes. Ana saw that the agents were waving a little blue car out of one of the two incoming lanes and into the secondary processing area. She put down her pen and went out.

Henry Million's dog was hopping around, excited by the presence of the car. The driver, a young woman in professional clothes, was out of the vehicle with a baby in her arms. Ana arrived in time to hear the agent in charge tell Plante to put the woman in holding.

The agent in charge's name was Artie Kopp. Ana knew him from the Pollens' barbecues. He was a thickset man with heavily graying hair and skin burnished a deep bronze by the unrelenting Presidio sun. He motioned for Henry to run Paco around the car again, this time with the doors open.

Paco scrambled up into the passenger seat of the car, sniffing enthusiastically. Henry encouraged the dog: "Get it, boy! Get it!"

The front seats were clean. Paco crawled into the back where a baby seat was securely fastened. He barked and scratched at the baby seat. Henry pulled the dog away and gave him a black rubber chew toy. Paco dug his teeth into the toy and immediately forgot the hit.

"Let's check it out," Kopp said. They were joined by another agent, one whose name Ana didn't know. The man stood around while Kopp put the driver's seat forward and leaned in to unfasten the baby seat. He brought it out and sat it on the ground. It was plain and blue and full of crumbs and stains. Ana saw nothing unusual about it.

Kopp stripped off the padding and found nothing. Then he turned the seat over and poked his finger into the cavities there. "Bingo," he said. He dug into a hollow and came away with a small bag of white powder.

"Coke?" Ana asked.

Kopp seemed to notice her for the first time. He shrugged. "Probably. Maybe. We'll test it. Henry, run the dog over the car one more time. If we have to, we'll break it down."

Ana followed Kopp back to the building. She waited while the CBP agent checked a sample of the powder with a self-contained testing packet the size of his thumb. The liquid inside turned blue for positive. "Coke," he said.

There was a scale on the counter near Ana's notes and the binders. Kopp weighed it out. "Forty-one grams."

Ana looked at the woman and her baby in the holding cell. The woman's face was fallen. The baby grabbed at her hair and gurgled. "*¿De dónde vienes?*" Ana asked her.

"Ojinaga," the woman said.

"You knew there was *cocaína* in your baby's chair?"

The woman nodded.

"It's not much weight, but she'd probably make a hundred bucks carrying it across," Kopp said. "If she turned out to be reliable, they'd give her more to bring over. That's the way it works."

The woman looked from Ana to Kopp and back again. Ana saw the resignation there. She would be taken in and fingerprinted and separated from her baby for however long it took to put her before a judge and pronounce sentence. Ana saw it all playing out as if it had already happened. Mother and child would only be together again when they were deported back to Mexico.

"How old is your baby?" Ana asked.

"Eighteen months."

"It's a girl?"

"*Sí.*"

"I'm sorry," Ana said.

"It is done," the woman replied.

"I have to log it now," Kopp said. "You want to mark it down in your book?"

Ana turned away from the cell. "I'll do it later. You need someone to take them back to the station?"

"I'll call one of ours to do it, Ranger. You don't need to bother."

It's not a bother, Ana wanted to say, but she didn't. Instead she looked out to the lanes again. The nameless agent was tearing into the rear bumper of the car with a pry-bar as long as his body. The front bumper was already off. They would break down the car piece by piece — taking out the dash, pulling up the carpet, checking the fuel tank — until they were sure there was nothing left to find. The hunk of a car that was left would be parted out, or maybe slapped back together and put up for auction; because it was used in the commission of a felony, ownership was forfeit to the United States of America.

In the other lanes, business went on as usual. No one even looked toward the woman's car. Henry and Paco were back at work, sniffing new cars. They roamed the short line of vehicles. Ana could almost hear Henry from here: *Get it, boy! Get it!*

"I'm going to go," Ana told Kopp. "I'll be back later to finish up."

"We'll be here."

Ana collected her notebook and went outside. The temperatures were already starting to pick up. She was glad she hadn't chosen to patrol today; she could feel that it was going to be searing.

She went back to her truck and sat a while behind the wheel. She did not know where she was going now. The CBP station awaited and she could get a head start transcribing her notes, but she didn't want to just yet. She was aware that the woman and her baby were bothering her, and she knew it would bother her all day. What she really wanted to ask the woman was why she would take such a risk with her child on the line, but she already knew the answer: because of the money. No one brought anything across the border except for money, and it was no different here than it was anywhere else along the river.

In the end she started up the truck and drove away, not sure where she was headed or what she would do when she got there. She kept on going until her phone rang and she learned that the autopsy report on her dead Mexican was ready.

15

The office of the Medical Examiner of Presidio County was located in a government building two blocks from the hospital where the actual cutting and sewing was done. Ana parked on the street and came inside, where it was cool and smelled good. She did not like going to the autopsy room itself, where the air stank of disinfectant and steady decay.

She had to wait a while in the reception area until she was ready to be seen. The secretary waved her in when it was time, and she passed through an inner door with fake oak veneer into the office of Joshua Mikesell.

Dr. Mikesell was on the phone. He motioned for her to sit down. "Uh-huh," he said. "Two hundred. That's right. Okay. Good-bye."

When he hung up, he smiled and came around the desk to shake Ana's hand. He was a middle-aged man, very thin, with a ring of hair around his skull and bald on top. When he smiled, he showed many teeth. "Ana, how are you doing?" he asked.

"I'm all right. Taking it easy today."

"I wish I could do the same. I'm only in the office for about an hour today and then it's back to the grindstone. You're lucky you caught me."

"They called and said my report was in."

"Yes, it's here," Mikesell said and searched his desk. "Dead Mexican with three bullet wounds. That was a pretty easy one."

Ana took the report when it was passed to her. It was on light paper, almost like onionskin. The top page had outlines of a human body, front and back, and the pictures were marked and numbered where the wounds were. She didn't read it yet.

"Cause of death was a bullet through the heart," Dr. Mikesell said. "Stopped his pump almost immediately, I'd say. If it hadn't, either of the other slugs would have done the trick: both of his lungs were perforated. He would have drowned in his own blood."

"Were you able to pull a bullet from the body?"

"One. It was deflected off the vertebrae. The impact with the bone deformed the metal extensively, but you can probably get ballistics data from it."

"We'll send it in for analysis."

"Here it is, then," Mikesell said. He passed Ana a plastic baggie fastened to a yellow sheet of paper. Ana added it to the rest. "Good luck with that."

"Was there anything else?"

"Well, I can tell you that he was in good shape, aside from the gunshot wounds. All of his other organs were healthy, he had low body fat and he didn't show signs of malnutrition. He took decent care of himself. And he had very good teeth."

"Does that mean anything?"

"Only that he had a nice smile."

"Did you fingerprint him?"

"Yes. Those got faxed over the CBP. I didn't hear anything, but they wouldn't tell me, anyway."

Ana got up. She was taller than Mikesell by an inch or two in her boots. "Thanks very much, Dr. Mikesell."

"Please, I told you to call me Josh."

"Okay. Thanks again. This will help."

"Any chance you'll catch the one who did it?"

Ana paused at the door. "Probably not."

"That's too bad."

"Yes, it is."

16

S he went back to the CBP station. No one looked up from their work when she went to her cubicle or paid much mind as she composed a report on the autopsy. She wondered idly if the mother and her baby had been brought in yet, but stopped herself from visiting the holding cells to see. When she was finished, perhaps, but only then and only maybe.

The bullet taken from the corpse would eventually have to go to Austin to be examined. Ana looked at it and saw what Dr. Mikesell already said: the metal was twisted into a random shape. There should be no way to cull lands and grooves from that slug. But perhaps she would be surprised. She had been surprised before. At least she had the shell casings; extractor marks on the brass were almost as revealing as a ballistics test, so long as she could find the weapon. Which was unlikely.

Ana called up the fingerprint report on the dead man. It was a blank, showing nothing. He was not in the system, whether for legal crossing or because he had been caught coming across illegally. Even now he remained nameless and would stay so, unless the Mexican government had files the US did not.

That reminded her that she would have to call Jorge Vargas at the consulate. She would have to put together a second report with the salient details of all of her investigations and deliver it with the body within the next few days. The Mexicans would want to know everything, but they were likely to be disappointed. There was nothing to know.

A shadow fell across her. It was Darren. "Hey," he said.

"Hey. What are you doing hanging around?"

"My turn to watch the fort while everyone else gets to go play," Darren said. "What about you?"

"Nothing new. Putting the dead Mexican into the system. He was clean on fingerprints. No priors."

"That's got to be frustrating."

"Doesn't it frustrate you?"

"I don't know. Someone dies out there from exposure or a snakebite or something like that, maybe I feel a little something, but when it's just *narcos* shooting *narcos*... not so much."

"He might not have been a *narco*."

"Well, we'll never know, will we? You send anything to Vargas yet?"

"I was just getting ready to write it up for him."

"No way he'll admit that it was crooks doing crooks out there," Darren said. "And you can forget about ever hearing back from their *policía* if they do come up with something. Information flows south across the border, never north."

"Since when did you get so negative?"

Darren shook his head. "I don't know. Lack of sex, maybe."

They both looked around, but no one seemed to have heard them. Ana put her finger to her lips and motioned Darren closer. He leaned in. "What?"

"If you want it so bad, when can you come around again?"

"Tonight, maybe. I'll tell Jeannie I'm going out with some of the guys. She'll never check up on that."

"Okay, then. And keep your zipper up until then, all right?"

Darren smiled. "Yes, ma'am."

He straightened up and made a show of fixing his tie. Ana looked again, but no one was watching them. "Thanks for letting me know about the fingerprints," she said.

"Huh? Oh, yeah, sure. No problem."

"I'll talk to you later."

"See you."

Darren went and Ana turned back to her keyboard. Her hands were shaking a little and she made fists to still them. When she looked again, Darren was out of sight, and no one was watching her. She had nothing to be afraid of.

It took the better part of an hour to draft a copy of the report that would go to Vargas. Ana made it as detailed as possible because she knew he would appreciate that. His superiors were like hers: always looking for more answers, even when there were no answers to give. She knew he was never glad to share the news of another death on the Texas side of the river.

The police on the Mexican side had done a good job keeping the carnage from spilling across the border, at least where Ojinaga and Presidio were concerned. Sometimes, when she was at the port of entry, Ana looked across the bridge and saw military vehicles parked there, watching the flow of northbound traffic. She didn't know how many men they had stationed in Ojinaga. The town was small, like Presidio. Ana could not imagine big-time drug cartels bothering with their port of entry, but there was a stack of narcotics in the evidence room that said otherwise.

She printed out the Vargas report and put it in a folder. Maybe she would deliver it today. There was still the matter of the body, but that paperwork came through Dr. Mikesell's office, not her. Ana wondered if she should mention the woman and her baby to Vargas. Perhaps there was something he could do for them.

Ana passed Darren on the way out, but they didn't look at each other. She was in her truck again when her phone rang.

"Torres," she answered.

"Ana? It's Mom."

Ana remembered she had planned to call. She switched the phone to speaker and put it on the dashboard. "Hello, Mom. How are you?"

"I hope I'm not bothering you at work, but you didn't call back, and—"

"It's all right. I'm not busy."

"I can call back if you are."

"No, really. Tell me everything."

They had not spoken in over a month, and her mother began a recitation of everything that had transpired between conversations. Ana heard about her uncles and her father, and what her mother was up to now that she was retired from working for the state of Texas. Ana did not have to speak because her participation was limited to listening. Eventually, she would be asked about her day, her life, and she would say the same thing she always said: *I keep busy. I'm keeping safe.*

Ana didn't mind the ritual of it. Sometimes she even took comfort in the way it played out. Once a long time ago, when she was younger and more impatient, she might have been a little short with her mother, or rolled her eyes when the stories grew too long, but she knew now that her mother said these things because she cared, and because she wanted Ana to be a part of the family, no matter how far away she went.

"How is Presidio?"

"The same. Not much happening here."

"Have they said anything about transferring you? Maybe back to San Antonio?"

"I haven't heard anything. They'll keep me here as long as they need me."

"Your father and I should come visit sometime."

"You can do that. But there's not anything to see. Mesquite trees. Cows."

"I heard on the news that the cartels are taking hostages along the border. People trying to cross into the US. Holding them for ransom and killing them if they can't pay."

"That happens a long way from here," Ana said.

"Do a lot of people come across there?"

"Not a lot. Some. The worst thing they have to worry about is the heat, not cartels."

"That's good to know. All they want to do is make a better life for themselves."

"There are legal ways to do that, Mom. Then they don't have to worry about Los Zetas or whoever. If the come across legally, they're not my problem."

"But Immigration makes it so *hard*."

"I told you before, Mom: it's as hard as it needs to be. Some of these people, they have criminal records. They're bad men." Ana thought of the *narco*-carrier who called her *chica*. It faded quickly. "The process weeds those kinds of people out."

"I just hope you're not too hard on them when you catch them."

"I'm not."

She was halfway to the consulate now, and she sensed the conversation drawing to a close. Whenever her mother talked about border policy, it meant she had run out of family news to share. They would never agree completely, but they would not disagree harshly.

"I guess I ought to let you go," her mother said.

"I need to get back to work, anyway," Ana said.

"You be careful, *mija*. Don't do anything foolish out there."

"I won't. I promise."

"I'll call you again."

"Good-bye, Mom."

The phone went dead. Ana put it in her pocket. She glanced at the folder on the seat beside her. If only her mother knew what she was doing now, what she had done for the last few days, she would never worry. Nothing ever happened in Presidio. Even when someone died, the danger was long past before Ana got there.

This place didn't need her.

17

In the end she decided the delivery to Vargas at the consulate could wait. She left the folder in the truck when she got home early and took the opportunity to have a nap. When she woke, she felt sluggish and wished she'd done something else instead. She waited out the time until Darren's shift would be over.

Ana heard his truck on the drive. She let him in and they kissed in the open doorway. His hands were on her immediately. She did not fight it.

In the bedroom they stripped each other and then had sex on top of the sheets. They took their time about it. Ana made Darren wait for her before she gave him what he needed. At last they were naked and sweaty, limbs tangled together, Ana's feet dangling off the edge of the bed.

"It stays good," Darren told her after a while.

"How long can you be here?"

"Another hour or so. Something like that."

It was still light outside, the long summer day seeming to hang on forever. Ana looked at shadows and brilliance on the ceiling, sweat cooling on her body, a few hairs plastered to her forehead and at the back of her neck. Night wouldn't come until after nine, which seemed far too long to her.

"She never asks after you?" Ana asked.

"No. Why?"

"You're gone a lot. Doubles, night shifts... you'd think she'd keep a closer eye."

"Good for us she doesn't," Darren said.

"Good for us."

Silence fell between them. With her arm across Darren's chest, Ana could hear his heat beating steadily. She had the smell of him in her nostrils, mixed with the odor of sex. A shower seemed good to her now, but she wouldn't move just yet.

"Go ahead," Darren said finally.

"Go ahead with what?"

"Say what you want to say."

"I don't want to say anything."

Darren shifted to make a little distance between them. Ana didn't move to take up the space. "You bring up Jeannie, you must have something to say. So just go ahead and say it."

"Really, Darren, I don't have anything to say."

He fell quiet for a few beats and then he said, "You want to call it off, don't you?"

Ana propped herself up on one elbow and looked at him. "What are you talking about?"

"I mean, I figured it was inevitable. This kind of thing can't last."

"Where is this coming from?" Ana asked.

Darren sat up and freed himself from her touch. His voice was flat as he spoke to the wall: "She does ask."

Ana didn't say anything. She wanted him to continue. The room was warm, breathless and expectant. She thought about pulling the sheets over her nakedness because the sensation of intimacy between them had slipped away.

"She asked me two nights ago if I was having an affair."

"What did you say?"

"I told her no. What else was I supposed to say?"

"Do you think she knows it's me?"

"Could be. Maybe. The list of available women at work is pretty short."

"But it could be anybody."

"I don't think she sees me taking up with a civilian."

Now Ana did pull the sheet over herself. She sat up with her back against the headboard and listened to the quiet that descended, the hum of the air conditioner in the next room. It was never cool enough in this house.

"What do you want to do?" Ana asked eventually.

The muscles in Darren's back were tense, she saw them move when he did. He was a handsome man, with good looks from an Anglo mother and a Latino father. He had drawn from the best parts of his parents, and he was strong and reliable and good in bed. The conflict in him was palpable.

He looked over his shoulder at her. "I don't want to stop seeing you."

"But Jeannie—"

"I don't care about that. She and I have been growing apart for a long time. We don't even touch each other anymore. But when I'm with you... it's different."

A shiver trilled through Ana. She kept her voice even. "What are you saying?"

"I'm saying I'm in love with you."

This was all wrong. He was saying things she did not want to hear and saying them with conviction. She saw the beginnings of tears in his eyes. Soon he would turn to her and want to hold her and tell her again and again that he loved her. She did not want that. Her mind rebelled against it.

"I said I love you," Darren said.

"I think you should go," Ana replied.

"What? Isn't that what this is all about? You want more and you thought I wasn't going to give it to you, so you were going to cut it off. Well there's no reason to cut it off because I love you. We belong together."

Ana got out of bed, conscious of her nudity, and fetched a robe from the bathroom. She pulled it around her and cinched the belt tightly in front. "I said from the beginning that this wasn't going to be like that," she said. "I said it and you agreed."

"Wait a minute: are you saying you *don't* want me to love you?"

"I'm saying... look, you should just go. We'll talk about it another time."

Darren's expression curdled. "I don't want to go."

"Well, you have to. This is my house."

"I want to hear you say that you love me first."

Ana put a hand to her head. An ache was forming behind her eyes. She shuddered again. It was difficult to keep from shouting, though she wanted to shout. *Get out! Take your things and get OUT!*

"Darren... you knew I wanted to keep this casual. Nothing has changed."

"You're wrong, everything *has* changed. I'm in love with you, Ana."

"Will you *stop* saying that? Everything you think about what I want is wrong. When I said I wanted us to be friends and nothing more, I *meant it*. Now you *have* to go. We will talk about this *another time*."

"Fine."

Darren left the bed and gathered up his things. He dressed in the front room, away from her, and she was glad of that. She didn't want to see him any more tonight. Eventually, the front door opened and closed, and his truck engine turned over. She waited until he was halfway down the drive before she ventured from her bedroom. He had left nothing behind. That was good.

She did not know how to feel, whether she should cry or be angry, and instead she walked the interior of the small house busying herself with little tasks like putting away dishes and starting the night's meal. A part of her expected him to call her, but by now he was at home with Jeannie, having a late dinner and pretending that nothing was off at all.

18

She forgot to set her alarm and overslept the next morning. The sun was already rising fast as she hurried to dress and eat breakfast and get out to the truck for the start of the new day. Because she had taken a break from patrolling ranch land, she was behind schedule and would have to make it up somehow over the following week.

She was halfway to the stables when her phone rang. At first she thought to let it ring, because it was probably Darren, but the number was not the same. She answered.

"Ranger Torres, this is Sheriff Sellner."

"Good morning, Sheriff. What can I do for you?"

"Well, I'm standing out on the Sheedy property and wondered if maybe you could come by."

"More bodies coming across?"

"Bring your horse. I think you're going to want to poke around."

"I'll be there. Give me forty-five minutes."

When she hung up, she was annoyed. Sheriff Sellner could be impenetrable when he wanted to be, and now he was. It would have been easier for both of them if he would just state his business, but he wouldn't and largely, Ana suspected, because she stepped on his toes with the handling of the Mexican body. Now he would only be happy if he could tug her string a little bit and see the Ranger hop.

It took her thirty minutes to get to the stables and deal with Rico and then longer to get out to the Sheedys'. Sheriff Sellner would notice she was late.

Ana saw Bill Sheedy's truck parked by the gate with Sellner's. The sheriff waved her down. She came up slowly and got out.

"Morning, Ranger," Bill Sheedy said. He looked glum, and for a moment Ana thought maybe they were dealing with another body. But even Sheriff Sellner would not keep that from her, and there would be more people on the scene.

"Good morning, Mr. Sheedy. How are you?"

"A little pissed off, if you don't mind me saying so."

"The action's a little farther in," Sellner said. "Follow us, all right, Ranger?"

"Lead the way."

They went through the gate caravan-style and drove a while. Ana wondered if they were going out to the spot where she and Trumble and Stender had rounded up the illegal crossers, but Bill Sheedy took a fork that cut across unfamiliar territory until finally they rolled to a stop.

Ana got out of her truck a couple of yards shy of a great explosion of cactuses that must have been ten feet across. There were still morning bugs calling to each other from the mesquite trees, but they would go silent as the day heated up.

"About a hundred yards that-a-way," Bill Sheedy said, and waved off south.

They walked together through the trees until Ana saw a high line of barbed-wire fencing. Once they reached it, they followed the fence another dozen yards until they reached their destination.

La Frontera

Half of the ten strands of tightly drawn barbed wire had
been cut, leaving a curling passageway through the fence. Bill
Sheedy spat in the dirt. "See what they did? Cut the fence
clean through."

"He was out checking fence-line this morning, ran across
it," Sheriff Sellner said.

Ana examined the ground on both sides of the fence.
Sheedy's bootprints were easy to pick out, but there were
plenty of others. "I can't tell how many came through here.
Probably a lot from the looks of it. Ten or fifteen."

"And you want to know the goddamned thing about
it?" Sheedy asked. "Not fifty yards further down I put a ladder over the fence just so's they wouldn't cut it if they came
through. Ladder cost five hundred bucks! And then they just
go and chop a hole right in it."

"He called me first thing," Sellner said. "Then I called
you."

"No offense, Sheriff, but what can I do? The damage is
already done."

"You check out the back-country all along here, don't
you?"

"Yes."

"Well, I figure you can take a gander at Bill's property,
maybe see what else those illegals tampered with. There's
other fence out there; maybe they cut those, too."

Ana frowned, but looked the other way so Sellner would
not see it. She hadn't planned on hitting the Sheedy place
today, and technically Sheriff Sellner was in no position to
say what she would do on any given day. But Bill Sheedy
was angry, and Sellner expectant, and Rico was already in the
trailer.

She turned back to Sellner and Sheedy and smiled. "Sure," she said. "I can do that."

"Much obliged, Ranger Torres," Sellner said. "You can do a better job on some of that ground with your horse than I could do with my truck."

And you don't have to go out of your way to take care of things. "Of course," Ana said. "Let me get Rico unloaded and I'll start right now."

Bill Sheedy offered his hand. "Thanks, Ranger. Maybe you can figure out where they came from."

"They came from Mexico, Mr. Sheedy."

Sheriff Sellner laughed. "'They came from Mexico'! That's a funny one."

The three of them said their good-byes back at the trucks, and then Sheedy and Sellner peeled away from the group to head back up the track to the gravel road and off the property. Ana brought Rico out of the trailer, checked his saddle and then mounted up.

"Come on, lazy," she said. "I guess we're on fence duty today."

19

She spent all morning and the first part of the afternoon making the rounds of Bill Sheedy's back forty. She found no more cut fence, though she followed miles of it as the heat notched higher with the sun in the sky. It was all a waste of her time.

Backtracking along the crossers' trail was easy enough to do, and by the time she was done, she figured there had been about thirteen altogether. They were moving fast, probably by night, guided by a *coyote* who knew what he was doing, cutting across open ground and moving through the fence line instead of along it. It was no surprise they missed the ladder; more than likely they could not see it in the dark.

Ana brought Rico back to the stables and spent a little time just watching the horse make himself comfortable in the corral before she moved on. She still had the report for Vargas in her truck and she swung by to drop it off before taking a late lunch and then going home early; she didn't want to risk seeing Darren at the station, and no one would notice anyway.

It was uncomfortable in her home, with the atmosphere of the night before still lingering. Ana went to the refrigerator for beer and remembered she still hadn't bought any. In the end she was reduced to putting up her sockfeet in front of the television the way she had done hundreds of times before, just letting the sounds and pictures flow over her meaninglessly.

When dinnertime came around, she went out again and had the evening meal at the same restaurant where she took lunch. She got a spot of barbecue sauce on her shirt and cursed.

There were any number of places she could have gone, things she could have done, but none appealed to her. At the same time, she wanted to get away from the TV and her empty house. She knew no one who would be happy to see her show up on their doorstep in the evening hours and had no one to call. Ana wandered the streets of Presidio, looking in storefronts and passing people she didn't know on the sidewalks, until finally the sun came down and she was forced home like the rest of the townsfolk.

That night she lay awake in her bedroom, remembering Darren there and the things he said and her response to them. She hadn't changed her mind, but she wondered if maybe she had handled things differently, he might not have left so angry. Even though he was gone more often than he was there, she missed him.

Sleep came late and wakefulness early. She had no dreams that she could remember. Putting on fresh clothes made her feel brand new, and when she came out into the early-morning chill, she felt more positive than she had the night before.

She got to the CBP station before most of the morning shift had reported in. At her cubicle she logged her activities from the day before, including the fruitless search of the Sheedy property, and neglected to mention that she spent most of her time idling instead of working.

One of the morning guys, Adam Ludden, came by her cubicle with a slip of pink paper. "This came through the main switchboard last night. Call from the consulate."

"Thanks," Ana said. She looked at the message and then she called Jorge Vargas. Her call was put right through.

"*Buenos días*," Vargas said. He sounded as if he had just sprung freshly from his bed, pressed and ready for the day, while people around the CBP offices were dragging through their morning routine, barely fueled by coffee. "How are you this morning?"

"I'm good, thank you. I just got your message."

"I wonder if we could meet to discuss it? If you have time, of course."

"I have time. I'll be right there."

"*Gracias.* I will be here."

Ana took her hat and left the station by the back door. She crossed town in just a few minutes; there was no logjam morning traffic in Presidio. When she got to the offices of the consulate, the same receptionist was working as had been a few days before. She smiled politely.

Vargas came out to greet her and took Ana's hands in both of his before sketching a kiss on her cheek. He invited her into his office and offered her coffee. She declined. "Then to business," he said and they sat across from each other in the comfortable leather chairs.

"I guess you wanted to know about the report?" Ana asked.

"Yes. I faxed it to my superiors in Mexico City. As usual, a very thorough job by your medical examiner. Thank you for being so prompt and meticulous."

"It's part of our job."

"I know and I told my superiors that when they called back to ask questions about the investigation into the death."

"Well, we ran fingerprints, but he wasn't in the system," Ana said. "We have the shell casings collected from the scene, as well as other evidence, but there's not much to go on. A few tracks that come from nowhere and lead nowhere. I think our investigation is pretty much closed."

"But do you have suspects in the killing?"

"The evidence points toward an internal dispute. Mexican on Mexican."

"I see, but did you pursue any other lines of questioning?"

Ana blinked. Vargas leaned slightly forward in his chair, waiting on her answer, but she didn't know what he expected her to say. "Well, no," she said finally. "It seems pretty clear-cut."

Vargas nodded and waved his hands as if to clear the air. "I apologize," he said, "but you're probably absolutely right. You see, I know you and I know that you are nothing less than completely methodical in your work. The Texas Rangers are the best the state of Texas has to offer, is that not so? Compared to the men from Customs and Border Protection... you do quite well."

"I try," Ana said.

"The thing is, my superiors are curious about *alternative* ideas concerning the crime."

"What kind of alternative ideas?"

"I hesitate to say. I don't want to insult you."

"That's all right, say what you need to say."

"They want to know if it is possible — even if it is unlikely, as you say — that our countryman was killed by an American."

With that, Vargas sat back in his seat, having released the idea into the room. Ana nodded slowly, but she was thinking about the land where she found the body, about the rape tree and the tracks and everything else that she had seen on that day. At last she spoke, saying, "I don't think so."

"You understand I have to pass these things along."

"I understand. But like I said, I don't think so. I saw no tracks besides the ones left by the crossers, and the disposition of the body and the evidence on the scene... no, I don't think so."

Vargas made a face as though he was in pain. He leaned forward again. "My superiors asked me to ask you to be absolutely certain."

"I am absolutely certain."

"But there must be some avenue you have not pursued. Some question that hasn't been asked. A suspect, however dubious. I only ask because then I can report back to Mexico City that everything that could have been done has been done. Then there will be no more inquiries."

"I don't know what you want me to do. The evidence is the evidence."

"Please, Ana. For me."

Ana frowned, still thinking. Vargas was making her doubt her own judgment, or at least opening the door to doubt. She reviewed the scene a second time, considered to whom she had spoken and everything that transpired, until finally she said, "I suppose there might be one more person I could ask."

"Really? That would be wonderful."

"It means losing some of the goodwill of the ranchers around Presidio," Ana said. "It's not something I would do if you weren't asking."

"Believe me, this brings me no pleasure."

Ana stood up sharply and Vargas rose with her. She went for her hat on a hook by the door. "It could take me a few days to do this," she said. "Can your people in Mexico City wait that long?"

"I can stall them so long as I can say you are doing something."

"I'll do something. Then the case is closed."

"Of course. I don't expect anything will come of this, whatever you have planned. You understand that I—"

"You're not the one who wants to know," Ana said. "Don't worry, I get it. I'll call you when I have more information. Or when I find out there's nothing to tell."

"Thank you, Ana."

Ana sighed and left by the door. She did not wait for Vargas' handshake or his kiss.

Out in her truck, she turned on the engine and ran the air conditioner to cool the cabin, though she wasn't driving yet. She was not angry, but she felt much the same way she had when Sheriff Sellner assumed she would be happy to mind the Sheedys' fences on a hot summer day. She did not like the sensation.

What she wanted to do was to march back up to the offices of the consulate and say that she knew what she was doing, that the crime scene was examined properly, that the evidence was interpreted correctly, and there should be no question of her conclusions. She wanted to say that, but it was impossible. She was as bound by the forms of duty as Jorge Vargas, and both of them knew it. Questions were posed, and she was meant to answer them quickly, completely and to everyone's satisfaction.

Ana thumped the heel of her palm against the steering wheel. "Goddamn it," she said out loud. There was nothing else for her to say.

She got on the radio to the CBP dispatcher. "This is Ranger Torres. Tell anybody who asks that I'll be out at the Bowder place for a little while. I'll keep in radio contact or you can always try my phone."

"Roger that, Ranger," said the dispatcher.

Ana put the truck in gear and made a u-turn in the middle of the street. She pointed herself east and drove out of town.

20

The Bowder house was quiet and still. Ana saw no sign of Claude Bowder's truck, or his wife's, and for a little while she entertained the fantasy that neither of them would be home and she could put this off for another time. Eventually she had to leave her truck and cross the little patch of grass to the front door.

"Hello the house!" she called. At the front she opened the screen door and stepped onto the porch to knock on the interior one. She used her official knock, the one they taught police officers everywhere: strident, hard and insistent.

She had to knock twice more before there was sound inside and the lock unfastened. Claude Bowder appeared in a t-shirt and sockfeet looking bleary-eyed as though he had been drinking.

"Ranger Torres? What's the commotion? I was having a lazy morning. Sleeping in."

"Sorry about that, Mr. Bowder. Can I come in?"

"Sure you can come in. Come in!"

Ana entered and took her hat off. Bowder closed the door behind her. For the first time Ana noticed there was the faintest smell of mothballs about the house.

"I'm going to fix myself some iced tea. You want some?"

"No, thanks."

"You prefer coffee?"

"I don't need anything."

"It's no trouble."

"No, really."

She followed Bowder into the kitchen where he took a pitcher of iced tea out of the refrigerator and poured a tall glass. There were lemons swimming in the pitcher and Bowder plucked one out delicately before putting it in his tea.

"My wife's out at her sister's place in Uvalde," Bowder said. "She won't be back for a few days. Thought I'd take it easy while she was gone."

"Sounds like a plan," Ana said.

"Now, what can I do for you? No more trouble on my property is there? Because I've had about all the trouble I can stomach for one month."

"No new trouble. The same thing," Ana said.

"That dead wetback?"

"That's the one."

"What about him?"

"Well, the medical examiner's all done with the body, and he's ready to be shipped back to Mexico. But the Mexican government has some questions about the way he died, thought maybe I could do something to answer them."

Bowder lifted his glass and examined Ana over the lip. He drank and swallowed and then he said, "What kinds of questions?"

"You remember he was back-shot?"

"I remember."

"From what I can tell, he was shot by his own people. All the signs point toward it. I have no reason to think otherwise."

Bowder's eyes narrowed. "But?"

"But... there're those questions."

"Shit," Bowder said and he put down his glass hard. "They're saying I did it, aren't they?"

"They aren't saying that exactly."

"But they think I done went out there and gunned down some wetback."

"They think maybe somebody did."

Bowder shook his head. "And you didn't tell them to take their damned speculation and stick it up their asses? Who's saying this stuff about me?"

"Nobody's saying anything about you specifically," Ana said. "The Mexican government just knows that there are some angry ranchers along the border and they want to make sure this wasn't one of them."

"'Angry ranchers,' what a crock. They let those wetbacks run wild all across the border and they blame *us* for being up in arms about it? I hope you told them where to go."

"Actually, I told them I'd look into it."

"*What?*"

Ana raised her hands in front of her. She could feel the ire coming off Bowder like waves of heat. *I hope you appreciate this, Jorge.*

"You're saying I'm suspect on my own land, Ranger?"

"I just saying I'm looking into it as a favor to the Mexican government. It isn't like I'm opening up a whole new investigation. We all know what went down out there. It was Mexican-on-Mexican violence."

"Now I *wish* I'd shot him."

"You don't want to say that," Ana said. "Listen: this is a simple situation to resolve. All I need to know is if you own a .45 and, if you do, I need to take it in for a forensic expert to examine it."

"What kind of gun do *you* carry, Ranger?"

"A .40 Glock."

"So you're off the hook."

"Mr. Bowder, you're not *on* the hook. This is just to eliminate you as a suspect. Now, do you have a .45?"

"Maybe I do and maybe I don't," Bowder said and he crossed his chest with his arms. "How you going to get it from me if I don't cooperate? Don't you need a court order?"

"I don't need a court order if you surrender the weapon voluntarily. That's what I'm hoping you'll do."

"What a bunch of bull*shit*."

"Please, Mr. Bowder. It'll make it a lot easier for everyone."

"Easier for you, maybe. I have my rights!"

"No one's taking away your rights."

Bowder grumbled something Ana didn't understand and then picked up his glass again. He drained it and held the glass uneasily, as if he couldn't decide what to do with it, and then he set it down. "I want you to know that I'm doing this under protest."

"I kind of figured that."

"Don't you go being smart now!"

"I'm sorry. Do you have a .45?"

"Yes, I do. A Colt Series 70. It has rosewood grips."

"Sounds like a nice gun."

"It is. And I don't want anything happening to it."

"I'll take it today, have it in El Paso tomorrow and bring it back the day after that. You have my word. Nobody's going to try and take it apart; we'll just fire a couple of test rounds and check the extractor marks on the spent casings."

Bowder left the kitchen and was gone for a while. When he returned, he had the pistol. It was a weapon with blued finish and it did have rosewood grips. With Ana watching, he dropped the magazine and locked the slide back, and then he handed it over.

"I'm believing you, Ranger Torres."

"You can trust me, Mr. Bowder."

"This'll prove I didn't shoot that wetback?"

"As near as we can prove anything. I'm not worried."

"You'll excuse me if I don't break out the party hats."

"I'll show myself out?"

"I'll see you to the door," Bowder said.

Back out under the sun, Ana adjusted her hat. She looked back to see Bowder behind the screen door, face sour, as she took his weapon away. She did not want to know what else was going through his mind. Ana raised a hand in farewell and went to her truck.

By the time she turned the engine over, Bowder had closed the front door. The house was quiet again, as if no one was home.

21

Ana left early the next morning with the pistol wrapped in a cloth on the seat beside her. She took US-67 out of town toward Marfa, some sixty miles away. That town was barely waking up when she passed through, just another little place on the wide Texas map. She went through Valentine and Van Horn, too, angling west through dry country until she could link up with I-10 and follow it all the way to El Paso.

She was a member of Company D, out of San Antonio, and she wouldn't have minded heading back east to see the familiar city. El Paso was the home of Company E, but it was closer by 200 miles. She entered the city before lunchtime and navigated her way to the District Company headquarters on Franklin Ave. A show of her ID got her a space in the parking garage.

It was a different sensation, being here. Ana had almost forgotten what it was like. There were many people working in many offices and still others passed her in the hallways. Hundreds of people worked in this building alone. Ana felt strangely exposed, as if the dust of Presidio had clung to her somehow and she was marked as a stranger.

The office she needed was on the third floor. It was a functional place, with a tall counter and a frosted-glass partition to keep prying eyes off the men who worked behind it. Ana showed her ID to the woman at the counter. "I'm here for Ranger Unrein. Ranger Torres from Company D."

"It'll be just a minute."

Ana took a seat in a straight-backed chair by the wall. She watched the ceiling fans turn while she waited. Eventually she heard voices and a tall man emerged from behind the partition. "Ranger Torres?" he asked.

"That's me."

"Come on around. I'm Lance Unrein."

She passed through a swinging door at the end of the counter and met with Unrein halfway. The Ranger shook her hand firmly, then steered her behind the partition to an area where several desks were arranged together to maximize working space. He seemed to be the only one in. He showed her a chair.

"What can we do for you today?"

"I have a gun I'd like to submit for testing, along with a slug and some brass for comparison. We had a shooting out in Presidio. Mexican national. Everything says he was shot by another Mexican coming across the border, but we have to rule out the rancher who owns the land. This is his pistol."

Unrein took the .45, weighed it in his hand. "We can certainly do that for you. The brass and the slug?"

Ana produced an evidence bag with the empty casings collected from the scene and another with the badly deformed slug. She was glad now that she hadn't sent it to Austin yet. "I'd like a full ballistics workup."

"Stay here and I'll make sure this gets into the right hands."

Unrein left her at the desk and disappeared into another room. A long while passed, but Ana was used to waiting. Most of police work was waiting: for the right moment, the right person, the right piece of evidence. This was doubly true when it came to forensics.

A half hour passed before Unrein returned. The gun and the evidence bags were gone. "I sent them out for analysis," he said. "I told them to bump you to the top of the pile, seeing as how you're visiting from out of town. It'll still be a few hours. Have you had lunch yet?"

"No, I came straight here."

"Then let me buy you something. I know a place."

They went to a Mexican restaurant a few miles from the headquarters. The owners seemed to know Unrein, and they gave the Ranger and Ana a good booth near the back, away from the noisiest parts of the restaurant.

"I guess I should have asked you what you like," Unrein said. "This is where me and some of the others like to go for lunch or after our shifts end. Food's good and the prices are right."

"This'll do."

Ana looked at Unrein. He was sandy-haired and had light eyes; a good-looking man. She ordered a beer and it came in a bottle with a wedge of lime in the mouth. Unrein had soda.

"Used to be we could have jumped the border and gotten some good eats that way," Unrein said. "But we don't do that anymore. Julio and Josefina, the owners, they're from Juárez and they don't even go back to visit relatives."

"How far are we from the border?" Ana asked.

"Not far. A mile, maybe."

"What's it like at the port of entry?"

"Always busy. But CBP has the manpower in place. They don't need us. Not like where you are. Presidio, right?"

"That's right."

"Got a partner?"

"No, I work it by myself."

"That's got to suck."

Ana let that one go past her. She had some of her beer. It was cold and clean-tasting, like the lime. She might not have had a beer in the middle of the day before her time in Presidio, but now it didn't seem to matter. For his part, Unrein hardly seemed to notice.

A waiter came and took their order. Ana found herself wondering if he had his documents on him.

"Still, it has to be better than working El Paso," Unrein said to fill the gap. "We've got every problem you can think of: illegal crossers, smuggling, gang violence... you name it. The local police are stretched thin. We do what we can to back them up, keep the overall crime rate down."

"Not too much gang activity in Presidio," Ana said. "We still get crossers, make drug busts, that kind of thing. Just think of it on a small scale. Like *really* small."

"I think I'd take it."

"You want to trade?" Ana said, and they both laughed though it wasn't funny.

"At least Ojinaga's quieter than Juárez. We got five, six killings a day happening on the other side of the bridge. Military and police patrolling the street in armored cars. We look across the river, we see a situation ready to blow. And El Paso's right on the front line. We'll get the worst of it when it comes."

"I'll give you that," Ana said. "Ojinaga's quiet. Everything's quiet."

The food came and they ate. Ana found herself watching Unrein and didn't know why at first. Then she realized it was because it had been a long time since she'd eaten with anyone besides Darren across from her. She was used to his way of sitting, of cutting his food. These were comfortable things, like a settling in, and the thought of it bothered her more than she wanted to admit.

"Tell me about your dead Mexican," Unrein said at last.

"Not much to tell. I found a rape tree out in the back country, those bullet casings you saw and then a corpse. Shot three times in the back. Don't know his name, don't know where he came from. As soon as this is done, I'll wash my hands of the whole thing."

"Rape tree?" Unrein asked.

"I guess you don't see them here, seeing as how you're in the city."

"No. Never heard of it."

Ana played with her food, looking for the words. She finished off the last of her beer. "Sometimes when the *coyotes* come across, they make a stop on the US side of the border. They separate the men from the women and... they rape them. Doesn't matter how old or young they are. And when they're finished, they put the panties in a tree like it's a trophy wall. They leave them there. I find them."

"Jesus. Does this happen a lot?"

Ana took a bite and chewed it for a while before answering. The image of the rape tree came to her mind and she shoved it off to one side, concentrated on the man in front of her instead of the memory. "Not a lot," she said. "But enough."

"Why do they do it?"

"Nobody knows for sure. Maybe they want to put a scare into the crossers. Maybe they just like doing it. I don't know. But I know I don't like finding them."

"Who would?"

She pushed her plate away. Her appetite had fled her.

"I guess we're not the only ones with problems," Unrein said.

"Like I said, if you want to trade, I'll be happy to."

"I can't imagine coming across something like that. And as a woman...." Unrein let it trail off.

"I like to think it'd shake a man, too."

"No doubt."

Ana signaled for the waiter and ordered a second beer, not caring what Unrein's thoughts about it might be. There was no reason for her to get behind a wheel, and two beers weren't enough to buzz her anyway. "Let's talk about something else," she said.

"Okay. How long 'til someone spells you out there in Presidio?"

"I don't know. It's been about two years, and they haven't said anything about rotating me out. I just take it one day at a time. Keep watch over what they tell me to watch and help round up bodies from time to time. Living and dead."

"The CBP guys work with you all right?"

Ana thought of Darren. "We get along. They know why I'm there."

"'One riot, one Ranger,'" Unrein said.

"I'd take a riot out there any day," Ana said. "Riots aren't boring."

They finished their lunch, and Ana left half of her second beer in the bottle. Unrein paid the tab — a courtesy of Company E, he said — and drove her back to the headquarters. Once there, Ana staked out a position on a long bench in the hallway outside Unrein's office and let herself fall into a waiting trance, looking neither left nor right, just letting the drone of activity lull her like the sound of cicadas in the brush.

She spent hours that way, thinking of nothing and scarcely moving a muscle. Unrein came out once to make sure she didn't need anything, maybe a cup of coffee, but she declined. Instead, she waited, and the time ticked slowly past.

Ana was almost completely detached when Unrein appeared again. He had a folder in his hand, and Claude Bowder's pistol and the evidence in the other. Someone had bagged Bowder's gun. He said something to her. "What?" she said.

"I said we've got your report for you. Sorry it took so long."

"That's all right."

"Come on in and we'll have a look."

They went into Unrein's office and sat at his desk. Ana opened the folder to find three sheets of thin paper and a couple of photocopies, images of the shell casings blown up and marked with pen, the same with the slug and its pristine counterpart, fired into a water tank in a ballistics lab. It did not take more than a few seconds to skim the report and find out what it all meant.

"So?" Unrein asked.

"Not a match," Ana said.

"Is that what you figured?"

Ana nodded. "I never had any doubt."

"Well, now somebody in Presidio gets to sleep a little easier."

Ana put the report away and offered her hand to Unrein across the desk. "I appreciate everything you did."

"Any time. Whatever you need."

"What I need now is to get back on the road so I can get these to the right people first thing tomorrow morning."

"You mean you don't want to stay over in beautiful downtown El Paso? You can hear the gunfire in Juárez in the night."

Ana smiled. "I think I'll pass."

"Your loss."

Unrein saw her to the door, and then she was on her way. She would catch the last few hours of sun on the way back to Presidio, but it would be dark by the time she got home.

Home. There was that word again. She didn't like it.

22

It was after ten, but when Ana stopped by the CBP station there were still agents on duty. No one bothered her while she ran off copies of the forensic report, or even said goodbye when she left. She got home a few minutes past eleven and brought Claude Bowder's gun inside with her. When she woke in the morning, it was waiting for her on the kitchen table, wrapped in plastic, ready to go home.

As she drove to Bowder's place, she thought a little about El Paso. They wouldn't make a production over one man's gun or one dead Mexican; they had too much on their minds. A cut fence wouldn't send them scrambling across dry country looking for phantom crossers. They had real problems, real crimes, with Ciudad Juárez waiting on the other side of the border like a malignant growth eager to expand across the river. But they did not have rape trees. That was something.

Both the Bowders' trucks were parked in front of the house today, and before Ana could even get out of hers, Elaine Bowder was out the front door and shouting. Claude Bowder came out behind his wife.

"Ranger! How dare you accuse my husband of gunning down some wetback? Is that what it's come to now? Treating ranchers like criminals because some Mexican kills another Mexican on his land? I'm asking you, Ranger!"

Ana put up her hands to ward Mrs. Bowder off. "Nobody's accusing anybody of anything. And here's Mr. Bowder's gun, just like I promised."

Claude Bowder took the weapon and turned it over in his hands inside the plastic bag. For the moment his wife was quiet and he grunted, "All right."

"Don't you think you ought to apologize for putting Claude through that?" Mrs. Bowder asked.

"Mr. Bowder, I apologize for any offense. I'm just doing my job."

"Your *job* is stopping those wetbacks from coming across the river!" Mrs. Bowder exclaimed.

"And to make sure no one's breaking the laws of the state of Texas," Ana replied. "Murder is a crime, even if it is a Mexican who got shot."

"Serves them right for coming across anyhow," Mrs. Bowder said, though she seemed to have lost some steam.

"The results of the tests were definitive," Ana told Bowder. "Your gun was *not* the same one used to kill our dead Mexican."

"I told you, didn't I?" Bowder asked.

"And I told you I didn't believe it, either. So let's all calm down."

"I *am* calm," Mrs. Bowder said.

"Okay."

"Are you going to the meeting?" Mrs. Bowder asked. "Are you going to explain to everyone that Claude was a suspect in a shooting? They'll want to know."

"When's the meeting again?"

"Tomorrow night."

"I'll be there. And he was never a suspect, Mrs. Bowder."

"Same difference."

"And maybe this will be a good thing," Ana said. "Everybody needs to make sure they aren't rushing to pull the trigger on any crossers that might come through their property."

"Or you'll throw them in jail."

"That's right, we will."

"Well, I'm going to be shut of it," Bowder said. "I got my gun back, the wetback's body is headed off to Mexico where it belongs, and things can go back to normal. As normal as they get, anyway. Seems like things are going backwards sometimes."

"I'm really sorry, Mr. Bowder," Ana said. "If there's anything I can do—"

"Just keep those goddamned wetbacks off my property! It's bad enough when they aren't shooting each other to death."

"I'll do what I can."

"See that you do. And see you tomorrow night. We're meeting at the Gaughan place."

"I remember."

Bowder put a hand on his wife's shoulder. Reluctantly, the woman turned away, as if she had more words for Ana, but could not give shape to them just yet. Ana took a deep breath and let it out slowly. Finally she went back to her truck.

Her next stop was the Mexican consulate. She thought to call ahead, or just fax the test report over, but she drove instead. It was still early when she parked in front of the building and went inside.

Jorge Vargas saw her immediately. Ana held the folder with the reports inside in front of her instead of offering a handshake. Vargas didn't seem to mind. He invited her in.

Ana waited while he examined the report. When he was finished, he closed the folder and put it on his blotter. "Well," he said, "it seems as though you were right about the culprit. Whoever he was, he was not this man, Sr. Bowder."

"I hope this can be the end of it," Ana said.

Vargas nodded quickly. "Of course, of course. As I said to you before, this was simply something my superiors in Mexico City had to ask. To be certain. I know you understand this."

"I understand just fine. Were you able to identify him on your end?"

"I don't know. That information wasn't passed to me. And I doubt it will be. He was not a legal visitor to the United States or an immigrant, so this office's interaction with him would be nil."

"So I guess I'll never know," Ana said.

"It is important to you?"

"He died on American soil. He ought to at least have a name."

"He'll get one. And if it matters, I will find out. Just for you."

"Thanks, but don't put yourself out."

"Consider it a favor from me to you."

Ana stood up. "I have to go."

"You can't stay a while?"

"No, I have work to do. I just wanted to make sure you got that report straight from me. Consider that a favor from me to you."

"I will. And I thank you again."

They parted as they always did, with phantom kisses and well-wishes. Ana left the office feeling lighter now that the deed was done. The dead Mexican was no longer her concern

in any way. She could get back to doing what she was tasked
to do. At least until the next body appeared.

23

The next evening she drove to the Gaughan place, a medium-sized spread given over to raising sheep and goats. The Gaughans had a windmill near their house that pumped a trickle of water from deep beneath the earth into a broad-mouthed concrete reservoir in their back yard. Ana thought that if they added a silo, it would be a perfect picture.

There were a dozen trucks scattered in front of the Gaughans' house and a pair of official vehicles, one from the Sheriff's Department and another from Border Patrol. Ana remembered that Darren had mentioned something about this month's meeting, and she found herself dreading seeing him.

The scent of barbecue carried over the roof of the house from the back yard. A big shade tree grew there, fed partly by water from the reservoir. A mesquite grill had been set up and a long wooden picnic table around which a collection of ranchers, mostly older folks with grayed hair, ate brisket, sausage and burgers. Ana saw Darren standing with Matthew Millwood from the Sheriff's office, eating a burger off a paper plate. Both of them were wearing ballistic vests, Darren's emblazoned with the words BORDER PATROL. When Darren looked at her, she avoided his gaze.

To a one the ranchers were dressed in camouflage gear, both men and women alike. They also wore ball-caps or armbands marked with a yellow outline of Texas and the words *West Texas Border Volunteers*. There were no weapons on display, but Ana knew that once they were away from the police, most of these people would arm themselves.

"Here comes the Ranger now!" called someone and there were hellos all around. Ana accepted a hamburger that was thrust into her hands. She saw Claude Bowder approaching her with an open bottle of RC Cola. He offered it to her. She took it, then looked for a place to put everything down.

The atmosphere was familial and there was plenty of talk. Ana spotted Mrs. Bowder across the table, looking at her reproachfully. Ana found somewhere else to look. For his part, Claude Bowder seemed unconcerned by her presence. He went to a spot by the trunk of the shade tree, this time with a thick ring-binder in his hands. When he found his place, the talk began to die down.

"I'd like to call to order this meeting of the West Texas Border Volunteers!" Bowder said. "All right, everybody, settle down."

The last voices died. Ana ate her burger though she didn't want it.

"We all know it's been a busy month," Bowder said. "Some wetbacks got caught out at Bill Sheedy's place, and you know about the Mexican that got himself shot on my property."

At this last, Bowder looked directly at Ana. She thought he was about to say something about it, but he moved on instead.

"The thing is, we've got to keep a sharp eye out because they're getting more daring. They caught those wetbacks at the Sheedys' in broad daylight. And who knows what happened to the one who killed the other on my spread. For all we know, he's planning to cross tonight.

"We have Ranger Torres with us again tonight, and Agent Sabado from Border Patrol, and Deputy Millwood. If you see anything on watch, it's them you call and them you let handle the situation. We don't need anyone catching a bullet.

"So in a minute I'm going to call out assignments. We're going to spread out over three properties tonight: mine, the Sheedys' and the Esteps'."

Bowder began to read from his binder. The Volunteers had a complicated map that stretched over the bulk of properties along the Rio Grande, broken out by "sectors" and given letters and numbers in a system Ana had never bothered to learn. That was their concern, and not the authorities'. It was the ranchers who would sit on lawn chairs or in deer blinds watching for any sign of illegal crossers. In the unlikely event that they did, they would call the uniforms in to intercept.

"How's the burger?" Darren spoke into her ear over her shoulder, and Ana flinched despite herself. He laughed and put a hand on her arm. "What, did I scare you?"

"No, you didn't scare me," Ana lied.

"You're not wearing your vest tonight. You know they like it when we come all kitted out."

"I decided to be comfortable instead."

"Well, you look good."

Ana looked away. "Not here."

"I just said you looked good, that's all."

"Not here."

"Yes, ma'am," Darren said, and he walked away.

When the assignments were done, the ranchers began to break up and head for their vehicles. Bowder lingered. "Where are you going to be?" he asked Ana.

"Close by. I'll stay on the radio so anyone can flag me if they need to."

"I'm going to carry that .45 you took from me. You aren't going to arrest me if I don't lock it up in a gun case before I get to my sector, are you?"

"No."

"Good. See you later, Ranger."

Ana, Darren and Millwood waited until all the ranchers were on their way before they went to their own trucks. They would park, strung out, along the highway that bordered the ranch land. They would keep in touch by radio, listening to the crosstalk between ranchers. These vigils lasted five or six hours, usually long enough for someone to grow cold and tired and bored. The infection would spread, and then it would all be over for another month.

"See you," Millwood said to Ana and Darren and climbed behind the wheel. He turned around in the dust and headed out. Sheriff Sellner offered overtime to any deputy willing to ride herd on the West Texas Border Volunteers.

"So," Darren said, "can we talk now?"

"We need to get going," Ana said.

"I'd really like to talk it out now."

Ana stopped on her way to her truck and turned on Darren. "What do you want to talk about? The same thing as before? Because I told you how I feel."

"You told me we could talk it out."

"Well, I was wrong. There's nothing to talk about."

"So you're saying it's over?"

"I'm saying... I'm saying maybe it's time to take a step back. It's clear that we're looking for different things, and that's not going to get any better the longer we keep this up."

Darren took a step toward Ana, but something in her look made him stop. "I'm not going to apologize for loving you," he said.

"Then don't. But don't ask me to love you back."

Ana saw fleeting whispers of emotion cross Darren's face. He opened his mouth to say something, closed it and worked the muscle in his jaw. When he was done, he stepped back. "Okay," he said.

"Just give it some time."

"Okay."

"Let's do this."

Ana went to her truck and Darren to his. She led him off the property and, after a few minutes of driving, he pulled around her and accelerated into the gathering darkness. His taillights disappeared.

She drove until she was roughly in the center of things and pulled over to the side of the road. Her radio was on and she tuned it to the channel the Volunteers used. Already there was talk going back and forth: reports on nothing from the back country. Ana killed the engine, put out her headlights and sat in the dark just listening.

After a little while the moon was up, almost full, casting ghost light on the surrounding ground. The Volunteers had grown quieter over time as they settled into their positions, watching through binoculars and night-vision scopes and all the other detection devices they had at their disposal. This ritual assured them somehow, though it was invariably fruitless.

It was stuffy in the truck's cab. Ana opened the window to let the cool night air in. The hairs on her neck prickled from the chill. It wasn't cold enough for her to see her breath, but it was enough to risk exposure if a person went out unprepared.

The change in temperature from day to night was the worst thing about this country, Ana thought.

Hours passed. The radio squelched. "This is Claude over in section 2A," the speakers announced.

"What you got, Claude?" asked someone.

"Not sure yet. Might be some lights and movement over here. I'm waiting to know for sure. Ranger, are you on the line?"

Ana unhooked the mike from the dash. "I'm here."

"I'm out a ways, back in that patch where you were looking that day you found the Mexican. I might have something."

Ana tensed in the darkness. "Darren, Millwood, you hearing this?"

"I'm listening," Darren said over the line. Millwood chimed in after him.

There was quiet except for the low hiss of static from the radio. After what seemed like a long time, Bowder came on again: "We definitely have movement. I saw a light. They're a ways out right now, but they're coming straight toward me."

"Understood," Ana said. "I'm rolling."

"I'm on my way," Darren echoed.

Ana started up the truck and wheeled it around on the tarmac, headed back the way she'd come. The demarcations between properties were familiar enough to her now that she knew them even in the dark, without signage. She was just minutes away from the gate to Bowder's back forty. After she arrived there, she looked back up the road and saw no headlights coming yet.

Through the gate and on the gravel track, she drove as quickly as she dared. There were white-tail deer out here and other good-sized animals that could jump out into the way of a fast-moving truck and make a mess. She called Bowder back. "You have GPS coordinates?" she asked.

Bowder gave her the coordinates, and she punched them in one-handed as she drove. He was right: he was less than a half-mile from where she found the rape tree and the dead Mexican.

"Can you see them still?"

"They're coming. Slowly but surely. How long are you going to take getting here?"

"I'm moving as fast as I can. Going off-road."

The truck jounced as Ana took it off the gravel and into rough country. There were trees and brush, and she dodged them as they cropped up in her headlights. She remembered that it got especially rutted the farther south she went, with treacherous gullies that could bottom out a vehicle, even one with four-wheel drive. But the crossers Bowder saw were on foot, and coming on more slowly than she could go.

"Darren, you out there?"

"I'm on the property a little ways behind you. I can't see your lights."

"I'm out here."

"I'm coming. Millwood, where are you?"

"Almost there. I missed the gate, I think."

"Well, hurry it up."

Ana was a diamond in the center of the GPS display. Bowder was a dot crawling little by little toward her. Her truck hit some deep ruts, and once she thought she was going to be stuck, but she kept on going. It was easier crossing this kind of country on horseback.

Eventually the trees began to thin out, and if it wasn't easier going, at least she was not called upon to weave back and forth through catching brush and scrabbling limbs. The rocky land was up ahead. Soon she would have to kill her lights or risk giving herself away to the crossers headed directly for her. She could drive by moon- and starlight, but it would not be easy.

"I'm about two miles out," she said at long last and doused her headlights. The glow of her dash reflected against the inside of the windshield, but she looked past it at the silvered landscape. Her tires were grinding little rocks and hauling up bigger ones. The truck's suspension was stiff and Ana felt every jarring impact as she drove. "Darren, are you still coming?"

"Still. Don't worry about me."

At last she was close enough to see a black patch on the back of a short ridge. A flashlight turned toward her and swung like a lamp. Bowder signaling her. She let the truck ease to a stop in the lee of the ridge and killed the engine. When she got out, she saw Bowder and his wife together at their makeshift watch station: folding chairs, blankets and a tripod-mounted night-vision scope. Bowder had a rifle and he came down to meet her.

"You're just in time. They're less than a mile off now, I figure."

"How many bodies?"

"I can't tell. Maybe ten or fifteen."

"Let me see."

Bowder let Ana take his place in his chair. She peered through the scope at a green-tinted landscape. It was barren and looked like the surface of the Moon. She spotted the lone mesquite tree and, beyond it, the movement of people in a group.

They were moving tightly together and fairly swiftly. Ana saw the glow of a flashlight turned toward the ground and then it switched off. An experienced *coyote* would only use the light now and again to confirm the way, but not enough to attract attention, even out here, where there should have been no one to see.

"You going to be able to handle all of them, Ranger?" Elaine Bowder asked.

"I won't have to do it alone. Darren's on his way."

"I can back you up," Claude Bowder said, and he brandished his rifle. He had the Colt pistol, too.

"You've done enough. There's not going to be any shooting tonight."

"What if they're armed?"

"We'll try to take them without it coming to that."

Ana watched the group of crossers come on steadily until, finally, she heard the sound of Darren's engine approaching. She left Bowder's scope and went down to meet Darren.

"Got about a dozen or more," Ana said. "I figure we come at them from two sides, try to contain any runners."

"You want to wait for Millwood?"

"Any idea where he is?"

"I think he got turned around again. I put in a call for backup, but it'll be a while before they get here. We can get a bird in the air if we have to."

"Then it's just you and me."

"All right. Let me get my shotgun."

Ana checked her belt. She had a pistol, ammunition, a flashlight and a half dozen plastic cuffs. Her hands shook a little, but she wasn't sure if was from the chill or the adrenaline.

Darren came back with his shotgun. It had a tactical light on the barrel that he switched on and off to test. "All right," he said.

"They're turning," Bowder announced under his breath. "Coming right at us."

"Darren?"

"I'm ready when you are."

"Then let's go."

They set off together across the moonlit ground. Ana was aware that they would be visible before long, but she hoped for surprise nonetheless. No one could expect the authorities to strike out here, in the dark. And not alone. They would expect horses or ATVs or trucks and a helicopter, too. Ana wished she had all those things.

Every time her boot scraped on a rock or she kicked over a loose pebble, it sounded like a hundred men marching through, and Ana flinched. She searched the land ahead for a sign, listened for a sound. When she saw the flashlight come on again, she saw the group was closer to her than she originally thought.

Darren was somewhere off to her left, creeping up the same way. Ana could see all of them now, marching resolutely along, and all of them carrying bulky packs. She drew her weapon with her right hand and her flashlight with her left. There it was: that tremor again.

They could not coordinate without giving themselves away. Ana advanced until she was just ten or fifteen yards ahead of the group, still invisible to them, and then she switched on her flashlight and rushed forward. "Texas Rangers! *¡Manos arriba!*"

She was aware of Darren's light coming on some distance away, of him yelling in Spanish for the crossers to put their hands up, *up!* They closed on the group fast. A commotion erupted among the crossers, a torrent of panicked Spanish.

The man with the flashlight turned its beam on Ana, and then she heard the gunshot.

"Gun! Gun!" Darren shouted.

The muzzle flash was like a spot of orange light blinking at her. A bullet whined off a rock to her right, and then suddenly she was knocked back sharply by a blow in the side. All the wind went out of her. More gunshots, but she was tilting over. The pistol in her hand went off, though she didn't recall pulling the trigger. Someone screamed.

Something buzzed past her ear. Another shot. She fired again, though her knee was giving away. The crossers were falling to the ground as one, singling out the man with the flashlight who did not stop shooting.

Darren's shotgun roared, and the flashlight went spinning into the air. Ana fell hard on her elbow, her pistol slipping from her grasp. The pressure on her chest was enormous and suffused with pain.

"Ana! Ana!"

"I'm all right," Ana whispered. She tasted salt.

Darren was over her now as she flopped onto her back. He spoke into the microphone tagged to his shoulder, screaming *officer down!* again and again. Ana could not take a deep breath, or any breath at all. The stars flickered.

"Keep your eyes open," Darren told her. He was pressing on her chest, and she was aware of the hot wetness under his hands. "Do you hear me? Just stay conscious. People are coming."

Ana turned her head. She could see the crossers cowering on the ground, and hear them lamenting in Spanish she couldn't understand. Even Darren wasn't making sense, though he was still talking to her. The words were warped, broken. God, she was in *pain.*

She saw one crosser laying in the dirt, his boot-toes pointed toward the sky. She knew he was dead.

Darren kept shouting at her, Ana looked up into his face and watched it dissolve into black.

24

"Darren?" she asked.

It was bright because the sun was coming through the window and casting gold onto her bed. Ana was warm beneath the sheets, though the air was crisp and cold. She saw the ceiling, the fluorescent lights.

"Darren's not here," said someone. "It's me, Julio."

Ana turned her head and found her neck was stiff and painful. Julio Stender was by her bed, dressed in uniform with his hat in his hands. The door to the room was open and a nurse walked by. When she breathed deeply, she felt something stiff and constricting over her right side beneath her gown. There were tubes running into the back of her left hand.

"Stender?"

"We've been taking shifts, all of us from the station. You missed Darren. He was here yesterday."

"Where am I?"

"The hospital in Alpine."

Ana tried to lift herself up, but fresh shocks passed through her side and she relented. Stender reached out a hand, but didn't touch her. She settled back into the bed.

"You caught a bullet in the lung," Stender said. "We had to carry you out of there so you could be airlifted. You lost a lot of blood. We thought... we thought maybe you weren't going to make it."

"How long have I been here?"

"A week or so. They've had you sedated most of the time."

Ana touched herself on her right side, gently, feeling the bandaging there. She didn't press hard. She tried thinking of the moment she was shot, but the images were mixed up, hard to follow, and gave her a headache.

"You want something to drink?"

"Sure."

Stender went away for a while, and Ana looked around her room. It was small and spare, with just one chair for a visitor. There was not even a telephone. She was attached to monitors, but they were all muted, and she could not read them, anyway. No balloons or flowers decorated the place, but at any rate they wouldn't have belonged. This was a sterile, functional space and in a way it reminded her of her house in Presidio. When she was gone from it, it would be as though she had never been there.

When he returned, he had a paper cup with water and ice. "They said this was okay," he said. He helped Ana lift her head to drink. Ana was thirstier than she realized and drained the cup.

"More?" she asked.

"I'll be right back."

Ana looked out the window, but she couldn't see anything besides pale blue sky and the sun. She waited until Stender came back and drank some more.

"They're going to check on you soon," he said.

"Tell me what happened."

"Darren ought to be the one, because he was there."

"He's not here now. Tell me."

"Well, when you came up on all those bodies, the *coyote* opened fire on you. Just like that, no warning. He tagged you, but you got him! Darren says he doesn't know how, but you clipped him right in the chest. Then Darren blew him away."

"How is Darren?"

"He's fine. He's been worried about you. We all have. The governor sent somebody down special to look into things. I'm sure he'll come by, too. Everybody's going to want to come by now that you're awake."

"That's nice," Ana said.

"I didn't tell you the best part."

"What's that?"

"The gun that shot you, they sent it to Austin to have forensics take a run at it. They matched it to the gun that killed that dead Mexican. He's the one! You got the guy!"

Ana closed her eyes. If she concentrated, she could still feel pain in her bound side, though it was deep and muted by drugs. She stayed quiet for so long that she heard Stender take a seat in the chair near her bed. Then she opened her eyes. "I'm not asleep," she said.

"I wasn't sure."

"I want you to tell everybody thank you. I really appreciate it."

"I'll tell them."

"Did the doctors say how long I'll be like this?"

"They didn't say anything to me. I'm sure they'll tell you soon."

Ana nodded. She realized that she had things to say, but no one to say them to. Stender was a nice enough man, but he wasn't the one she wanted to see now. "See if you... see if you can get Darren to come out and visit," she said.

"I will. He'll want to. He carried you all the way to his truck and drove you out of there."

"Tell him... I want to see him."

"Of course."

That was all she was willing to share with Stender. If she could have rolled over and turned her back to the man, she would have. Everyone could come visit her and wish good things for her and congratulate her or whatever they wanted to do. She knew what she wanted to do now.

PART TWO
LUIS

1

Luis González awoke to the sound of scratching. He opened his eyes and without moving his head looked around the room. Soft light filtered through the bedroom window. The clock on his bedside table ticked. Everything was as it had been when he turned in for the night.

The scratching came again. Luis levered himself up and listened. He wore a t-shirt and his arms were chill in the room. The window was half-open and the night air came in freely. By noon it would be different, the room would become stuffy and overheated, but for now it was almost cold.

He put the sheets and blanket back and swung out of bed, his bare feet on the concrete floor. He made the quick walk to the wardrobe across the room and put on a plaid robe. He had no slippers.

The house was small and filled with things. Pictures adorned the walls and there was too much furniture for the space. Most of it had belonged to his parents and, when his mother died, there was nowhere to put it all, and he could not bear to throw any of it away. Luis went down a short hallway to the kitchen as the scratching began anew.

He opened the back door and confronted the dog on the other side of a screen door. The dog was white with large brown spots and was dirty from sleeping on the ground. The dog lifted a paw to scratch again.

"Good morning, *señor*," Luis said. "Is there something I can do for you?"

Other dogs began to gather until there were nearly a dozen collected before the door. They were different shapes and sizes and all mutts. They assembled themselves behind the white-and-brown dog, expectant.

"May I have coffee first?" Luis asked.

The dogs were mute. He closed the door.

Luis put on a pot to boil. He went to an open-faced pantry where rows of dog food cans organized themselves beneath shelves of human food. A large bag of dry kibble sat to one side with a long-handled scoop in it.

The dog food bowls were large and set to one side of the sink where he had put them the night before. There were six altogether. He arranged them on the little kitchen table with its checkered tablecloth, then started opening cans from the pantry.

When each bowl had been filled, he scooped generous portions of kibble into them before mixing everything together with his hands. There was renewed scratching at the door.

"I'll be there soon enough!" Luis called.

He washed his hands in the sink and dried them. When he opened the back door, the dogs were all still there. He brought out the bowls, three balanced on one arm. The dogs swirled around him, tails up and wagging.

The area behind the house was shaded with a broad awning bleached through by the sun. A few plastic chairs were scattered about and there was a grill, though it was rarely used.

Luis put the first three bowls down and the dogs pressed in. "No fighting," he admonished them. "There's more coming."

He fetched out the last three bowls and put them away from the first. The pack split into two groups, each jockeying for a better position, but they obeyed him and there was no growling or snapping.

The dogs were fed twice a day. Luis went through pounds of kibble seeing to their needs. It was his only outstanding expense. As for himself, he ate little. Like his dogs, he was lean.

They all had names, of course. He could not simply refer to them as *perro* and get away with it. He played with them and ran with them, and in the evenings, before supper, he brought out a tennis racquet and some ratty old balls and rocketed them out toward the wilderness. The dogs chased the balls as a pack, but they fell into line behind whichever got his jaws around the prize first.

His dogs were all male. When a female tried to join the pack, he saw to it that she found a home elsewhere. He did not want puppies. That would complicate things too much for him and his friends. They were far enough outside of town that his dogs didn't stray looking for females in heat. Instead, they stayed close to the house, lounging in the shade beneath the awning, or chasing down the odd rabbit that risked coming near. Luis saw a deer once, when he came out to feed his dogs, but the pack ran it off.

He stayed a little while to watch them eat, but the chill forced him inside. His pot was boiling. He made instant coffee and while he drank it, he made eggs and browned chorizo for his own breakfast. The dogs were pushing the empty bowls around outside by the time he sat down to eat. They would lick until there wasn't even the smell of food left.

A shower in lukewarm water followed and he took time to shave. He wore a goatee and prided himself on keeping it clean. Looking at himself in the mirror, he saw more gray hairs joining the many others that had already taken root. He was forty-two.

He dressed in jeans and sneakers and a short-sleeved shirt with buttons that he ironed the night before. When he went outside again, the sun was fully above the horizon and the air was not so cool. He gathered up the empty bowls while the dogs watched expectantly, as if today was the day he would change his mind and serve them a second helping.

The bowls he washed in the kitchen sink, and then he set them aside to dry. He was still early and there was no rush. Outside again, he saw the dogs were already taking up familiar positions around the back of the house, staring off at nothing, but always testing the air with their noses.

Luis liked the view from his back door. He got to see the sun rise over the tree-spotted landscape and turn the dirt gold and red. There were no other buildings to the east of him except an old shed that he barely used, so it was easy to imagine that he was the last man on Earth. Just him and his dogs.

"Working time," he told the dogs. He locked the back door, petted Papi and Amigo on the heads when they came close and walked around to the front of the house where his old pickup truck sat in the square shadow of the house.

It was more than a mile from his place to the nearest house. Ojinaga lay farther still to the west, close enough that he could see the lights at night, but far enough away that it was invisible by day. The drive took him nearly half an hour.

Behind the wheel, he cranked the engine and negotiated the gravel drive. None of the dogs came around to watch him go. They knew he would be back.

2

Ojinaga was not a large town. In all there were fewer than twenty thousand people living there, which suited Luis well enough. He had grown up here, and very little had changed over the years. More lights, a few more houses, more brand-name stores, but at heart it was a farming town, a ranching town and if all went well, it would remain so.

From time to time there was talk that Ojinaga could become a larger through-way into the United States. For years out of mind the Puente Ojinaga had served as a link to Presidio and Texas to the north. Not a big bridge and not a bustling port of entry. This, too, was good.

Most of what farmers produced in Ojinaga sold south of the border, not like the industrial farms that did their business primarily with the States. Those trucks came rumbling along the Bulevar Libre Comercio from the south, day and night, though thankfully never in numbers.

Once Luis had been to Nuevo Laredo and he saw all the trucks there. He did not want that for his home. Nor did he want the *maquiladoras*, the factories that manufactured goods for American buyers, to proliferate. So far there were only two, and they did not spew pollution. One of them made prefabricated houses.

He did not have time to think about these things anymore. He passed a group of shops and pulled around the block to park behind them. Then he let himself into one through the back door. The metal was rusted in the pattern of an exploding star.

The storage room at the back of the store was quiet and dark. Luis found the switch panel by feel and put on the lights. He did not keep much stock back here, so the wooden shelves were mostly empty.

Luis preferred to keep as much product in the front of the store as possible and the shelves there were piled high. He walked down an aisle that had shoes on one side and energy drinks and protein bars on the other. There was camping equipment and batteries and backpacks. He even carried CamelBak water systems, though these were high-priced and did not sell well. There were t-shirts and windbreakers and lined jackets, too. At the register he had displays of caffeine pills and energy shots.

The safe was behind the counter, built into the floor. Luis brought out the cash drawer and counted it out of habit. His bank was on the drive home and he dropped off the deposit every night after closing. He put the drawer in the cash register.

After he unlocked the front door, he also unlocked the shutter that closed it in. Then he went out on the street and unlocked the three other shutters that secured his display windows. When that was done, he cranked open the short awning that spanned the front of the store. At the height of the day, a person could be cool under there.

He flipped the sign in the door from CLOSED to OPEN, and then he went outside. There was no one on the walk in either direction. He went to the next shop, where there was the strong smell of coffee coming through the open door.

Tomás Hernandez was behind the counter of the little convenience store, restocking cigarettes into an overhead hopper. The old man smiled at Luis when he came through the door. "*Buenos días*," Hernandez said. "How is the Dog Man this morning?"

"Good. *¿Y tú?*"

"I will survive."

"The papers here?"

"Of course they are. They always are."

Luis took a copy of the *Ojinaga Hoy* from a wire rack and brought it to the counter. It was a thin paper, barely long enough to read in twenty minutes, but it was a habit Luis had kept for many years.

"You should subscribe," Hernandez said when he took Luis' money.

"Then I wouldn't be able to see you every morning."

"Is my company that good?"

"It's good enough," Luis said. "Thank you for the paper."

"*De nada.* What do you have planned for today?"

"The same as every day: sell some things, make some money. You?"

"I think I'll do that, too. Yesterday was terrible."

"It's the heat. People don't like to come out and shop."

Hernandez shrugged. "I don't mind the heat. It's better than being cold. People should head south a thousand miles if they want to feel real heat."

"Then who would we sell to?"

"You'll always have customers."

"Maybe."

"Maybe nothing. Everyone comes to see the Dog Man."

Luis waved away the suggestion with his newspaper. "You act like I'm famous."

"You are, don't you know?"

"Oh, never mind, old man. I have to get back. See you tomorrow."

"Tomorrow, Dog Man."

The sidewalks were still deserted when Luis went back to his store. A truck carrying a half-dozen workers in the bed crept by, headed somewhere Luis could not know.

He read the newspaper from front to back, including all the advertisements. When he was done, he went to the front windows and looked out at the empty street. Across the road, a hairdresser's was opening for the day, and beside that the lights had gone on inside a dentist's office.

Luis sighed, and then he read the newspaper again.

3

It was half past eleven before he saw his first customers. They came hesitantly up the sidewalk, slowing when they reached the far end of the front windows to look inside. The man was in his early twenties, with a wispy mustache, and the girl he was with seemed just as young. They walked close together, as if they were afraid to let any light fall between them.

Luis let them come on slowly, watching them from behind the counter as they advanced along the displays to the entrance. The two of them paused at the open door, and then they came in together, arm in arm.

"*Hola,*" Luis said and he offered them a smile. "*Bienvenido.*"

The young man nodded stiffly. "*Hola, señor.*"

"Feel free to look around," Luis told the man and the girl. "If you need anything, come talk to me. I'm Luis."

They turned away from Luis and proceeded down the first aisle. Luis heard them whispering to each other, and from time to time they checked the price tags on items they found. They did not hurry, and once in a while they both cast glances over their shoulders at Luis behind the counter.

Once a long time ago, Luis would have figured them for shoplifters, but by now he knew their type. They were not from Ojinaga — that much he could guess without knowing anything about them — and they were unsure of their place in the scheme of things. They didn't know whether Luis would bark or bite, though he planned on doing neither.

He let them browse and busied himself straightening up the things around the register though they didn't need it. They would react badly if he had his eyes on them all the time, and he wanted them to feel at home. When they were ready, they would come to him.

They looked around the store for fifteen minutes and sometimes they were brave enough to take something off the shelf and examine it before putting it back. Luis was aware of them drawing nearer by inches until, finally, the young man stood before him at the register, empty-handed. "*Perdóneme, señor*," he said.

Luis looked up as if he was pleasantly surprised to see the young man there. "There's no need to call me *señor*," he said. "My name is Luis."

"Excuse me... Luis. My wife and I have some questions."

"I'm here to help."

The young man gathered his wife up until they were fused at the hip again. Luis revised his estimate of their ages downward. They were probably only nineteen. "We... we're going to make the crossing. What will we need?"

Luis nodded. "You came to the right place."

"That's what we heard."

Luis came out from behind the counter. He was not a tall man, and the young man was an inch or two larger, but he stood with his shoulders stooped. Luis wanted to grab him and straighten him out. *Stand up, man!* He looked the couple up and down, at their windbreaker jackets and jeans. They looked as though they hadn't changed clothes in days, and maybe they hadn't.

"What are your names?" Luis asked.

"I am Joaquín. This is Sofia."

"Joaquín, Sofia, I'm glad to meet you."

Luis offered his hand to them. First Joaquín shook it, then Sofia. They seemed almost afraid to grip too tightly.

"The first thing you need to have are shoes," Luis said. "Let me see your soles."

They turned up their shoes one at a time and Luis examined the tread. He also looked at the tops of the shoes for holes or tears. "Will we need new ones?" Joaquín asked.

"No, I think you'll do all right. They aren't new shoes and they aren't too old. To be truthful, new shoes are more trouble than they are worth. You can get blisters, and the deep tread leaves better tracks for the Americans to follow. These are the clothes you'll be wearing?"

"Yes."

"The windbreakers are warm enough at night?"

"If we keep moving, yes. They get cold when we try to sleep."

"You won't have any time for sleeping," Luis said. "Good enough. You are going with a *coyote*?"

Joaquín nodded. "Of course. We're going with—"

"Don't tell me. I don't want to know."

"Why not?"

"Because it's none of my business who you deal with. My concern is that you get across safely and, once you are there, that all goes well. You have packs?"

"What we brought with us from Torreón."

"What are you carrying?"

"A few things. Mementos. A change of clothes."

"Only one?"

"That's all we had room for."

"Don't worry, you did right. Sometimes people try to bring too much with them. You want only what you can fit in one backpack. And if you have to go into the water, you'll need those extra clothes."

"They say there will be boats."

Boats. If these two were lucky, there would be a rubber raft or two, heavily overloaded with crossers, and at worst, a collection of inner tubes. In the latter case, they would be soaked to the bone and likely all their things along with them. Hiking the land on the other side of the border in sopping clothes was not something Luis would want for himself.

"Are you going at night?"

"Yes."

"Then you will want something to keep you awake. Some caffeine pills or a drink. Adrenaline will do much for you when you make the crossing, but you'll need more than that when you're hiking to the highway afterward. I can sell you some. You'll also want to bring water. Even a sports bottle will do. People still sweat in the nighttime when they walk a long while. You'll want something to wash your mouth out, at least."

Luis guided them to the appropriate places in the store. They came to the counter with just a few things, only a few hundred pesos worth of merchandise. He could have sold them more, things they would have no use for, but this was enough. He put their purchases in a paper bag.

"Thank you, *señor*," Joaquín said.

"What did I tell you about that *señor* business? It is Luis."

"May I ask another question?"

"You can ask me all the questions you like."

"They said that you used to take people across the border."

"Yes, that's true."

"But you don't do that anymore?"

"No, I don't. I run this store now. For people like you."

Sofia spoke up for the first time: "Will we make it?"

"That depends on your *coyote*. And some luck. The Americans are very good at what they do, but they can't catch everyone. The odds are good."

"Thank you again, Luis," Sofia said.

"You're welcome. Where do you want to go when you get there?"

"Baltimore, Maryland," Joaquín said. "We have relatives there who can find us work."

"That's a long way to go."

"The hardest part is at the beginning."

"This is true. I wish you the best of luck."

"Good-bye, Luis."

"Good-bye."

Luis watched them go, the paper bag tucked under Joaquín's arm. He wondered if he would have another customer today. It was always slow in the hottest months.

4

Luis put down the shutters for lunch and was locking
the front door when he heard a truck's horn on the
street. A big Ford with an extended cab rolled up on the far
side of the street and made a looping u-turn to come up in
front of Luis' shop. The passenger-side window came down
and the driver leaned over. His eyes were hidden behind
wraparound sunglasses and his hair was thick with styling
gel. He gestured with a hand full of rings. "Dog Man! Hey,
Dog Man!"

"Ángel. What do you want?"

"Going to get something to eat?"

"Maybe."

"Come on with me. I'll buy you something."

"That's all right. I can pay my own way."

Ángel peered over the tops of his sunglasses at Luis. "Don't
be that way, Dog Man. Come on. It's just a little food."

Luis hesitated. "All right," he said finally. "Meet me in
back."

"Whatever you say!"

He finished locking the store and went to the back room.
He shut off the lights and let himself out the rear door. Ángel
was waiting there, the big engine of his truck idling.

"*¡Muy bien!*" Ángel exclaimed when Luis opened the passenger side door and climbed in. Ángel wore a white shirt with an open collar to show the gold cross he wore there. A .45 automatic was jammed into his waistband for anyone to see if they cared to look. "Going to get some tacos!"

Ángel left the shops behind and turned out onto the road. The windows of the truck were heavily tinted and warded the sun away. Luis put on his seat belt.

"How are things back at your shop, my friend?" Ángel asked.

"Good. A little slow."

"I pass by there every day. It looks like a tomb. How do you manage to pay the rent on that place?"

"It's not so hard. The landlord is reasonable."

Ángel nodded as if to a music beat, but the radio was switched off. Luis looked at the ornaments hanging from the rear view mirror, including a picture of the Virgin of Guadalupe. He sat with his hands in his lap.

"It would help me if I knew what you wanted," Luis said.

"What makes you think I want anything?"

"You don't come around otherwise."

"Didn't I just tell you I drive by your place every day? You are always on my mind, *amigo*. I don't send a load of bodies across the river, I don't think of you. Francisco, too."

Ángel guided the truck to the main thoroughfare, headed straight on toward the border bridge. They passed several restaurants, but he slowed for none of them. His head angled back and forth as he scanned the road, always watching.

"I had two of your customers in my shop this morning."

"What makes you think they're mine?"

"You're putting everyone else out of business."

"Wrong. I'm putting them *in* business. With me."

Finally, Ángel slowed and pulled off the road to parallel park in front of a little taquería. There were a few other trucks there, but Ángel's was the largest and the fanciest. He killed the engine and the air conditioner stopped humming. Immediately the air seemed to grow thick.

"Let's eat."

Ángel led the way in. The taquería was small, with plastic tables and chairs, but it smelled richly of spiced meat. Two men were eating at a table against the wall. When they saw Ángel and his gun, they quickly wrapped up the rest of their meal and left. Luis wished he was going with them.

He stood to one side while Ángel ordered for them. It was a big meal, but Ángel was tending toward fat. He already had the formation of a second chin, and his waist pressed against the visible butt of his pistol. When he was finished, Ángel pointed toward a table. This was where they would sit. Luis obeyed.

A man came from behind the counter and delivered two tamarind-flavored Jarritos to the table. Ángel sat down across from Luis. He cracked his knuckles. "So," he said.

"So," Luis replied.

"Why do you have to be so difficult, Dog Man? Is it something I said that offends you? Do I smell?"

"It's nothing like that," Luis said. He drank some of the soda. "I decided to retire from the business before you and Francisco even started doing it. I like running my store."

"And staying with your dogs outside of town."

"That, too."

Ángel eyed Luis warily and took up his own bottle. He drank half of it and put it down again. The glass sweated onto the table. "What's the matter, you don't like money?"

"I like working for myself. Not Los Zetas."

"Am I one of Los Zetas? I'm an independent businessman."

"Everyone pays a toll to the Zetas."

"So you're smarter than you look."

Luis rolled his bottle between his hands, drawing a pattern of condensation on the table. It was hot in the taquería, with only a fan blowing toward the counter to stir the air. The front door was wide open, letting the summer in. "When I was working the border, I didn't have to answer to Los Zetas. When they came around, things changed. I didn't want to be a part of that. You can understand what I'm saying, can't you?"

"I can understand it."

"Then you know why I must say no to you."

"It wouldn't have to be a permanent thing. Just share some of your old routes and tricks with my people. You have the experience. They don't. The fucking Americans are all over us when we cross the border."

"Things are different there, too. People are paying more attention to the border now."

"But you never got caught."

"I'm sure you have *coyotes* working for you that haven't been caught even once before, too. And there are only so many ways to cross the river. There's nothing I could teach your people that they haven't learned for themselves."

"What if I said that you could work for me without ever having to deal with Los Zetas?" Ángel asked.

"And how would you manage that?"

"I know how to be a middleman," Ángel said.

The food came: plastic baskets with wax paper in the bottom and tacos aligned neatly side by side. Ángel had spicy chopped beef in his tacos, while he'd ordered barbacoa for Luis. Ángel had a good memory; barbacoa was Luis' favorite.

They ate together without saying anything for several minutes. New customers wandered in and made their orders. When they spotted Ángel, they made sure to give his table plenty of space. There was a zone around Luis and Ángel, invisible but tangible. Luis did not like being inside that bubble.

"What do you say?" Ángel asked at last.

"The same."

"Even if I keep the Zetas off your back?"

"I told you: I've had enough of that life."

"So it's just you and the dogs now."

"It looks that way."

Ángel shrugged. He finished off the last of his tacos and wiped his mouth with a paper napkin. "Well, I did what I could. You're just too pigheaded for me. I'll tell Francisco you're out for good. He told me he was sure I could talk talk you into it, especially if I offered you big money."

"What's big money these days?"

"Enough to keep that shop of yours afloat for a while longer, at least."

"I do all right."

"Hmm. Maybe. Finish up, I need to get going."

"I'll take it with me," Luis said.

"Pigheaded, all right. Fine, take it with you. I have to go."

"Maybe I could just walk back," Luis suggested.

"You really *don't* want anything to do with me, do you?" Ángel asked.

"It's not that."

"Okay, I'll go. But my door is always open if you change your mind."

Ángel got up from the table and stretched so that everyone could see his gun, then he headed for the door. After a while Luis heard the rumble of Ángel's engine and waited until it faded away. He wrapped his tacos up in the wax paper, finished his soda, and left.

5

He walked along the storefronts, passing in and out of shade as the sun beat down and scoured the street. Today he would take a long lunch, he decided, and leave the store closed for another half-hour or so beyond what he usually would. It would take twenty minutes to get back there anyway, so what was the point in rushing? Chances were he would have no customers.

Ángel was right, though Luis would not admit it; business was poor and sometimes the shop was like a tomb. Things had been better when he was still known as a first-class *coyote*. People would come to buy his wares and get his advice often, though he always turned them away when they asked if he would guide them across the border.

Being a *coyote* was more than just being an escort across the river and the open land to the nearest highway; it took connections and money and all the things Luis did not have anymore. A *coyote* could bring a group of crossers over the Rio Grande, but unless he had already arranged for a vehicle to pick up his people on the main road, or for a stash house in Presidio where everyone could take a rest and be shuttled away a few at a time, that *coyote* was doing nothing except guaranteeing he would be caught.

It had been long enough now that Luis didn't know the first person to contact on the American side to transport or hide crossers. Ángel and his brother had all the connections now. Even if he wanted to take up the life again, he would be beholden to them from the start.

He looked up the street as a large, green truck trundled into sight. It was a military vehicle with an open back, hoops of bare steel exposed over the bed from which a canvas roof could be draped. As the truck drew closer, he saw that there were soldiers in the back. They had weapons, barrels up, beside them.

Luis stepped into the shade of an awning and stopped as the truck moved past him. The soldiers in the bed did not spare him the slightest glance. A couple of them were talking to each other, and Luis caught a few tattered fragments of words as they went by. The others were stolid, baking under the sun on the metal pan of the truck.

There were something on the order of four hundred troops stationed in Ojinaga. They could be seen at the bridge into the United States or patrolling, like now, the main streets of the town. Occasionally, they would travel on foot in groups of six or more, marching along the sidewalks or on the dusty shoulders as if they were on patrol in a foreign land.

The government said the soldiers were there to do battle with Los Zetas, but Luis had never heard of them doing battle with anyone. They went about their business, and Ojinaga went about its business, with neither affecting the other. Sometimes they would help the police make arrests, but these weren't violent affairs. The carnage of the big cities along the border seemed a long way away from Ojinaga.

Luis watched until the truck had progressed two more blocks and then made a right turn off the thoroughfare before he went along his way. It was an old habit with him: watch the authorities and don't make a move until you know where and why they're going. These soldiers were just making themselves known, reminding Ojinaga that they were still around and still a force to be reckoned with.

He wondered what the Zetas made of these soldiers. Los Zetas were powerful along the border, and Luis knew that in the cities to the east they were not afraid to engage the military in open combat. Here they hardly seemed to bother. Perhaps it was because so little happened in Ojinaga that it wasn't worth the effort. Certainly Ángel Rojas and his brother were not kingpins of crime. They smuggled people and sometimes marijuana across the border, but they were small fish.

After he walked a little further, he crossed the street and headed for a little office with a sign bearing the word DENTISTA over the door. The sign lit up at night, but in the daylight it was almost washed out by the summer sun. Opening the door, Luis received a blast of cold air in the face that made his skin prickle.

It was a small office with a waiting area scarcely large enough for three people. There were a like number of chairs crammed into the space, as well as a tiny coffee table on which were scattered a handful of magazines. A receptionist sat behind the counter eating a sandwich from a brown paper bag. She looked up when Luis came in.

"Luis!" she said.

"Adriana. I hope I'm not interrupting anything."

"No, no. Come in! I was just having something to eat. The doctor is out to lunch."

Adriana Segura was a slight woman with delicate features and long, straight hair she kept pulled back at work. She dressed like a professional in a blouse the color of spring flowers. When she smiled, she showed brilliant white teeth. She worked for a dentist, and it only made sense.

"I have a little something to eat, too," Luis said. He showed her the wax-papered tacos. "Mind if I stay for a few minutes?"

"Of course you can. Come around here and sit by me. There's a stool."

Luis came behind the counter. Everything was neatly arranged: appointment books, message tablet, pens, pencils and rubber stamps. Adriana was an orderly woman, and Luis tried to be the same when he was around her. He sat beside her on a three-legged stool and carefully unwrapped his tacos. Suddenly he wished for napkins.

"I didn't think I'd see you today," Adriana said.

"I happened to be close by."

"It's nice. Thank you."

Doctor Guzman, Adriana's employer, was one of many dentists in Ojinaga. They were crowded up against each other and competed fiercely for business. Dentistry was one of Ojinaga's main attractions to those across the border, and Americans came over to have their teeth examined and treated even with the soldiers and the Zetas and the threat of violence.

Luis ate his tacos and Adriana ate her sandwich. Luis was content just to watch her because he thought she was the loveliest woman in Ojinaga. Or perhaps that was overstating it. She was younger than him by more than ten years, but she didn't seem to mind, and so he didn't let it bother him, either. Still, she was beautiful.

"I'd offer to share my apple with you, but I don't have a knife," Adriana said.

"It's all right. I've eaten plenty."

"Did I tell you it's good to see you?"

"You mentioned it, yes."

Adriana laughed lightly at herself. "I was thinking earlier that something was missing from my day. I didn't realize it was you. How are things at the shop?"

"Slow," Luis admitted, but he didn't want to get into that now. "How about here?"

"Slow, too. I've caught up with all my paperwork and I have nothing to do. Doctor Guzman is about to go crazy with boredom. He's been doing those puzzles with numbers and boxes? You know them? Sudoku? It's Japanese."

"I don't know them."

"He does them all day sometimes. It distracts him when business is bad."

"I suppose I could come in for a check-up."

"How are your teeth?"

Luis clicked them together. "Sharp."

"Like your dogs."

"Like my dogs."

Adriana started her apple. She took a large bite and checked herself as juice escaped down her chin. She flushed. "I forget my manners."

"I didn't even notice."

"I told my mother about your dogs. She wants to know what it's like, living with so many."

"I like it. They keep me company when I'm feeling lonely."

"Are you feeling lonely?"

Luis looked at his hands. "Only sometimes."

"We should do something about that."

"How is your mother?" Luis asked.

"Fine. Well, as fine as can be. They say she may need dialysis soon. I feel so badly for her. And she's so far away. I wish I could visit more often, but I don't have enough left over after I send money to her."

"Doesn't the government pay for her care?"

"Only the doctors. She has to pay expenses to live and for a nurse to visit."

"That can be a lot?"

"Very much."

Luis nodded. "You should have her move to Ojinaga to be near you. We have a hospital here. She could be cared for."

"I don't think she wants to move from our home. That's where she lived with Papa all those years. Moving would be too much."

"Still, you should think about it. You have a good job here, and it would be less expensive if you could live together."

Adriana looked thoughtful for a moment, and Luis thought he caught a hint of moisture in the corner of her eye before she turned away. She put her apple aside unfinished and began folding her paper bag up neatly. It would be used again.

"It's just a thought," Luis added quickly.

"Thank you," Adriana said, and she put her hand on top of Luis'.

Luis glanced at the clock on the wall. "I should be going," he said. "I can't leave the store closed for so long. Who knows who might come by?"

"You have to leave?"

"I'm sorry. But I will make it up to you: how about we go dancing on Tuesday night? There's music at the hall. We could have a good time."

"I'd like that very much," Adriana said. She smiled. All trace of tears was gone from her eyes. "What time?"

"I think they open the doors at seven o'clock. There will be food."

"Pick me up?"

"Of course. If you can stand to be seen in my truck."

"Your truck is fine."

"Okay. We'll do it."

Adriana rose from her seat and gave Luis a peck on the cheek. "Thank you again for coming by. It would have been boring without you."

"*De nada.*"

Luis put the stool back in the corner and came out from behind the counter. At the door he paused and looked up and down the street. He saw no sign of Ángel or the soldiers or of anyone else at all. Chances were good it would be the same at his store: another empty afternoon spent waiting for customers who never came.

"I'll see you tomorrow night," Luis said.

"I look forward to it."

When he left the dentist's office, the heat swatted him like an open hand, but he didn't mind. Already his mind was turning on the next night — what he would wear, what they would do, the things they would say — and was away from the dusty street. By the time his thoughts returned to the present, he was nearly to the store, where he would stand sentinel until closing time.

"Dancing," he said out loud, trying to prod himself back into the future.

Dancing.

6

On Tuesday business was better than it had been for the past few days. Luis had customers in the morning and the afternoon, and one man even bought one of the expensive CamelBak packs that Luis had for sale.

In truth, it was not that terribly far across the ranch land north of the river until one reached the highway, but Luis always recommended more water than was strictly necessary for the journey. Sometimes crossers would be forced to wait long hours in the blistering heat until their pick-up arrived, and it was not unheard of for a group cut loose of their *coyote* for whatever reason to meander across dry, hot land, succumbing to temperatures that sometimes exceeded one hundred degrees.

There were some on the north side that tried to help. They left stations in the roughest areas, stashes of drinkable water for crossers to refresh themselves. The ranchers hated them and it was not rare to find one of these stations torn apart, the plastic jugs shredded and all the water dried up.

Luis led his crossers across some difficult terrain, but never so rugged that it would risk the group. Once upon a time he knew the ranch land least likely to be defended by the Border Patrol, the ways with the fewest number of fences to deal with, the byways that kept his people far from prying eyes, but still got them quickly to their destination. He doubted his knowledge was much good anymore, despite what Ángel Rojas might say. When customers came to his store asking for advice about such things, he deflected their questions back toward more concrete matters like equipment and supplies. Too often would-be crossers came into his store with broken-down shoes or clothes inappropriate for the weather and the rigors of the crossing. These people he sold to knowing they would be safer for having crossed his path than they would have been otherwise.

The *coyotes* under Ángel would not care about these issues. However a person came to them, that was how they would be crossing, even if their shoes would be filled with sharp rocks before a mile of hiking was done. So long as they delivered their people to the appointed place at the appointed time, that was good enough. Anyone who could not take the pace or the terrain would simply be left behind.

Luis closed the shop a little early that night so he could make the trip to his house and still get back to Adriana with plenty of time. The dogs stirred as his truck climbed the rise to the house, barking greetings.

He took time to pet them all and let them smell him, then he went inside and set about fixing their evening meal. It was before time, but he would be out until late and he did not want his friends to go hungry. The dogs didn't care one way or another; they tucked into the big bowls as if they had gone unfed for days.

After he took a shower, he laid out his clothes on the bed. He would wear a fancy shirt and a nice pair of pants, along with a pair of shiny boots he only brought out for such occasions. The pants were wrinkled and he hurried through ironing them before dressing. He looked at himself in the mirror. "Not bad," he said.

A few of the dogs trailed after him when he drove away, but eventually they turned back toward the house. They were used to his comings and goings and, so long as he returned in time for their next meal, they were satisfied to let their pack leader have his peculiarities. He would come back with strange smells, as well. A real treat.

Adriana lived in an apartment complex just a half mile from Dr. Guzman's office. Her apartment was on the second floor, and Luis swung around in the little parking lot and honked his horn twice to call her down. She appeared after a moment and came fast down the stairs to him. Luis got out to hold the passenger door for her.

She wore a light cotton party dress with lace and a pattern of blue flowers on the breast and skirt. She wore it off the shoulders. The lace made it seem delicate. Her hair was done, falling around those bare shoulders in waves. Luis caught the scent of her as she brushed past him and closed the door. He smelled it again when he got back behind the wheel. It was a perfume she only wore on a special occasions, like this one, and he liked it very much.

"I'm sorry I'm late," Luis apologized. "I should have left the store earlier."

"It's all right. I was only just finished getting ready."

"Shall we go?"

"Yes."

Luis drove them across town to the dance hall. The parking lot there was busy and he waited for a spot. There was a charge to get in. Luis paid for both of them.

Inside, the music was already playing and people were on the dance floor. A distinct cloud of cigarette smoke had already begun to gather in the rafters, but the smell of fresh cooking overwhelmed anything else. A number of the tables were already occupied, but Luis found one fairly close to the band. "Eat first?" he asked Adriana. She nodded in the affirmative.

He went away and came back to their table with two plates stacked high with food. They ate enchiladas and *refritos* and rice and wiped their plates with flour tortillas. A man came around with a platter of beers, and Luis paid for two bottles. He toasted Adriana and drank.

"Now we dance!" Adriana said and she rose from the table. When she took Luis by the hand, he had no choice but to follow.

The *norteño* music played, and Luis and Adriana danced to every tune, fast or slow. Other couples swirled around them, driven by the music, and there were smiles on every face. The dance floor only cleared when the band took a break and recorded music came from the speakers. Luis bought more beer.

There was a light sheen of sweat on Adriana's face, but Luis thought this made her look more radiant. He was perspiring, too, from the collected body heat in the hall and the dancing itself, but it was good.

"I like the band," Adriana said.

"I'm glad. They're from Chihuahua, I think."

"How are your feet?"

"I can still dance if you can."

"Of course!"

Eventually the band returned and the music began once more. This time it was Luis who led Adriana out. They were the first couple on the floor. They danced as if for the pure joy of it, and maybe that was true. Luis felt the rest of the people fall away from him when he turned around the floor with Adriana, until there was only her and only him, and even the band vanished and their music played from the vibrating air itself.

The dance lasted for hours until finally the last song was played. The long table of food was exhausted, and even the beer-sellers had put away their platters. Luis and Adriana retired from the dance floor pleasantly exhausted. People were already filing out the door.

"Thank you for this," Adriana said.

"I should thank you. I haven't danced like that in a long time."

"It's late, though. I should be getting home."

"Let's go, then."

The sun was down and the moon was up, shining among glittering stars. The evening cool had already started and Luis liked the way the breeze from the open windows buffeted his face. He looked over at Adriana and saw her hair blowing. He wanted to kiss her.

When they reached Adriana's apartment, Luis got out quickly and came around to get Adriana's door. She smelled as fresh now as she had at the beginning of the night.

"This is where I leave you," Luis said.

"*Buenas noches,* Luis." She kissed him on the lips then, a quick kiss, and then they were parted. Luis felt himself flush.

"Good night," Luis said.

He waited until she had mounted all the steps to her apartment before returning to his side of the truck. Upstairs, Adriana paused in the half-open door and waved to him. He waved back.

Luis pulled out of the parking lot and drove away. The cab seemed emptier than it should have been with her gone.

He wanted to look over and see her again, see her hair blowing from the open window. Instead, he thought of the dance and the music, and he made his way home thinking good thoughts.

7

The next day he woke even before the dogs began to stir and fixed himself a simple breakfast with coffee in the little kitchen. He sat at the kitchen table watching the sun rise through the drawn curtains at the window. When he was finished, he went to his bedroom and changed into sweat pants and a sweatshirt and put on running shoes.

Outside he stretched, first one leg and then the next, and then loosened up his back. The dogs milled around him, knowing what the routine meant and ready for the next thing.

"*Vamos*," he said to them when he was done, and he set off jogging at a gentle pace away from the house. The dogs followed.

Luis went along a dusty trail that the dogs had made for themselves. It cut out across the broad, open ground and went straight a long way before it hooked back onto itself. The dogs had their own ideas about how much land belonged to them.

They kept up with him easily, even when he increased the pace, the small ones running dangerously close to his heels, darting in and out like pilot fish. The big ones loped alongside, tongues lolling as they worked themselves up. They watched him for the changes. He was their focus, their lead dog.

Eventually he reached the limits of the trail and followed it left as it began the slow loop around. Despite the cool he was sweating, but his breath came steady and even. His heart beat quickly, but it too remained under control. He could keep this up for as long as he liked.

The trail came close to a mesquite tree and he dodged out of its way. The dogs simply passed beneath its branches. A jackrabbit broke from cover and fled at top speed, but Luis' pack did not leave him. Maybe when they were on their own, they would stop to chase the animal down, but for now they were engaged in serious business.

His house was a scratch on the horizon as he turned back toward home. Elsewhere people were waking and stumbling through their morning routines, but Luis was out with his dogs. He liked to do it, though he did not run with them every day. Their company now was the kind of friendship he could easily understand and appreciate. Wherever he chose to go, they would follow unquestioningly. When he left them at home during the day, he could be sure they would be there when he returned, and they wouldn't hold it against him that he had been gone. That was the power of the dog, and he was surprised so few people understood it.

They closed the loop and headed along the same path along which they had come before. The bigger dogs were really panting now. He should run with them more often; they were getting fat and lazy. He resolved to get up early the next three days in a row and take them with him on this circuit.

Back at the house he paced a little until his heart no longer raced. He did a few more stretches to avoid cramps before he went inside and prepared the dogs' morning meal. They were ravenous and crowded each other to get at the bowls.

Luis stripped and took a shower and dressed. He had set aside his dancing clothes from the night before. In a day or two he would hand-wash them and press them out for the next time he and Adriana had a celebratory evening together. It occurred to him that he should buy a few shirts to vary things a bit, but he could not justify the expense when there were other things to consider, like his dogs.

The dogs had finished their meal by the time he came out again. He petted those who came to him and bid farewell to those who didn't. Then he was behind the wheel of his truck, steering into town.

He had just turned onto the asphalt roadway that led to the heart of Ojinaga when he saw the army truck pulled over by the side of the road. A few uniformed men strolled openly across the lanes and someone had put flares down. Luis approached them slowly.

A soldier waved for him to stop and he obeyed. Three of them converged on his truck, each of them carrying an automatic weapon casually, their faces impassive. "Identification," asked the one at the driver's side window.

Luis produced his identity card. He kept his hands on the wheel, even though the soldiers did not seem especially jumpy. Instead of smiling, he tried to put on the same blank face he wore in his ID photograph.

"Where are you going?" asked the soldier. He held on to Luis' ID.

"To work."

"Where do you work?"

"I have a store in town. El Mercantil. Off De La Juventud."

Luis noticed that one of the soldiers had moved around toward the back of the truck and was peering into the bed.

He had only a few things there: a section of plywood, a spare tire and a wrench. The soldier reached in and lifted the plywood to look under it.

"I don't know your store."

"It's a very small store."

"It must be."

The soldier seemed reluctant to give Luis his identification card. He matched eyes with the other soldier poking around in the back and after a moment he nodded ever so slightly. He gave back the card.

"I can go?" Luis asked.

"Yes. Go on. Move it."

Luis put the truck in gear and drove on, quickly leaving the roadblock behind. He watched them in the rear view mirror as if expecting them to suddenly hit the road in their heavy vehicle and rush to overtake him. A trembling passed through him.

This happened sometimes. Not enough for Luis to grow used to the imposition, but often enough that he knew how to behave when it did. He did not understand how they could throw up such obstacles and yet let Ángel Rojas and his brother moved about freely. The gun Ángel liked to show off in his waistband was enough to win him prison time, but no one said a thing about it. Francisco Rojas was less obvious than Ángel, but certainly he, too, could be found guilty of something without too much work.

Perhaps it had to do with Los Zetas. Everyone feared the Zetas. The Zetas had turned the border into a killing zone. Of course they were in Ojinaga — they *had* to be, because they were everywhere else — but they did not wantonly murder here. Maybe, Luis thought, there was an equilibrium that had been established that neither side was willing to upset.

If the highway came through the way people kept saying it would, things would change, but for now Ojinaga was more potential than asset.

Meanwhile, Luis would have to live with roadblocks or street stops or just the simple action of block patrols by armed soldiers. They all, the people of Ojinaga, would have to put up with it. The alternative was giving the town completely over to Los Zetas, and without the counterbalance of the military and the police, intricate though their dance might be, that would be no good.

Luis kept checking his mirror until the truck was out of sight. Only then did he allow himself to let out his breath and drive.

8

H e worked three days and did steady business. Maybe the rough patch was past.

On the third day he spent the morning restocking from the back room, straightening displays and dusting. A light-bulb needed replacing and he brought out the ladder to deal with it. While he stood on the second step from the top, the front door opened and the little bells there jingled.

"*Un momento*," Luis said. He was careful with the burned-out bulb, lest it fall and smash all over the floor. Once he had the new bulb in, it flashed brightly, and he could feel the heat from it. He climbed down.

The man stood as the counter with his back to Luis, look-ing at the items displayed behind the register. He wore a base-ball cap and a t-shirt with SAN ANTONIO SPURS and a basketball emblazoned on the back.

"May I help you?" Luis asked.

The man turned around. "I hope so," he said.

"Alberto! Why didn't you tell me it was you?"

Alberto Pérez was a slight man, shorter even than Luis and rangier. His legs were gangly in knee-length shorts and he wore Nike sandals. He smiled and offered his hand. "Luis," he said, "it's been a while."

"I heard you moved to Nuevo Laredo," Luis said.

"I did. Now I'm back."

"For how long?"

"About a month now."

"And you only come to see me now? What's the matter with you?"

Luis went behind the counter and dragged out a stool. He offered it to Alberto first, but the man declined and Luis sat on it instead.

"I had to get myself oriented again," Alberto said. "It's been a while. Things have changed. I needed to see what was what."

"Things haven't changed that much. You haven't been gone that long."

Alberto shook his head. "No, they've changed a lot. The first thing I find out, you're not leading crossers over the border anymore. That you opened up a shop. What happened there?"

"Never mind that," Luis said. "How have you been? How was Nuevo Laredo?"

"Crazy. The Golfos and Los Zetas are all over the place, shooting it out with police and the army. Blood in the streets. It got so bad it was impossible to do business there anymore."

"People stopped crossing?"

"No, they still cross, but it's hard. Los Zetas will snatch someone right off the street and hold them for ransom. They can't pay, they don't make it out alive. The lucky ones just lose everything and get dumped on the streets. They can't even pay their *coyote* anymore. And don't get me started on the Americans."

"I hear they're cracking down in Presidio, too," Luis said.

"You hear? Since when does Luis González not know *exactly* what's going on along the border? I tell you, I couldn't believe it when they told me you quit."

"I thought I could do better with a business," Luis said. "I get by."

"Did the Zetas get to you, too?"

"No, no, nothing like that. Believe me: the story is boring. You'd laugh at me, probably. Besides, I like this. I keep regular hours, I make steady money and no one bothers me."

"No one bothers you? Sounds nice."

"Is someone bothering you?" Luis asked.

"I thought I'd come back west to see if there was somewhere a man could ply his trade without having to worry about getting a bullet in the back of the head," Alberto said. "Like I said, it's just too dangerous in Nuevo Laredo, and it doesn't get any better when you cross. A gunshot or jail, and who needs that?"

"I understand."

"Anyway, I thought Ojinaga might be the place for me again. Someplace small. I mean, we used to do all right together before."

"We did," Luis agreed. "But...?"

"I think you know what I'm going to say next. The Rojas brothers. Ángel and Francisco. I had no idea they would take over like they have. You know most of the other *coyotes* are tied up with them now? It's better than dealing with the Zetas, sure, but a man can't scratch his ass without getting permission first. How'd it happen, for God's sake?"

Luis frowned a little and shrugged his shoulders. "Little by little. I was out of the business before they really started to make their move. I thought there were still some independent operators, though."

"All gone," Alberto said. "Or, at least, I can't find any. Everybody we used to know is paying tribute to the Rojas brothers or working for them directly. I found out in a hurry that new faces aren't welcome around Ojinaga anymore."

"You're not exactly a new face," Luis said. "You have history here."

"I might as well have come from another planet, the way people are treating me. I understand the new guys don't know me, but you'd think the old-timers would be willing to let me in. Instead it's, 'Go see Ángel Rojas.'"

"Did you go see him?"

"Sure. He laid out the deal for me. I said no thanks."

Luis considered. Ángel had not explained all the details to him, but Luis knew enough to know that a deal with Ángel Rojas was going to be a bad one, or at least unfair. And he knew Alberto Pérez; he was not the type to leave money on the table. "How much does he take?" Luis asked.

"Seventy percent."

"Off what kind of price?"

"He says he's only charging three thousand a head, but the going rate everywhere is at least five thousand. I figure he's lining his pockets with the extra he doesn't tell you about. Him and his *brother*."

"That two thousand might be going to the Zetas," Luis said.

"Ángel is in with Los Zetas?"

"He says he is. I believe him."

Alberto swore. "You can't get away from those guys!"

"He might just be saying so," Luis reasoned, "but I don't know if they'd let him do business like that. Using their name. And he says he can keep the Zetas off your back. Maybe he's paying them off the top, maybe with part of his percentage. Who knows?"

"There has to be a better way," Alberto said.

"Like what?"

"Like maybe two old friends going into business together."

Luis saw Alberto's eyes flash and immediately his heart fell. It did not take much effort to work through to the end of that line of thinking, and already he knew the answer he would give. "I told you I gave it up," he tried. "I'm no good at it anymore."

"No good? You used to be the *best.*"

"That was before I let it go. Trust me, Alberto, you don't want me as a partner. I'll only drag you down."

Alberto held his hands up to stop Luis' thought. "Wait until I tell you the rest, okay? I made a contact in Presidio who'd be willing to let us stash our people, and I can get transportation out of town, too. The whole thing, from start to finish. We work together, we split the take evenly. No need for the Zetas and no need for Ángel Rojas."

"Everybody pays Los Zetas," Luis said.

"Then we pay them! They probably don't care one way or another if it's the Rojas brothers coming up with the money or two men working independently. If the Rojases can do it, so can we."

Luis shook his head slowly. He got up from the stool and walked around. He busied himself straightening a shelf of protein bars. "I don't want to get caught up in that. I'm sorry."

"*¿Por qué no?*"

"It's just not the same," Luis said. "It was different before you left. Now you can't turn around without bumping into the police, the army or Ángel Rojas. And the Americans... you know the pressure they're under to catch us. They'll stop at nothing. It's not just a couple of *vaqueros* against the world anymore. The odds are against us."

"I can't believe I'm hearing you say this," Alberto said.

"If you'd asked me before, I wouldn't believe it either, but times change. It's too complicated. I told you, I like my business. I like what I do. If I were to go back to all of that, then what becomes of this? I can't have it both ways."

"I'm disappointed."

"I'm sorry. I truly am."

Alberto sighed and leaned heavily on the counter. He kicked the floor idly with the toe of his sandal. Finally he straightened up. "I can see coming back to Ojinaga was a mistake," he said.

"It's not so bad."

"Sure, if you have your own business and don't run with the *coyotes* anymore. How do you spend your days now?"

"I read. I take care of my dogs. I know a woman."

"Those damned dogs. You still have all of them?"

"Plus a few more since the last time you visited," Luis said.

Alberto smiled reluctantly. "Think you can spare some time one of these nights to come out and have a few *cervezas* with an old friend? If you're not too busy with your dogs or your woman."

"I'm sure I can manage it."

"Then we will."

The smiles were gone. Luis wanted to say something to Alberto to lift the weight from him, but he could think of nothing. An awkward silence descended between them, until Luis said, "What will you do?"

"What can I do? I don't have much money put away, so I won't be buying my own store anytime soon. Besides, what would I sell? No, I'm not cut out to be a businessman like you."

"Then...?"

"I guess I'll have to go back to Ángel Rojas and tell him I reconsidered. I won't like doing it, but that's the only thing I know. Being a *coyote*. And I'll be starting at the bottom of the heap. There will be young kids who know the other side the border better than I do."

"You'll get it back."

"Maybe." Alberto kicked the ground again. "I should go."

"It was good to see you, Alberto. Just tell me when you want to have those beers, okay? We'll have a good time."

"Sure. Okay. *Adiós.*"

The bells jingled when Alberto left. It seemed very still in the store after he was gone.

9

Luis parked his truck in the lot outside Adriana's apartment building. He lingered a bit, still thinking about Alberto, then shrugged off that pall and got out of the truck. He went up the steps to Adriana's door and by the time he got there, he was ready with a smile.

He heard the lock disengage and the door opened hesitantly. A little girl stood in the gap, looking up at Luis. She wore a white dress with green and red flowers on it and was barefoot. "Hello, Isabella," Luis said. "May I come in?"

Isabella turned from the door. "Mamá!" she called. "It's Sr. González!"

"Let him in!" Luis heard Adriana say. She sounded like she was in the kitchen.

The little girl opened the door wider and stepped aside to admit Luis. He passed through the doorway and into a small front room with a throw rug on the floor and a few paintings on the wall. A little television droned away in the corner. Luis didn't recognize the show.

"He's inside now, Mamá!" Isabella yelled.

"Okay. Tell him I'll be right there."

"Mamá will be right here," Isabella said, and she closed the door behind Luis.

Isabella was seven years old with the same light skin and the same dark eyes. Luis had not known her father, so he wasn't sure what features Isabella shared with him. All he saw were the similarities between her and her mother. Even now Luis could tell that Isabella would be very pretty when she grew up.

"How are you today, Isabella?" Luis asked her.

"Okay."

"What did you do all day?"

"Drew pictures. Do you want to see them?"

"Of course."

Isabella vanished into the next room. Luis sat down on the narrow couch. Everything was crowded in the apartment. There was barely enough room for the scant furniture Adriana owned. Luis thought there was only one bedroom, as well.

When the little girl returned, she had a sheaf of drawing papers in her little fist. She knelt down on the far side of the diminutive coffee table and spread them out a few at a time. The pictures were drawn in crayon and meticulously colored, even when that meant the trees were purple and the sky hazed with green. Isabella's figures were blocky and awkward, but it was clear she had put much effort into them.

"I like this one," Luis said. "What is this?"

"That's Mamá's work. That's Doctor Guzman."

"Of course. He's smiling to show his nice teeth."

"Yes," Isabella said seriously.

They went through the whole selection. Luis was effusive with his praise, but he wasn't sure if Isabella was buying into it or not. Finally they came to one that showed a house surrounded by animals, all colored brown.

"What is this?" Luis asked.

"That's your house. Mamá says you have lots of dogs."

"But you've never been to my house."

"I *imagined* it."

"Ah. Where am I?"

"You're visiting us."

"Okay. Well, if you want to color it, my house is blue and white."

"I will," Isabella said and she vanished again, only to reappear with a cup filled with crayons. Without any further prompting, she went about adding the colors to Luis' house. She was not totally wrong.

Eventually, Adriana appeared. She was changed out of her work clothes and into jeans and a simple blouse, though she wore an apron over them. "*Hola*," she said. "I'm sorry, but dinner isn't ready yet."

"I'm in no hurry."

"Good, because it will be a while. I worked late for Dr. Guzman."

"Don't worry," Luis said. "Take your time."

"Okay."

"Do you need any help?"

"Only if you want to keep me company."

Luis stood up. "Isabella, I'm going to talk with your mother in the kitchen, all right? My house looks beautiful."

Adriana retreated to the kitchen and Luis followed. The space was as restricted here as it was elsewhere in the apartment, though there was a little nook where a table and three chairs could be squeezed in uncomfortably. The kitchen smelled of spices and cooking meat and the two-burner stove was occupied by two big pots that steamed.

"Thank you for being patient." Adriana gave Luis a brief kiss on the cheek.

"I really don't mind."

"How was your day? Mine was crazy. Busy, busy."

Luis made a noncommittal gesture. "The same. An old friend dropped by to say hello. He's back in town after a long time away."

"Is he disappointed that everything is the same?"

"Something like that. We'll go out and have a drink some night to celebrate his return."

"Excuse me, I need to get into that drawer."

"Of course. I'll stay out of your way."

"You're not in my way. I'm just disorganized tonight."

Adriana used a cloth and lifted the lid off one of the pots. There was an explosion of rich aroma in the close room, carried on a billowing cloud of steam. She used a long-handled spoon to stir, then put the lid back on.

"Everything seems like it's going to be great," Luis offered.

"It's simple. Like me."

"I'm the simple one," Luis said. "It's just me and my dogs."

"I've been meaning to ask you," Adriana said. "Why do you have so many dogs? You know they call you 'Dog Man,' right?"

Luis nodded and smiled a little. "They've been calling me Dog Man since the time I had five dogs. Now I have even more. It's because I like dogs and they like me. I understand them. It's a natural fit."

"How do you mean, you understand them?"

"Dogs are a lot like people: they want certain things and in return they give you loyalty. So long as you don't let them down, they will always love you."

"But what about people who beat their dogs?"

"Fearing someone isn't the same as being loyal to them," Luis said. "And no one would beat my dogs. I would beat *them*, maybe, but they won't beat my dogs. My dogs are my family."

"There's just dogs, though. Aren't they?"

Luis struggled to find words. It was always the same when someone asked him about his dogs. He could tell them so much, but eventually it became a matter of feelings and emotions that could not easily be explained. When he saw a dog, he felt a kinship with the animal and, more often than not, the dog would respond to that. How could he interpret that for someone who did not feel the same?

"I hope you don't mind me asking," Adriana said.

"No, it's not that. It's just... I mean... dogs don't abandon each other. I know they will always be there for me. Maybe it's as simple as that."

"You need a good woman."

"I thought I found one."

Adriana smiled, as if to herself. "*Tal vez*," she said.

"You should come and see my dogs sometime. You'd like them."

"Maybe I will. But will they like me?"

"A dog can sense if a person is bad or good. I think you have nothing to worry about."

"You're making me blush."

"I didn't mean to."

"Go back in the living room and let me finish here. Then we'll eat."

10

They ate and afterward they crowded onto the little couch to watch television until it was time for Isabella to go to sleep. Luis wasted time watching the news while Adriana disappeared into the bedroom, and after a half an hour she emerged. She turned the TV off and sat down beside him.

"Full?" she asked.

"Very."

"It tasted good?"

"It was excellent," Luis said.

Adriana settled against him, and he put his arm over her shoulders. Her head pressed against the side of his chest. "I'm so tired," she said.

"If you want, I can go."

"No, please stay awhile."

"Okay, I will."

She stayed like that, leaning into his body, for a long time, and Luis thought maybe she'd fallen asleep. But then she said, "I heard from my mother today."

Luis stayed still. "How is she?"

"Not good. She needs more money."

"Do you have money to send?"

"Maybe. It will be difficult, but I think we can make it work."

"You could ask Dr. Guzman for a raise."

"I couldn't. Business isn't that good. Besides, he already pays me more than he probably should."

"I don't know about that," Luis said. "You work hard. You're reliable. What more could he want?"

Adriana fell silent for a while longer. Luis was conscious of her breathing. This time he knew she was awake, just wrapped up in their embrace unmoving. "Do you think I should go to the United States?"

This time Luis looked down at Adriana, but he couldn't see her face. "What? Why?"

"Everyone I talk to says the pay is better in America. And I have skills. I can do office work just like I do here. I've even been working on my English when patients come in."

"It takes a lot to work in the United States. Lots of paperwork, and even then you're not guaranteed to find good work. Mexicans in America do all the jobs no one else wants to do. Do you want to be somebody's maid? Cleaning out toilets? Because that's what they'll have you do."

"You've been to the States?"

"A few times."

"Was that... before?"

The question made Luis frown. He wanted to change positions, but Adriana was still tucked neatly under his arm and showed no inclination to move. "You know I don't like to talk about that."

"Okay. Just tell me what it was like, then. We don't have to talk about the rest."

Luis breathed deeply. "It's very busy, especially in the big cities. But it's always going by too fast for a Mexican to grab on. That's what I'm telling you: it's not a life you want. Every Mexican I saw in the States was picking up garbage or mowing lawns. They say there are some success stories, but I didn't see any of them."

"But the money—"

"There's money to be made right here. I make my money here. Dr. Guzman does the same. There are thousands of Mexicans right here in Ojinaga who work every day and provide for their families. People just like you. They don't have to settle for being second-best."

Luis heard something and realized that Adriana was crying. She did it quietly, but it did not escape him. "Hey," he said and he urged her to sit up. "Hey, don't cry. I don't mean to make you cry."

Adriana slipped out from beneath Luis' arm. She wiped at fresh tears on her cheeks. "I'm sorry," she said. "It's only that I don't know what to do. It's not easy."

"No one said it was going to be. Some days, I'm not sure if I will be able to keep my shop open, but I make it. You will, too."

She nodded and dried her eyes with the back of her hand. The tears made her makeup run, and Luis saw the rising self-consciousness in her face. "I didn't mean to upset you," she said.

"I'm only upset because you are."

"It's just... she's my mother, and I have to look out for her. Like you and your dogs."

"I would never compare your mother to one of my dogs."

"It's not that. It's what you said about loyalty and love."

Luis tried to smile for Adriana, but his heart was heavy. He touched her hair and wanted to pull her to him and hold her tightly until she was well again, but the moment for such things had passed, replaced with something pained and awkward.

"Excuse me," Adriana said, and she left the room. When she came back, she had wiped away the mascara streaks and had a tissue in her hand. Luis stood up.

"I should probably go."

"You don't have to. We can still sit."

"No, I have to be up early tomorrow and you need your rest."

They hugged delicately, as if each feared the other might break. When Adriana kissed him, Luis could smell her tears. He let her show him to the door. "I will see you again soon," Adriana said.

"Maybe we could go dancing again."

"Maybe. Good night, Luis."

"Good night."

He waited until she closed the door and locked it before he descended the stairs to the parking lot. A few of the other apartments had lights in their windows and he caught a snatch of a news program playing loudly on someone's television.

After he left the parking lot, the headlights clearing space ahead of him, he thought about Adriana. On a good night, he would remember her as being exuberant and full of life. On a night like tonight, he could not get past the tears and the things she'd said about the States.

Luis wasn't lying about the things he'd seen there. So many crossers had passed over the river with him, all of them hoping for the same thing, and he had never had the courage to tell them what they were headed toward. It wasn't just that they were criminals, but that they were beneath the attention of Americans even when they held down jobs and added to society. Mexicans were invisible there, and when they weren't invisible, they were despised.

He did not want that for Adriana or Isabella. They would cross together, of course, under the guidance of one of Ángel Rojas' *coyotes*. They would hike across the harsh land to the highway, or until they could steal their way into Presidio to be hidden like a stash of illicit goods. Eventually someone would come to carry them away to one of the big cities: to San Antonio or Dallas or outside the state entirely. They would have no one but each other, and once they were dumped off at their final destination they would be entirely on their own.

It was better to scratch out a living south of the border than to face what waited to the north. Luis was convinced of this. A Mexican did not have to apologize for being Mexican in his own country, whereas he would be judged by that measure every day in the United States. In Ojinaga, working for Dr. Guzman, Adriana wore pretty blouses in an office where she did important work. Luis could not imagine her trading that away for a maid's uniform and a toilet brush.

He made his way to the road out of town. On both sides of him, Ojinaga began to fade away into dusty scrub land. The last of the street lights passed behind him, and ahead there was only darkness.

11

Luis awoke with the idea in his head, as if he had been thinking on the problem all night while asleep. He considered the idea while he ran the dogs and when he made their breakfast and while he showered and dressed.

When he was a *coyote*, Luis knew other *coyotes* who squandered their earnings on their vices. Alberto's sin of choice was alcohol, and at his height he could drink for days on end without coming up for air. Sometimes Luis was with him, but most times he was not, preferring to spend time with his dogs in the little blue-and-white house outside Ojinaga. He saved his money, and when the time came that he would make no more trips across the border, he had enough for the store and some more besides.

Something was better than nothing. Luis would take the savings he had left and give it to her.

He couldn't just *do it*, of course. The subject had to be broached first and delicately. Adriana was a proud woman and would not want to impose on him that way. And there was the question of what it would do to their relationship. They had not yet even made love and he wouldn't make her a whore.

It would hurt him to do it. When the store did well, it took care of itself. When times were slow, he had the savings to dip into as an emergency measure. Any time he earned more than he needed, he paid his savings back. This would take away his safety net, the thing he had built up so steadily for so long.

Regardless, he would do it, and he would do it soon. He would allow for some time to pass before he saw her, let the embarrassment of that evening fade so that it didn't seem he was doing it just to placate her. They would go down to the bank together, and he would have them cut her a check in the full amount. He'd hold back just enough to keep the account alive, but she was welcome to the rest. He did not want her to cry anymore.

12

Luis dreamed the kind of dream that was mostly memory. He was aware that he was asleep and that the broad, dry landscape he saw around him was just a construct of his mind. He was not really hot, it had not been a long time since his last drink of water and the people who were with him were not real.

The crossing at the river had gone smoothly. The waters of the Rio Grande near Ojinaga were deep enough to cover a man's head and drown him if he wasn't careful, but Luis *was* careful and he let no one drift away when they made their way across on big inner tubes. Shivering and wet, they were all safe on the American side of the border.

He knew his way across the blank-featured land, even in darkness. He had been through there many times before. Eight people trailed along behind him as the eastern sky turned colors. They had gotten a late start and now they would pay for it.

Of the eight, seven were adults. The last was a little girl, seven years old, who walked hand in hand with her mother. Both of them were wearing bad shoes for the terrain, but such things weren't Luis' concern; he had to bring them to the rendezvous point within a certain window of time, and that was all that mattered.

He urged them to walk faster during those predawn hours, and faster still when the sun rose for real. Soon they reached a long stretch of barbed-wire fence and they followed it for more than a mile before reaching a locked gate. One by one they climbed over. The mother helped her daughter make it across, as she had helped her at the river.

When finally they reached the highway, the sun was already well on its way into the sky. No one was wet anymore, though maybe the absorbent inner soles of their shoes squelched with moisture when they walked. Some of the crossers didn't wear socks because they didn't want to get them wet. That was an invitation to blisters, and surely there were a few to go around.

The highway stretched east and west until it touched the horizon in both directions. There were no signs here, no mile markers or anything at all to make this length of road remarkable. Luis checked his watch. The van would be here before too long.

Coming across was Luis' part of the deal. Others picked up the task from here. He would not accompany these people to their final destination. In fact, he had no idea where they were headed after this. Maybe they'd make a jaunt into Presidio to be hidden in a house somewhere along a quiet residential street, or maybe they would be taken to points east.

The danger was the Border Patrol. Luis knew that they had sensors that could detect crossers' footfalls as they came out of the river. The sensors weren't obvious, buried in the ground as they were and mobile, so that different sections of the river were monitored at different times. Luis had only God to trust whenever he came across that this time the Border Patrol hadn't chosen *his* spot to surveil.

But the crossing had passed without incident and the hike across empty ranch land had likewise been easily done. Now there was just the van.

Time passed and the sun climbed higher. The air grew drier and the temperature spiked. The road was raised slightly from the terrain around it and Luis had his crossers sit at the bottom of this little rise while he kept an eye out for the van. He was sweating and so were they, but he hadn't wanted to waste time and effort dragging water jugs along with them. They were supposed to be on their way by now, and the van had air conditioning.

Eventually, the sun hung directly overhead. The temperature was over a hundred. Waves of heat rose from the baking asphalt. If Luis put his hand on the blacktop, it would certainly be burned. He checked his watch again, as he'd checked it every ten minutes, but doing so didn't bring the van.

He took a plastic bag from his pocket with his phone sealed inside. He freed the phone from the bag and dialed out. Javier answered on the fourth ring.

"It's Luis. What the fuck is going on? Where is the van?"

"Where are you?" Javier asked.

"I'm waiting at the spot! The van is late!"

Luis had never met Javier face-to-face. They did business only by telephone, and then only rarely. Javier was the one who arranged for the vans, and he was the one who knew where the crossers went when they were no longer Luis' responsibility. Without Javier, Luis could not bring people across successfully. They would be stranded, roasting under the sun, with nowhere to go. Like now.

So far no one had driven past. Luis considered himself more than lucky. All it would take was one driver to spot a group of Mexicans by the side of the road and a call would go to the Border Patrol. They were exposed here, without so much as a bush or a tree to hide behind. Eventually someone would come, and the van would have to be there before that happened.

"Are you sure you're in the right place?" Javier asked finally.

"Of course I'm sure! This is bad, Javier. I have eight here."

Another pause from Javier. Luis thought he heard talking in the background, but it was muffled and he couldn't be sure. "The van should be there," Javier said.

"I know this. It should have been here a long goddamned time ago!"

"Maybe they were delayed, I don't know."

"You need to call and find out."

Luis imagined how it could have happened: the van headed out from wherever it came from, its driver pulled over by the police for some traffic violation or maybe just because. After that, they might run the identity of the driver. Perhaps he had a record. Maybe they figured out where he was going. Maybe he was telling Border Patrol right this moment where he was supposed to meet his crossers.

"I'll call. You stay."

Luis glanced at the people. They were not listening to him, or at least they pretended not to. He saw the mother trying to shade her daughter's eyes with her hands. "I don't know how much longer I can do that."

"Stay ten minutes."

"Don't make me wait any longer than that."

"I won't. Ten minutes. I promise."

Javier broke the connection. Luis weighed the cell phone in his hand, willing it to ring instantaneously with his answer.

He could not be caught with them. Of that much he was certain. Watching the highway in both directions, he expected a vehicle with the green stripe of the Border Patrol to appear, closing fast. They would know he was the *coyote*. They would take his fingerprints. They might even put him in jail. What did they call it? *Human trafficking.* That couldn't happen.

Ten minutes lasted a lifetime. The phone rang. Luis answered.

"There's a problem," Javier said. "The van is not coming."

"What do you mean?"

"I mean it's not coming."

A dark spot formed at the far edge of sight, bubbling up until it became the shape of a car headed quickly west along the highway. It ticked toward Luis, driving fast. He couldn't tell yet if it was a police vehicle. He felt his stomach tightening.

"I have to go," Luis said. He closed his phone and put it back in the plastic bag.

It occurred to him to simply run, but if he did then the people might follow. The car was closer still, close enough that he could make out individual features like the windshield. He didn't think it was the police, but as before he knew that being seen by anyone would spell the end of the game.

He turned to the crossers sweating it out on the side of the road, unaware of the speeding car bearing down on them. "I know a place where there's water," he announced. "I'm going to bring some back for everyone."

A few nodded. The rest were withering in the heat. The little girl had sat down in her mother's lap and leaned against her, and though her mother still tried to shade her, Luis knew it would do no good. The gritty, sandy dirt was a cooking surface.

The car roared past them, carrying hot air in its wake. Luis got only a flash of the driver, but he knew that the man had been looking and that he had seen them. Right now he could be dialing.

"I'm going now," Luis said. "I'll be back."

He set off back the way they'd come and walked a mile without looking back. When he finally did, they were lost in the heat haze along with the black ribbon of the highway.

Luis turned away from them again, and this time he did not look back at all.

13

Upon waking he felt a terrible thirst. His mouth was barren. In the dark he passed from the bedroom into the tiny, functional bathroom and drank water from the tap. A part of his brain warned him from drinking too quickly or too much, as if he really had just come in from the heat.

He returned to his bed and sat on the edge of the mattress. The house was completely still and the country beyond the walls likewise hushed. Even the dogs weren't moving around. Luis rubbed his legs with his open palms, chasing away a marching ache that he did not really feel.

It might have reflected better on him if he thought of those people often, but he did not. Occasionally, there would come a dream where snatches of memory combined with other phantasms and drove him into wakefulness, like now, but most often they were simply something he tried to forget and had largely succeeded in doing.

Luis couldn't even remember all of their faces. If he could recall that much detail, then it would be one thing, but he couldn't. Tonight's dream couldn't be relied upon, either, because for the most part the crossers were just brown faces that looked alike, their shapes barely glimpsed.

The little girl he remembered, and her mother. Of the lot of them, they were the two that occurred to him most often. Maybe he had been watching them more carefully, he couldn't recall. He would not admit that what he felt regarding them was guilt, and that guilt made them appear to him more readily and more completely than any of the others.

Whatever the case, he had not taken another group of crossers across the river again. He settled his accounts with Javier through a third party, took his money and stayed home with his dogs for six months before finally making arrangements to open his store. The day the store opened he swore he wouldn't live with regrets. Guilt was regret's sworn companion. He relinquished that, too.

They hadn't been the first crossers he'd abandoned. Some he left right on the far side of the river, when it seemed that Border Patrol was closing in on them. Some made it to the open land before they were cut loose. Abandonment was part of the trade. Knowing when to leave when it became necessary, that was the sign of a true professional. Everything else could be learned, but the will to turn away was born to a select few. Those who didn't were caught, and being caught meant ultimately becoming less valuable.

When the Americans arrested a crosser, whether *coyote* or his follower, they took fingerprints and photos and stored them away forever. If a crosser was arrested again, they would be punished with jail time. At first it was not too bad, but for each failure, more time was added. Luis did not relish the thought of imprisonment.

Countless times he'd made the journey north and not once had he been caught. There were close calls, when he could hear the shouts of Border Patrol agents in the dark and see their lights, but he had always slipped away. Back into the embrace of the river. Back to Mexico.

It crossed Luis' mind that once he had seen a crosser one time, he had never seen that crosser again. Surely some of them, maybe even most of them, were caught eventually and of course some would never try to make the crossing again, but he would have expected at least one face to reappear in Ojinaga. He knew of people who'd crossed dozens of times, never allowing failure to deter them from another go, but none of them had been *his*. Luis didn't know if this was a good thing or a bad thing.

He lay down and stared at the ceiling in the dark. To force his mind away from the memory, he concentrated on Adriana and Isabella. They were his concern now, not people from his past, people he had never seen again and never would. He thought again of the money, of how he would sell it to her. Because he was selling something to her, most definitely. Like someone browsing his shop, Adriana didn't know exactly what she was looking for, but she knew she needed something. He was there to provide that now.

Sleep tugged at him again. When he closed his eyes, he did not see the little girl and her mother on the side of the road anymore. In their place were Adriana and Isabella. They needed him. He would not abandon them.

14

The bells at the shop door jingled. Luis looked up from his newspaper.

"*Hola*, Luis," Adriana said. She had a paper bag with her and was dressed for work. The door swung shut behind her and there was a brief gust of heat that swirled and died in the air conditioning.

"Adriana, this is a surprise," Luis said. He came out from behind the counter and gave her a hug, careful not to crush her bag. She gave him a brief kiss on the lips. "What are you doing here?"

"Bringing you food," Adriana replied. She produced containers from the paper bag and put them on the counter. There were plastic forks and knives and paper napkins, too. "I didn't think about drinks. I'm sorry."

"If you like water, then I have plenty."

"Water is good."

Luis went to fetch a couple of bottles from the shelves. He considered shuttering the store for lunch, but he thought maybe Adriana would find it too much like eating inside a prison. It wouldn't matter: business was usually slow in mid-day anyway.

She had paper plates out now and served *arroz con pollo.* There was a separate container with beans and she put corn tortillas by each plate.

"It's not hot," Adriana apologized.

"That's okay. It smells delicious."

They ate across from each other, standing at the counter. Luis watched her, considering how he could introduce the topic of money, then dismissing the thought. It was too soon.

She caught him looking at her and made a face. "Do I have something on me?"

"No, no. I just like to look at you, that's all."

"You'll make me self-conscious."

"I don't mean to."

"Talk to me, instead. Then at least you aren't staring."

"What should I talk to you about?"

"Anything. Tell me about business."

"It's good. It will be better when the weather's milder, but I'll get through the hot months all right." This made him think of money again and he pushed it from his mind. "I'm sure it's the same for Dr. Guzman."

Adriana made a noncommittal gesture with her hands. "It's different day to day. Some days it's crazy. Other days, like today, it's not so bad."

"That's why you were able to escape?"

"It's a good surprise, then?"

"Yes, very good."

They cleared the containers of their food, and then brought out a bundle of *coyotas* stuffed with brown sugar. Though there was nothing to making them, Luis thought they were the best *coyotas* he had ever had.

When they were finished, Luis said, "I'm stuffed. That's more lunch than I'm used to."

"That's why you're so skinny. We'll have to fatten you up."

"You'd like me better that way?"

"I like you whatever way."

Luis smiled. "I'm glad to hear you say that."

He gathered up the paper plates and napkins and the plastic cutlery and took them to the big trash can in the back room. When he returned, he caught her straightening out her blouse as if primping herself in front of the mirror. She blushed.

"I wanted to tell you something," she said once they were together again. "And you must realize that I've wanted to say it for a little while, only I've been too embarrassed."

"You don't have anything to be embarrassed about."

"Maybe so, maybe not. I wanted to tell you the other night when you came for dinner, but I was too caught up thinking about my mother. I'm sorry for that, by the way."

"No, don't apologize. She's your mother and family is important. My mother is passed away, but if she were in trouble now, I would do anything to help her, so I understand your sadness." Luis paused and then continued. "In fact, if there's something I can do to help, you have only to ask me."

"I couldn't ask you for help with that," Adriana said, and Luis' heart fell a little. "We've only known each other a few months."

"Still, I—"

"Don't worry about that. I heard what you said to me the other night and I'm not going to do anything foolish out of panic. You're right that Isabella and I have a life here."

Luis nodded, but kept silent.

"It's because of Isabella that I haven't... well, I haven't seen any men since Ernesto passed away. I don't want to confuse her. It's why I've wanted to go so slowly with you. I hope you understand."

"Of course."

"When we talked the other night, when we had a meal together, I thought I saw the chance to make things better for Isabella and me. That letting someone in was not necessarily a bad thing. That maybe you are the right one for us... for me."

"I feel the same way," Luis said.

Adriana took a deep breath, looked at her toes for a moment and then said, "I've made arrangements for Isabella to stay with a friend on Friday night. I'd like to have you for dinner again. Just the two of us. We'll have the whole evening to ourselves."

Luis exhaled sharply and smiled. "I wasn't sure where you were going with that," he said.

"Does that sound like something you would want?"

"Yes. Yes, it does."

Adriana sidled toward him hesitantly and Luis put his arms out for her. They embraced and this time when they kissed it lasted a long while.

15

He considered for some time what to bring Isabella as a present and finally settled on a soft doll. It was a girl in a peasant dress with long hair made of yarn. Luis hoped it would be well received.

At the appointed hour he arrived in the parking lot of Adriana's apartment building. He wore a clean, white shirt left unbuttoned at the collar and a pair of new denim pants. He'd chosen to wear the same boots he'd worn when they went dancing. He put on cologne.

Luis had flowers for Adriana. He gathered up the bouquet and the doll and climbed the steps to Adriana's apartment. His heart beat quickly and he steadied himself outside the door for a minute or two before knocking.

Isabella answered as before. She was not dressed up for dinner, but in shorts and a t-shirt for play. "Hello, Sr. González," she said. "Is it time already?"

"I think so. I might be a little early."

The little girl let him in and he was standing in the small front room of the apartment. Suddenly he remembered the doll and presented it to Isabella. "For you," he said.

Isabella received the doll with a serious face. "Does she have a name?" she asked.

"No. You'll have to name her."

"Hmm," Isabella mused. "I think a good name would be Cecilia."

"That is a good name. You like her?"

"Yes, thank you, Sr. González."

Luis crouched down so he could better speak to Isabella. "You can call me Luis if you want. We are friends, aren't we?"

Isabella nodded and the corner of her mouth quirked as if she might smile. "Yes. But is it all right for me to call a grown-up by his first name?"

"It's all right with me if you want to. I won't complain to anyone."

"Okay. Luis, then."

Luis touched Isabella lightly on the shoulder and smiled. "I'm glad we got that out of the way," he said. "Now, where is your mother?"

"She's in the bedroom, getting ready."

"Do you think you could help me with these flowers? Do you have a vase?"

"I don't know. I'll have to look."

"You do that and I'll wait here."

Isabella vanished into the kitchen area, leaving Luis alone. After a handful of minutes, Isabella returned with a white vase decorated with blue flowers. It was a little small, but Luis figured he could make the bouquet fit. "Is this all right?" Isabella asked.

"Yes, very good. Let's take these flowers to the kitchen and put them in water."

They went to the kitchen and saw to the flowers and vase. When they were done, they brought the vase back into the living room. The vase went on the undersized coffee table.

Adriana emerged from the next room. Luis saw that she had dressed up to the occasion, as well, and put on a pair of pearl earrings he had never seen before. He wondered if they were real. She wore makeup and her hair was done. "I'm sorry," she said to Luis, "I'm always running behind schedule."

"It's all right. Isabella kept me company."

"Are these flowers for me? They're beautiful, thank you. And is that a new doll, Isabella? Did you say thank you?"

"Yes, Mamá."

Adriana kissed Luis on the cheek briefly. "You're very thoughtful."

"Is it time for me to see Hector and Marta now?" Isabella asked.

"Yes. Get your bag."

Isabella vanished with Cecilia in tow.

"Hector and Marta are the neighbor children," Adriana explained. "They're about Isabella's age."

"She should have a good time."

"I hope so."

When Isabella returned with her small bag of things, Adriana ushered her daughter and Luis out of the apartment and locked the door behind them. She took Isabella by the hand and brought her to the third door down on the second floor. Luis waited while she spoke to the mother of Hector and Marta. It would be light for a couple more hours and there was a little grassy area near the apartment building with a pair of swings and room enough for a game of tag.

Adriana returned without Isabella and tried on a smile. "That's it," she said. "Are you ready? Where are we going?"

"I thought we could get some food and then maybe drive around a while before... before we come back. If that sounds like a good plan to you."

"I like it."

"Then after you."

They went to Luis' truck and he drove them to a restaurant not far from the international bridge. It was a clean, open place that served good food made with a home cook's care. Both Luis and Adriana had a couple of beers. Not enough to make them drunk, but enough to put a softer edge on the tension they both felt and neither talked about.

After that Luis drove aimlessly along through the town, past shops and offices and homes, not particularly caring where they were headed or how long it would take them to get there. Along the way he thought of mentioning the money he intended to give her, but dismissed the idea as coming too soon. They were both nervous enough, and something like that could spoil the mood completely. *Soon,* Luis promised himself.

The sun was going down by the time he put them back on course for home.

Luis saw no sign of Isabella or the neighbor children outside when they returned, but the twilight was deepening and likely they had been chased indoors. He parked and looked over at Adriana. She looked back hesitantly and he saw her bite her lip.

Then they were kissing in the shadowed cab. Her hands were on him and he touched her more urgently than he ever had before. She was yielding beneath his hands. He felt her hot breath on his skin when they broke at last. "Let's go in," she said quietly.

She held his hand up the stairs and let go only long enough to unlock the front door and see them through. After that they were on the couch, arms and legs twined together insistently. They didn't turn on the lights, but Luis could see her well enough in the dark: hair tousled, her blouse rumpled. "The bedroom?" he asked.

They passed down a short hallway and into another room. A little light from outside leaked through the curtains, showing two beds crammed into too small of a space. Adriana led him to the larger of the two and pulled him down on her.

He stripped her slowly in the unlit room before hurrying out of his own clothes. Then they were together on the narrow bed, on top of the sheets, her legs around him. It didn't seem to last very long, but they were together again twice more before finally they lay on their sides facing each other, Luis' back against the wall.

Luis rested his fingertips on Adriana's ribs, feeling the rise and fall of her breathing. He was aware of her watching his face and he wondered what she could see.

"Was it what you wanted?" Adriana asked him.

"Yes."

"I'm glad."

"Are you all right?" Luis asked.

"I'll be fine. I wanted it, too."

"You didn't have to," Luis said. "I would have waited."

"I know. But you waited long enough. It was time."

He wanted to ask her what changes would come now. Some he knew were coming. They would do this again. But would they still do the innocent things? Luis did not intend to let this alter his way of looking at her and he hoped it was the same for Adriana. Things were different, but they didn't have to disintegrate.

"How long until you have to bring Isabella home?" Luis asked.

Adriana checked the glowing bedside clock. "We still have another hour."

"What shall we do until then?"

"I'd think you were too tired to do *that*."

"You're probably right," Luis conceded. "It was just a thought."

"I like this," Adriana said. "Just being with you. I don't need anything else."

Luis let the room fall into silence. He traced the curve of her hip in the darkness, the bend of her leg as it extended slightly toward him, then back up to her arm, her shoulder and then her neck. Her hair was stuck there, the locks pasted down by sweat that was still drying. He plucked it away, leaving the skin bare.

"Do you love me?" Adriana asked then.

"I do."

"You don't have to say yes if you don't really."

"I'm not lying. I do love you."

"I wanted to tell you I loved you before, but it wasn't the right time. I was afraid of scaring you away. But now that we've been together it seems right to say."

"You wouldn't have scared me away," Luis said. "I don't scare so easily."

"Only it hasn't been that long, and—"

Luis put a finger to her lips, shushing her. "You don't have to explain anything to me. Love is a serious business, but you're a serious woman. You wouldn't rush into anything. That's not like you. And I'm careful, too."

She put her hand on his hand and pulled his finger away. "You don't think I'm too careful?"

"You can't be too careful. Not when it comes to this. You have Isabella to think of. It wouldn't be right for her to see man after man in her life. All those faces coming and going. You did what you had to do to make her safe, to know that I could be trusted to stay."

"Then you will stay?"

"As long as you'll let me."

"Thank you, Luis."

"You don't have to thank me."

Adriana was quiet, and then she said, "Do you think you could make love to me one more time before you go?"

"I can try."

"Then let's try."

16

L uis sat outside with his dogs as they ate their morning meal. They ignored him all but completely, focused instead on licking every last morsel of food from the bowls and then pushing the bowls around when there was nothing left to eat. Then they wandered around him, sensing his thoughtful mood, each coming for a turn nuzzling his hands or to press their bodies against his leg.

He wasn't unhappy. The night before had gone as well as he could have hoped, and he left Adriana's apartment full of life and energy despite the hour and the demands of lovemaking. He hadn't even been able to sleep right away, though by rights he should have been exhausted. When he finally slept, he dreamed the blank nothing only extreme tiredness could bring.

That was why he rose late and why he would be later still to get to the store. Luis did not feel like rushing things today. It seemed more like a day to mull things over than hurry.

Of course he would call her today at the office to check in on her. He wouldn't keep her long; he merely wanted her to know that he was thinking of her still and that last night had been important to him. Luis was very concerned that she understand he wasn't going to disappear, that the things he said were true, that he would be there again for her.

It occurred to him that he had not had Adriana and Isabella at his home. His trips to Adriana's apartment had been frequent enough, and she was always a gracious host. He was embarrassed now that he hadn't extended the same courtesy to her.

The house could stand a cleaning. Luis had a tendency to leave things as they were so long as they didn't get in his way. He'd grown used to the clutter and used also to being the only one called upon to deal with it. He wasn't even sure what he could do with everything even if he was to clear it all away; the things he owned weren't trash, and discarding them seemed a waste.

When he thought about spending real time together with Adriana — if they were to be married or just committed to living together — he considered the house and its potential. It could be emptied to the point where three could live there in comfort, if not grand style. Unlike where Adriana and Isabella lived now, mother and daughter would not have to share a room. A girl deserved her own space, Luis believed.

He owed no money on the house or the land. It belonged to his parents and they had settled ownership years before they died. The money Adriana saved on rent she could afford to send to her mother, or could be paid into savings for Isabella's future. All of this could be done eventually, once their relationship matured to that point.

"What do you think?" Luis asked the dogs. Ramiro, the ugliest of all his mutts, sat in front of Luis and licked his lips in response. He had no easy answers to provide.

It would be dinner, then. He would take a couple of days to clear the common areas, likely stacking things up in other rooms as a stopgap measure, and prepare to make a meal for Adriana for a change. They could come early and play with the dogs. Isabella would like that, he hoped. He had never asked if she had a pet dog when she was smaller, or how she felt about dogs now. Adriana herself seemed fine with the idea of them.

A meal at his home would also be a good time to talk about money. Though Adriana hadn't mentioned it, Luis knew the issue still had to be at least in the back of her mind. Her mother was not going to suddenly recover from her illness, and there was no extra income to be had in Ojinaga. Adriana was lucky to have one job, let alone two.

Luis had checked his account book and he had more than 100,000 pesos he could give Adriana right away. He would hold back only a little, just as he planned, as the seed from which a new cash reserve would grow. In a year's time he might be able to lend her still more.

It would be best of all if Adriana could bring her mother here. The old woman would not be able to live in that tiny apartment, but with a housing allowance from the state combined with Adriana's income and Luis' money, they could find something better. And when the time came that Adriana and Isabella could live with him, there would be plenty of places Adriana's mother could live comfortably on her own.

But he was thinking too far ahead again. Adriana hadn't even accepted the money yet, let alone decided where her mother could best live and be treated. And as inevitable as it might seem, there were no guarantees she would ever come to live with Luis.

"One thing at a time," Luis told himself and he went inside to get ready.

He got on the road twenty minutes later, still ruminating despite himself. He went on thinking about things even as he bought his morning paper, and they distracted him while he tried to read. Eventually he was forced to put the paper away and busy himself with mindless tasks around the store. Anything to still his brain. It almost worked.

At lunchtime he called Doctor Guzman's office, but the phone rang for a long time instead of being answered. Finally, a machine picked up and Luis closed the call without leaving a message. Now he had something new to fret about: where was she?

It wasn't that he was jealous. Instead, it was a kind of low-grade worry that something pressing might have come up and Adriana was forced to deal with it on her own. Maybe Isabella had taken sick. Maybe she wasn't feeling well herself. Or maybe, Luis considered, she was on her way to the store with another meal to surprise him.

He waited through the lunch hour hoping she would appear, but she didn't. Finally he called Dr. Guzman's office again and this time Adriana answered. "You're there," he said.

"Of course. Where else would I be?"

"I tried earlier and you weren't."

"Oh, I had to pick up a package for Dr. Guzman at the post office. Dental alginate. Do you know what that is?"

"Not really."

"It's something he uses to make models of teeth. He orders it from the States once in a while, and I always have to fetch it for him."

Luis felt stupid for worrying. She was at the post office, picking up something. Neither she nor Isabella were sick. Everything was well.

"I was hoping you'd come by and see me," Adriana said.

"I was hoping the same for you."

"Then we missed each other! Maybe tomorrow?"

"I'll be sure to come."

"That's good. I look forward to it. But I have to work again now. *Cuidate.*"

"Take care of yourself, too."

Luis hung up the phone and looked at the empty store. Worrying for nothing. Was this what happened when a man was in love? It had been so long he could hardly remember.

If he wasn't careful, he'd begin turning over the ideas of the morning in his head again and there would be no end to it. He looked forward instead to seeing Adriana tomorrow. He would bring food. They would talk. It would be good. And that was enough for now.

17

He spent two days cleaning the common areas of the house, mostly stacking up items in the second bedroom until there was barely space enough to move around in there. The floors were swept and polished and he put a new checkered tablecloth he purchased on the kitchen table.

There was little he could do for the outside of the house, which he realized for the first time was drab and run down. It had always been good enough for him, and appearances didn't mean much when the interior was comfortable, but he wished now that he had the time to repaint the exterior and maybe mend a few of the window screens.

Luis even made an effort to tidy up the dogs' area, filling in some of the deeper holes. The dogs had no idea what he was doing or why, but they stood by and let him do it without interference. He figured they would simply dig the holes again when the fancy struck them, but at least for now the dirt patch looked less like a bombing range.

It was a week later that he went to Adriana's to pick her up. They drove out of town with Isabella between them in the truck, heading out past the farthest edge of town and into the quiet countryside where he lived. Luis would have liked it if there were more trees, more green, and not just dirt and the occasional hardy plant or cactus. Ojinaga squatted in a dry land and there was nothing he could do about that.

He watched carefully for their reactions when the house came into view. When he didn't see looks of distaste, he relaxed a little. Things would be all right.

The dogs gathered to the truck as he pulled up, barking, knowing already that he wasn't alone. Luis parked and helped Isabella get out on his side. The dogs converged on the girl, pressing their noses forward. He interposed his body so they wouldn't crowd her too much. "They're curious," he told her. "Just let them sniff and then they'll get used to you."

Some broke away from the pack when Adriana came around from the passenger side. She held out her hands to them and they snuffled and licked. Luis could feel the excitement passing through them, but they weren't aggressive and he was glad of that.

"Can I pet them?" Isabella asked.

"Of course you can pet them," Luis replied.

He led Isabella by the hand away from the truck, the dogs moving with them. Isabella patted a brown-and-black dog named Franco, and soon the others were jostling for an opportunity for the girl to pat them, as well. A couple peeled off and went back to what they were doing before the truck arrived, their inquisitiveness satisfied. The crowd around Adriana and Isabella loosened somewhat.

"Come inside," Luis said. "We can play with the dogs in a little while."

Luis let them into the kitchen that he had so scrupulously looked after. He went into the refrigerator and produced a pitcher of *limonada*. Glasses came from an open-faced cabinet that had lost its door a long time ago. Everyone got a drink.

It was a little stuffy and Luis opened a window. Some of the dogs pressed up against the screen door to the kitchen, looking for another sniff or a pat on the head. Franco made a whining sound.

"So, this is it," Adriana said.

"Yes, this is it. My home."

"Will you show us the rest?"

"Come in the sitting room," Luis said. "The rest of the house we can save for another time. You don't want to see the bedrooms."

He had cleared out the sitting room completely except for a small couch and a rocking chair. His television set was tiny, with a twisted wire antenna that provided a fuzzy picture. There were photographs on the wall, mostly in black and white, but some in color.

"Is this your family?" Adriana asked.

"Yes. That's my mother and there's my father. These are my grandparents."

"And this little boy must be you."

"It is."

"You were a cute one. And look, you had a dog."

Luis blushed a little. "Always," he said.

Isabella sat on the rocking chair. Her feet dangled. "Will you teach me all of their names?" she asked.

"There are a lot of names to remember. Are you sure?"

"Yes!"

"Then I will. And we can play fetch with them. They love to play fetch."

"When will we eat?" Adriana asked.

"Not long. I have a lot prepared already. I just need to get to the kitchen and do the rest."

"Would you like some company?"

"Of course."

"I want to see the dogs again!" Isabella exclaimed.

"All right," Adriana said, "but don't get your dress dirty."

They gravitated back to the kitchen. Adriana sat at the table and Isabella went outside to the dogs. Luis busied himself with dinner. A long, flat cooking dish with carefully folded and sauced enchiladas came out of the refrigerator and went into the oven. He started on rice.

"My house isn't that impressive," Luis said after a while.

"It's nice. And it must be very quiet out here."

"It is. And a good place for my dogs. They get to run free and no one bothers them. It would be different in town. I would have to have a big yard and even then they would be fenced in."

"I knew you had them, but I didn't know you had so many."

"They don't call me Dog Man for nothing."

Adriana watched him, sipping from her glass now and again. She seemed a natural fit to his house. Luis had worried before that she would seem *wrong* here, that it would not be the same on his own ground as it was when he visited her. When he heard Isabella laughing outside, though, the image was complete and it was good.

"I'm glad to have you here finally," Luis said. "I'm sorry it took so long."

"It's all right. But my apartment was getting too small, I think."

Luis thought of them together in the darkness of her bedroom. They hadn't repeated that since. Luis felt presumptuous asking for more, knowing Adriana wanted to take things slowly, but having the urge nonetheless. "There's plenty of room here," he said. "Even though I have many things that belonged to my parents taking up space. I need to find a place for it all."

"How long has it been since your parents died?"

"A few years now. My father died when I was younger. My mother lasted a while longer. She died here, at home. It was what she wanted."

Luis saw a shadow pass over Adriana's face. She put her glass down.

"How is your mother?"

"You don't have to ask."

"No, I want to know. If you want to tell me."

Adriana sighed. "She's no better."

Luis stirred the rice. Heady steam rose from the pot. "I may have an idea about how to help you," he said. "With your mother, I mean."

"How?"

He cleared his throat and without looking at Adriana, he said, "I have some money put away. I could—"

"No, Luis. No."

"But I want to. And it's no trouble, really."

He felt Adriana looking at him, and he stared into the rice pot as if to escape her gaze. "My mother is my problem," Adriana said. "I won't drag you into it."

Luis ventured a glance in Adriana's direction. Her face was not unkind. "I feel like I'm involved," he tried. "You and Isabella and your mother... all the same. This isn't charity from me."

"Of course it is, and I won't have you putting yourself out for me."

"Maybe some charity *is* what's called for," Luis said with a little more force. "You need money for your mother. I have more money than I need. It makes sense."

"I don't want to talk about it now."

"All right," Luis said and he went back to cooking.

They had dinner around the kitchen table and did not speak of Adriana's mother even in passing. The meal was good, though Luis could have benefited from more practice and some of Adriana's special touch. He was used to making bachelor meals and he thought he could taste his inexperience.

Afterward they went outside with the dogs. Luis brought out the tennis racket and the collection of ratty balls and showed Isabella how to make the dogs chase them. This delighted Isabella and she clapped her hands as the dogs competed for the balls and then came rushing back to drop them at Luis' feet. Despite Adriana's admonition, the hem of Isabella's dress was dusty and dirty from playing with the dogs. Adriana didn't reprimand her.

When the sun went down, they retreated indoors to the sitting room where they talked. Isabella quickly grew bored and then tired, and before long she was snoozing on the end of the couch. Luis and Adriana left her and went to Luis' room.

They didn't undress. Adriana lifted her skirt and leaned over the bed and Luis came in behind her. They made sure not to make any noise that might wake Isabella in the next room. Later they lay side by side on the narrow bed, surrounded by Luis' things in the dark.

"Thank you for offering to help," Adriana said at last.

"I still want to."

"I know you do, but it's not right. I won't make those kinds of demands on you. Not now, when things are going so well."

"It won't change anything."

"Yes, it will. We will try not to let it affect us, but we'll know that things are different. If we were married...."

Luis stroked Adriana's bare arm. The softness of her skin was luxurious. "Then maybe we should get married."

She stiffened against him. "What?" she asked.

Immediately Luis regretted saying anything. He stared resolutely at the shadowed ceiling, trying to bore himself into it and escape his own stupidity. Adriana was a statue in his arms. "Forget it," he said.

"It's too soon to talk about such things," Adriana said.

"I know. I'm sorry."

Adriana was quiet a while. "I shouldn't have told you I love you."

"There's nothing wrong with that," Luis said.

"I knew it was too soon. I should have waited."

"It wasn't too soon," Luis said. "You love me. I love you. It's natural that we should say it."

Adriana sat up in the bed and straightened her skirt. She made to get up, but Luis caught her by the arm and held her there. "Let go," she said.

"Don't leave."

"You should take me back home. Isabella needs to sleep in her own bed."

"I don't want you to go. Stay here with me. Please."

Luis relaxed his grip on her arm and she didn't flee, but neither did she lay down again. She kept her back to him, and soon after he felt her shaking, though he couldn't hear her tears.

"Are you crying because of me?" Luis asked.

"No. I'm crying because it isn't fair."

"What isn't fair?"

"This. I should never have to ask you for this."

Luis sat up behind Adriana and put his arms around her. She was warm and pliant in his embrace and he could smell the scent of perfume from her neck. Adriana had done everything to be pretty for him tonight and he had made a mess of it. "You didn't ask me," he said. "I offered."

"I shouldn't have told you what was happening, then."

"I don't want you to hold anything back."

Adriana cried harder and Luis held her. She didn't try to escape him and he wouldn't have let her even if she had. They were bonded in the lightless room. He wanted her here forever if he could. Finally, she turned in his arms and kissed him and he kissed her back, tasting tears. She let herself be lowered into his lap and he cradled her until the crying ultimately stopped.

"Take the money," Luis said after she was silent.

"I can't."

"Take the money," Luis insisted. "Please. For me."

Another long quiet passed between them. "All right," she said.

"We'll go to the bank tomorrow."

"All right."

"And if you feel like you must repay me, then you can take your time. Like I told you, I have more money than I need. The store takes care of itself. This is something *you* need and I want to help you with it."

"All right."

"Go in the bathroom and check your makeup. You don't want Isabella to see that you've been crying. I'll take you home after."

She got up from the bed and went into the bathroom. Light flashed under the closed door. Luis listened for more crying, but she was spent of her tears. When she emerged, they held each other close and kissed, and Luis knew it would be all right.

18

They did as they planned. Luis had a check made out to Adriana and she took it, though she could not look the bank manager in the eye. Luis made sure she got to work after that. They didn't speak. And then went to his store.

He was opening the last of the shutters when he heard Ángel Rojas' truck creeping up the road. Luis tried to ignore the sound, but Ángel sounded his horn and Luis could disregard him no longer.

Ángel parked on the curb. When he came around to the , Luis saw the pistol again, worn openly, and wondered why the soldiers or the police hadn't seen fit to take it from him. A gun meant going to prison for someone like Luis. Ángel was surrounded by a ring of grace.

"Dog Man!" Ángel said. "Just the one I wanted to see."

Luis went into the store and Ángel followed. The man seemed wrong among the displays because he was not the type who would ever come here. Luis' customers were the poor, the desperate, the hopeful. Ángel Rojas did not fit any of these labels.

"What is this?" Ángel asked. "No 'hello'? No 'how are you doing, Ángel?'"

"Hello, Ángel," Luis said. He retreated behind the counter to put some space between himself and Ángel, but then Ángel simply bellied up against the other side. "How are you?"

"I'm doing very well," Ángel said.

"What can I do for you? I don't think you came to buy supplies."

"No, I didn't. But you might notice you're doing more business lately because of me. I've been sending my crossers to you, telling them they need new bags or new shoes or something. You should thank me."

"Thank you."

Ángel smiled. "You're welcome."

"If it's not supplies, then what do you need?"

"I wondered if you've given any more thought to what we discussed a while ago."

"If you mean about crossing the border, then no."

"Even though you talked with Alberto Pérez?"

Luis paused before answering. He thought about who might have told Ángel Rojas about his meeting with Alberto. No one had seen them together. It had to have been Alberto himself. "Alberto came to visit me."

"Alberto wanted to get back into the *coyote* business again in a more relaxed environment than Nuevo Laredo. He worked some difficult jobs back there, you know. The Americans are all over traffic across the border."

"They're not ignoring us here, either."

"But it's not like there. Even I would think twice about trying something in Nuevo Laredo. All those Border Patrol. All the expenses. I like things the way there are here: peaceful. I can do my business without having to worry so much."

Luis nodded, though he wasn't agreeing so much as letting Ángel talk. This was all leading one place, and Luis knew exactly what Ángel would say before he said it, just as he knew what his answer would be. They were merely playing out a scene.

"Alberto is a smart one," Ángel said. "He saw the situation in Nuevo Laredo and figured he could do better. Of course, he thought he could work without going through me, and that was his mistake."

"What did you do to Alberto?"

"Do? I didn't do anything to him. What kind of a man do you think I am?"

"But he didn't want to go into a partnership with you. He said so himself."

"That's what he said to me, too. I told him he was better off letting me be his middleman, but like I say, Alberto is a smart one. Too smart for his own good."

"Where is Alberto now?"

"Right now? Probably in his apartment. I told you, I didn't do anything to him."

"But something happened."

"Yes, something," Ángel said and his eyes glittered with amusement.

"Is Alberto working for you now?"

"The short answer? Yes. He's seen that he can't do business in Ojinaga without dealing with the Rojas brothers. And I'm glad he came to his senses before anything else happened to him."

Luis' mind turned, trying to draw more out of Ángel's words than the man was giving up. So far he hadn't heard of Ángel or Francisco using force against anyone who refused to work with them, but he supposed it wasn't impossible. But if Ángel had done something himself, why wouldn't he just say it?

"I wanted to offer you another chance to reconsider my offer," Ángel said.

"To work for you? I've said it before: I'm no good to you. All I do is sell supplies and advice now."

"You do more than that. I hear you help widows with their money problems."

Luis felt his face flush. He wanted to shout, but he didn't. "Who's been talking to you?"

"Haven't you heard? I know everything that's going on. And when you're giving out that kind of money, I figure it has to be some first-class *chocha* we're talking about. The kind that gets expensive."

"You get out! You get out of my shop!"

Luis boiled out from behind the counter, pointing at the door. Ángel was bigger than he was and heavier and he had a gun, but Luis disregarded all of those things. He pushed Ángel in the chest and the man fell back a step.

"You're being a hothead now!" Ángel said, and his face was dark.

"You get the hell out! You get out now!"

"Don't be stupid, Luis! You're better off working with me!"

Luis pushed Ángel again and then again until Ángel was at the door. "I don't give a shit what you have to say! Don't come back here again!"

Ángel halfway out the door. "You're going to end up just like Alberto," he said, and before Luis could say anything in return, he left. A few moments later the truck started up and rumbled away from the curb.

Luis was breathing hard and his vision was sharp from hyperventilation. He kicked the door hard enough to make the bells jingle. "*¡Pinche culero!*" he shouted at the empty store.

It was a while before he was calm enough to stand still, time spent pacing the aisles and cursing at random, half-hoping Ángel would come back through the door and Luis could take that damned pistol and beat him with it. He wanted to call someone, but he had no one to call. He didn't know how to reach Alberto, and Adriana did not need to be burdened with this.

"Goddamn it," he said. "Goddamn it."

19

He was in the storeroom when the soldiers came. They smashed through the front door, tearing the bells off their mount and cracking the glass, eight men in green uniforms with weapons. Luis had an armload of shoeboxes with him; he dropped them when they began to tear the store apart.

"Wait! What's going on?" Luis demanded as one soldier tipped over a display at the end of one aisle, spilling packages of caffeine pills and energy shots across the floor. Another raked his arm along a shelf of goods, sending all of it crashing. Luis tried to stop them, but two soldiers grabbed him by the arms and shoved him back against the counter.

They were methodical and they said nothing at all. Luis could not tell if they were even looking for anything. All they did was destroy, aisle after aisle, stepping over the fallen piles of merchandise to wreck the next set of shelves. One used the butt of his assault rifle to break the shelves themselves, bending them out of shape or snapping them off their pegs. Luis hollered for them to stop, but a soldier punched him in the mouth.

When they were finally done, they returned to the front of the store. One of them, a man with sergeant's stripes, stood squarely before Luis and shouted into his face: "Where are the drugs?"

"I don't have any drugs! Please, what are you doing?"

The sergeant kicked Luis between the legs. Luis went down halfway, supported by the arms, retching with pain. "The drugs!" the man demanded. "Where are you hiding them?"

"I don't... I don't have any," Luis said.

"Hold my weapon," the sergeant told one of his men. And then, to the ones holding Luis, "Get him back up."

The sergeant had fists of stone and he drove them into Luis' body. He was careful not to smash Luis in the face. Probably so he wouldn't break his hand. Once Luis did throw up, and he spattered the sergeant's boots. The man's face was a black cloud.

"Pliers!" the sergeant called.

The soldiers holding Luis' arms turned him around and forced him against the counter. His ribs were swelling against his flesh and it was hard for him to breathe. He could not resist as another soldier unfastened Luis' belt and yanked his pants down. Cool air played on Luis' legs.

"Get him spread!" the sergeant ordered.

They forced his legs apart and then a hard, sharp cold seized his scrotum from below. Luis screamed as it twisted and yanked. He felt blood.

Again the demand: "Where are the drugs?"

"I don't—!" Luis tried to say before the pliers bit flesh again.

"You're a fucking liar! Where are the drugs?"

The sergeant hurt him, the pain ballooning up through his body and blocking his throat so that he couldn't answer even when they asked him questions. They threatened to crush his balls and once he thought they were doing it. When the agony finally stopped, he fell to the floor among his things, shaking uncontrollably, his chin slick with spittle and his eyes full of tears.

The soldiers took turns kicking him into a ball, then marched out through the cracked front door to the waiting truck. He was bleeding onto his thighs, but he felt himself and everything was still there. His hand came away sticky with red.

He couldn't get up; his muscles wouldn't obey him. He lay there as two customers came to the door, then fled when they saw the scene inside. The police would come, he was sure, but no police came. In time, he dragged himself to the door and locked it. It took longer for him to pull his pants up around his waist and longer still to limp through the chaos to the back door and out to his truck. Twice on the way to the hospital he nearly passed out, but he made it there before the shakes kicked in again and he was unable to drive.

The nurses didn't ask him what happened. There was gauze and tape and they took an x-ray that showed one of his ribs was cracked. A doctor came to see him and he, too, didn't want to know the story. They left Luis on a bed in the corner of the emergency ward, shuddering under a thin blanket, until at last they had prescriptions for painkillers ready and sent him on his way.

At home he barely greeted his dogs, though they swarmed around him, smelling the blood on him, sensing his distress. He made it to his bed and collapsed into it fully clothed and, once there, he cried as if he were a child.

In his own bed he could sleep and when he woke again it was the middle of the night. The dogs scratched at the door, hungry for their evening meal, but he ignored them. He undressed himself carefully, thankful he couldn't see himself clearly in the dark. The knot of sterile dressing in his crotch was uncomfortable, but it contained the swelling he could feel with every movement.

When he could sleep again he was unconscious until daylight. The dogs were more insistent than ever. He dragged on his robe and staggered into the kitchen to make their meal. He was careful not to look at his body.

After that he took a dose of the painkillers and went back to bed. Hours passed into hours this way until it was nightfall again. It seemed to be easier to move when he prepared the dog's food, but he knew it was just his imagination. More painkillers brought more sleep.

He spent three days like that. Once or twice the phone rang for a long time, but he didn't get up to answer it. On the fourth day he dared to remove the gauze from his scrotum and saw the discolored marks, the broken skin and the swelling that hadn't yet gone away. Walking was still torturous, especially if he closed his legs.

On the fifth day he called Adriana.

"Luis, where have you been? I've been calling you. I went by the store and it looks like you were robbed! Are you all right?"

Luis wanted to cry into the phone, but he did not. "I'm all right," he said. "I'm going to come back to the store soon."

"What happened?"

"It was nothing. A misunderstanding."

"I'm coming to see you."

"No, don't come. I'm fine."

"I can tell you're lying. I'm coming out."

She hung up before Luis could argue more.

20

Adriana got a ride from a friend. Luis heard her arrive, the dogs barking. He didn't rise from his bed. She came in through the kitchen and made her way to the bedroom. When she saw him, he heard her catch her breath. His robe was open and the thick pattern of bruises was plainly visible.

"*¡Dios mío!*"

She came to him and would have embraced him if he hadn't flinched away. When she opened his robe further, she saw the rest of it and Luis saw her eyes began to tear.

"What happened?"

He told her everything. About the visit from Ángel and then the soldiers. About the sergeant and his pliers. At times both of them cried. Luis hated himself for being like this, for Adriana's upset, for all of it. He hated Ángel, too. He hated Ángel most of all.

"What will you do?" Adriana asked him.

"I'm going back to my store."

"What if they come again?"

"Then they come again. There's nothing I can do."

"They'll kill you," Adriana said.

"No, they won't."

"Then Ángel Rojas will."

"He won't, either."

"How can you know?"

"I know."

Adriana fell silent until finally she said, "Would it be so bad, working for him?"

Luis searched her face, but he saw nothing hidden there. Now he hated himself for suspecting her, even for a moment. "Is that what you think I should do?"

"I don't know what you should do. I just know I don't want this."

"I stopped doing that. I opened my store. I never wanted to go back."

"But he won't leave you alone, will he?"

"No."

"Then you have to do what he wants."

"That's not the man I want to be. For you. For Isabella."

Adriana cried again. Her tears fell on his cheek. "I only want you to be there for us."

"I always will be."

Luis wiped her eyes. He felt his own tears coming again.

"I'll look after you until you're better," Adriana said.

"I can take care of myself."

"No, I'll look after you. I'll come after work and be sure you eat right, that you're resting. I'll feed your dogs for you."

"How will you get here?"

Adriana smiled. "I'll use your truck."

"Don't you think you should ask first?"

"I just did."

She left him then and let him sleep. In his dreams he heard her busy in the kitchen and when he woke there was warm soup to eat. He told her how to make the dogs' meals and she did that, too. It was nearly dark by the time she left.

The next week was a cycle of the same. She came to him after work and only left him when she could stay no longer. Sometimes she lay in the bed beside him, careful not to touch him where he was still tender. He was glad of her presence and missed her when she was gone.

One day he heard the truck early and he left the bed to greet her. He met Ángel Rojas at the kitchen door.

"What do you want?" Luis asked.

"I came to see you. Your store has been closed for a while now. I thought maybe you were dead."

"You knew I wasn't."

"You're right, I knew. May I come in?"

"No."

"That's all right. I'll stay out here with your mutts."

The dogs milled around, but none of them came near Ángel.

"Is this what happened to Alberto?" Luis asked.

"Something like that. The police heard he was a courier for Los Zetas. They had to check him out thoroughly."

"You're a *pinche cabrón*."

Ángel smiled broadly. "I won't argue that."

"Then I'll ask you again: what do you want?"

"I want to know if you're feeling better about our partnership."

"Why do you even need me? You have plenty of *coyotes* in your stable. Young guys. I'm not young anymore."

"This is true, but you're also a role model for my boys. Everybody knows the name of Luis González. You can teach them all your secrets."

"I don't have any more secrets, don't you understand?"

"Then you'd better come up with some," Ángel said, "or you're going to get more visits. Maybe next time they break your *cojones* off at the roots."

"Goddamn it, Ángel, why are you doing this?"

"Because I can, you fucking *mamón*! Because this is what I *want*." Ángel's face congested, but then it cleared again. "But I'm in no hurry anymore. Take your time. Get better. And when you're good and ready, you come see me. We'll take it from there."

Luis felt hollow inside. "All right," he said. "All right."

21

I t took a month to undo the damage from the soldiers' visit.
Luis repaired the shelves as best he could and ordered new
ones where he could not. Business was slow to pick up again.
Luis did not ask Adriana for his money back.

His body healed. Adriana came every day for two more
weeks, then just twice and then not at all. He felt good enough
to make love to her again. He handled her delicately, as if she
was the one who had been hurt.

She called him at the store.

"I have to go," Adriana said.

"Go where?"

"To my mother. She's not doing well. They say she doesn't
have long."

Luis stood in the empty store. Everything was the way it
had been. Whenever a big truck went by, he shriveled inside,
expecting it to stop and for more soldiers to burst in, but they
never did. The crack was still in the glass of the front door.

"How long will you be gone?" he asked.

"I don't know. I've already asked Dr. Guzman for leave
and he's agreed. I'm going tomorrow."

"So soon?"

"I have to, Luis. It could happen any day."

"What about Isabella?"

"She'll come with me. She knows her *abuela* is ill. She's ready."

"I'll miss you," Luis said.

"I'll be thinking of you also."

"Can I see you before you go?"

"I don't think there's any time."

"Adriana—"

"I'm sorry, Luis. I don't want to go, but my mother needs me."

"Maybe I can come with you," Luis said impulsively.

"You have your store to keep track of. We'll be all right."

"Okay."

"Good-bye, Luis."

"Good-bye, Adriana."

He put the phone down. A clutch of four people were peering through his front window, talking to one another. Ángel was sending customers his way again. He knew he should smile for them and wave them inside, but he didn't feel like being cheerful for strangers. Instead he went behind the counter and stared at the phone, hoping it would ring again, that Adriana would have changed her mind and that she wanted him to come with her. To hell with the store.

The crossers came inside. "*Hola, señor,*" said the eldest one. Luis thought maybe they were all related. An uncle and three brothers, or maybe a cousin among them. They looked very much alike.

"*Hola,*" Luis said without enthusiasm.

"We were told... that is, we were sent here to get some supplies. For the crossing."

Luis could barely muster up enough energy to reply. "Who sent you to me?"

"His name is Alberto. He's going to help us with the crossing. Do you know him?"

"I know him."

"You'll help us find what we need?"

"I'll help you," Luis said, and he did.

They were out the door in less than twenty minutes, burdened with things they didn't really need. Luis sold them premium items they could have done without, not because he had any good reason to, but because it pleased him in some small way. Everyone was taking their cut from these people — Alberto, Ángel, Los Zetas — and why not Luis González? They'd land on the far side of the river with nothing left in their pockets, vacuumed clean by the people they paid to bring them to a better life. Some of them would bargain for more and carry debt they would never be able to repay. Luis couldn't bring himself to care.

It was the same for the crossers who came into the store after that, and then the ones after that. Luis fleeced them of every peso he could, all the while feeling a growing sense of sickness with himself that became open loathing. By the time he closed the shutters at the end of the day, he hated himself more thoroughly than he had ever hated anyone, even Ángel Rojas.

He didn't drive for home, but drove north toward the border until he saw a neon sign with big red letters proclaiming EL VAQUERO. His truck slotted in among a handful of others, including Ángel Rojas' shiny ride.

Luis had no trouble finding Ángel inside. Both the Rojas brothers held court in a corner booth facing the bar. On a small stage, a woman danced without much zeal, her top removed but her bikini bottoms still on. Luis wondered how she was able to move so well in high-heeled shoes. Scattered around the stage were men with drinks, tossing 20-peso bills at the dancer's feet like well-wishers.

"Dog Man!" Ángel called when he saw Luis. He waved for Luis to come closer. "Sit down with us!"

The man who had been sitting with Ángel and Francisco left, opening a spot for Luis. Francisco was like his brother, though thinner and slightly devilish looking with his goatee. Luis had never seen Francisco outside of El Vaquero.

"Dog Man, you know my brother," Ángel said. "Francisco, Dog Man."

"Hello," Luis said.

"Something to drink?" Ángel asked. "Have something to drink."

"No, thank you."

"You here for business?"

"Why else would I come?" Luis asked.

Ángel smiled at Luis and then he nudged his brother. "I told you he would come around eventually. Dog Man may be many things, but he is *not* stupid."

"Do you have crossers going over?"

"All the time. When do you want to go?"

"Soon."

"I can do soon. How is two nights from now?"

"All right," Luis said.

"It'll be a dozen people. You don't mind handling a big group your first time back?"

"No, I can handle it."

"I'm glad to hear that. Meet me here on Thursday night around seven o'clock. That is, if you don't mind closing your store early."

Luis was a machine. He felt Francisco watching him. He nodded. "I can do that."

"Thursday night, then. And Dog Man? It's good to have you working with us."

22

That Thursday night he did close the store early, putting out two customers who were still browsing the aisles. They stood by as he put down the shutters and finally left as he locked the front door. When he pulled out onto the street in his truck, they had disappeared.

He drove to El Vaquero and parked on the side. There were fewer vehicles there than had been gathered two nights before, but it was still early. Ángel's truck was among them.

Luis pulled a blue windbreaker from behind the seat and put it on. He zipped it up halfway, like armor, before he ventured through the red door of the club.

There was a different dancer on the stage and only one man sitting close to watch her. Ángel was alone in his booth, nursing a beer. He raised a hand in greeting as Luis drew near. "Dog Man," he said, "glad to see you."

Luis stopped at the booth, but didn't sit down. "I'm here. When do we go?"

"Soon, soon. Don't be in such a hurry. Sit down and drink with me. Flaco! A beer for my friend!"

"I don't need anything to drink," Luis said. He slid into the booth, conscious of Francisco's absence and the general emptiness of the club. They stood out here and it made him uncomfortable.

"You'll drink with me," Ángel said.

The beer came. The bottle sweated, the beer golden. Luis put out his hand just to touch the glass with his fingers. It was chilly in the club, but the beer was chillier still.

"Go ahead," Ángel said. "Drink up."

Luis fisted the beer and raised it to his lips. He drank, and the beer was cool and strangely satisfying, despite everything. When he put the bottle down again, he pushed it away from himself; he did not want to go into this with anything less than a clear head.

"It's good that you're ready to go," Ángel said.

"I want to get it over with."

Ángel laughed and shook his head. "We haven't even started yet and you're thinking about going home already! Don't you know you have to keep your head in it? I shouldn't have to tell you this."

"When will we go?"

"In a few hours. There's no rush. We have all night."

"Then why did you ask me here so early?"

"Because I wanted to take some time with you! Is that so bad? Just to talk."

Luis grabbed at the bottle again and drank angrily, quickly. He did not want to be in a temper with Ángel, not so close to a crossing, and maybe a beer would take the edge off. When he finished the bottle, Ángel called for another one. Luis drank that, too. He chided himself for being foolish. *A clear head. Remember?*

"Slow down," Ángel said. "Don't be in such a hurry."

"What did you want to talk with me about?"

"Just things. Like how you're feeling. All healed up?"

"Yes."

"Good. Your store is back to normal?"

"Yes."

"Even better. So it's like nothing bad ever happened."

Luis wondered if Ángel could see the hate in his eyes. Briefly he considered another drink, but he'd done enough damage. He was being foolish and he could not afford to be so.

"You know, I didn't like having to put them on you. There didn't seem to be any other way to make you come around."

"Well, you got what you wanted."

"Yes," Ángel said. He smiled a little. "Yes, I did."

The conversation withered. Ángel finished his beer slowly. His eyes were on the dancer, a short woman with small breasts and boyish hips. Luis could not be bothered to look at her.

"You know that girl over there?" Ángel said finally. "I'm going to fuck her tonight before we go."

"I'm glad to hear it."

"She'll fuck you, too, if you want it."

"That's all right."

"I forgot: you have a woman. What's her name again?"

"Adriana."

"And she's got a kid, right? That's a lot of trouble. I don't waste my time with women who have kids. Not when there are so many others to screw. Ah, well. There'll be time enough for that kind of thing later. Excuse me, Dog Man."

Ángel slid out of the booth and approached the stage. He tucked a bill in the girl's bikini bottoms and applauded loudly when she left the stage. When she vanished into the back room through a cascade of beaded strings, Ángel followed. Luis stayed where he was.

He found he couldn't sit any longer and he left the booth. A new girl was on the stage. Luis brushed past a couple of men entering as he left, escaping to the parking lot where the air was clearer.

Luis got into his truck. It occurred to him to simply drive away, but he had nowhere to go. If he hid at his home, Ángel would find him there, and the store was no safer. He was tethered to El Vaquero by an invisible rope and to Ángel by a chain.

After a while Ángel emerged from the club. He approached Luis, his boots crunching on the gravel lot. "I thought you ran out on me," he said.

"I'm here."

"Well, since you're ready, we might as well go. Follow me."

Ángel guided his own truck away from El Vaquero, and Luis trailed obediently behind. They crossed town and stopped at the very eastern edge of Ojinaga at an apartment building that looked as though it could fall down if the wind lashed it too hard. There was a big truck like the army used parked in the lot.

"Come inside," Ángel commanded when they were out of their vehicles. He led the way to a ground-floor apartment and unlocked the door with a ring of keys.

The crossers were waiting inside, some in the front room and some in the bedroom. The floors were scattered with mattresses, but no other furniture. There was no television or even a radio. The smell of old sweat was thick in the stuffy apartment; no one had so much as cracked a window.

"Your clients," Ángel said.

They gathered from different areas of the apartment. Seven women and four men and one little girl. Luis could not tell her age, but she was young, maybe as young as Isabella.

Her clothes were dirty. Many of the crossers' clothes were dirty, as if they had come a long way without access to soap or water, and maybe they hadn't.

"This is your guide," Ángel told the assembled crossers. Luis could not keep his eyes from the little girl. He remembered a hot afternoon and a strip of asphalt running to the horizon in both directions.

Ángel went on: "What he tells you to do, you do and you don't ask questions. It's the same for me: if I tell you to do something, you damned well better do it or I'll leave you out there."

Luis dragged his eyes away from the girl. "You?" he asked. "What do you mean?"

"Not in front of the children," Ángel said.

They passed outside and Ángel closed the door behind them. Luis felt a fresh anxiety plucking at his nerves. "What are you talking about?" he asked.

"I'm coming with you," Ángel said.

"When was that part of the deal?"

"You've been out of circulation a while, Dog Man. Someone has to watch over you, make sure you're still sharp. I would send Francisco, but his prints are already on file over the river and he can't afford to be caught again. So I'll do it myself. You wouldn't let me get caught."

"I thought you trusted me."

"Of course I trust you. This has nothing to do with that. Think of it as an on-the-job inspection."

"I also don't like that there's a kid with them."

"What's not to like? She's a little tyke. She won't be trouble. Her uncle is taking her to the States."

"Her uncle," Luis said.

"That's right. What are you worried about?"

Luis saw himself walking away from the crossers by the side of the road, passing to the south until they were gone for good. He crossed the river back to Mexico alone. "I just didn't know there would be any kids."

"I tell you don't worry. Ah, look, Ignacio is here."

A young man in a beat-up white Ford pickup cruised to a stop in front of the apartments and got out. He was lean and dark brown from a long time in the sun, his hair trimmed so closely to his scalp that it was just a shadow. The mustache he wore was thin. Luis thought he couldn't even be twenty.

"Ignacio," Ángel said. "Come over here and meet the Dog Man."

The kid approached, his eyes flickering up and down Luis, measuring him. He extended a thin-fingered hand. "*Mucho gusto*," he said.

Luis shook Ignacio's hand. "Who is this?" he asked Ángel.

"I just told you: this is Ignacio. He's one of my boys. He'll be coming with us."

"Wait a minute," Luis said and he raised his hands in protest, "you didn't say anything about bring one of your people along with us, either."

"Is there a problem?"

"Yes, there's a problem. We're already bringing across a big group and now there's you and Ignacio to think about. How many more of your people are you going to send over with us?"

Ángel shook his head. "You're getting excitable again. It's just going to be me and Ignacio. What's the matter, don't you like getting help? You said yourself that you're rusty. Ignacio has run a couple groups across the border on his own."

"Ángel tells me you're good," Ignacio said. "That I can learn from you."

"I don't know about that," Luis said.

"Don't be modest," Ángel said.

"Twelve people. One kid. You and Ignacio. That's it?"

"That's it. Besides the *mota*."

Luis felt a weight bear down on him and he reeled. He took a step back, steadied himself, and tried to bring some steadiness to his voice when he wanted to shout. "What marijuana?"

"Everyone carries a load," Ángel said. "It's part of their deal."

"Goddamn it, Ángel, I don't run dope! That wasn't part of *my* deal!"

"Your deal is whatever I say it is!" Ángel barked.

Luis opened his mouth to say more, but a look from Ángel silenced him. The weight did not leave him. The corner of Ignacio's mouth turned up in a smirk, and Luis knew exactly what he was thinking. Luis' face burned.

Adriana, why didn't I go with you?

"Are we clear?" Ángel asked, his voice taut.

"Okay," Luis said. He hung his head. "Okay."

"That's better," Ángel replied and the anger bled from his face. "There's no reason for this to go anything but smoothly. All you have to do is lead the way, Dog Man. Let us worry about the rest."

PART THREE
MARISOL

1

She woke to cock crowing in the dim early morning, but at first she did not stir in her bed. Instead she lay quietly, listening to the sound of nothing — empty streets and sleeping homes — and her own heartbeat.

It wasn't until she heard the distant noise of a car engine turning over that she pushed back the sheet and rose from her bed: a low, metal-framed construction that had belonged to her grandmother. Gentle light filtered in through the lace curtains on the window.

Still in her nightdress, she went to a wooden stand where a broad-mouthed enamelware bowl sat beside a matching pitcher of water. She poured out a measure into the bowl and washed her face and hands in it without soap.

The house was small: just three rooms, with the main one boasting both front and rear doors. She unlatched the back door and crossed a little space with a green garden to the outhouse where she did her business for the morning before retreating indoors again.

Her kitchen was a round-edged room dominated by an earthen stove fed with wood. There was also a single electrical socket into which she had plugged a hot plate. She heated a skillet on the hot plate and made eggs for herself. She ate in the main room at a tiny table with two chairs.

The light from outdoors was stronger when she returned to her room and dressed for the day. Her clothes were simple: a blouse and a skirt and sandals for her feet. The floor of the house was made of bare wood and sometimes the planks splintered, so the sandals protected her.

She went out in the front of the house and saw one of her neighbors unchaining a bicycle from a wooden post. "*Buenos días*, Marisol," the man said.

"*Buenos días*, Sr. Martínez."

"Have a good day," the man said, and he biked up the road past Marisol's house.

There was a clutch of houses in this corner of the village of Perquín, all of them small but all of them sturdily built. Deep forest grew up all along the road opposite them and the road itself was steep. They were in the mountains of Morazán in El Salvador, more than a hundred kilometers from the first city of size, San Miguel. Some of the houses had space enough in back to keep animals like goats and chickens. Marisol used hers for the garden.

A large bucket waited by the front door. Marisol locked the door with a padlock and took up the bucket. She followed after Sr. Martínez, up the incline toward the center of the village, though she wouldn't have to walk that far.

The sun shone in the morning, but there would be clouds by midday and showers. Late July was in the rainy season and they could expect rainfall once or twice a day. It was good for Marisol's plants, though it made for terrible humidity that clung to the skin in a clammy layer.

A mile from her house she came to a well. It was surrounded by a waist-high wall and there was still a framework for lowering and raising buckets, but there was a hand-pump which everyone used.

Marisol filled her bucket nearly to the brim. She took a moment to drink a few handfuls of water straight from the pump, then picked up her burden for the walk back home. Already there were others repeating her journey. Some would come twice or three times a day.

Perquín was not a large village, but it had its areas of lesser or greater affluence. In some places there was running water and indoor plumbing, but that was not where Marisol lived. She made the trip to water daily and used it sparingly. When she lived with her grandmother there had been more trips, but now she provided only for herself.

Back at the house, she unlocked the front door and brought the bucket inside. She used it to refresh the water in her bedroom pitcher and filled a large glass jar with water and tea leaves to put outside in the sun to brew.

Today she had no work, but she could not stay at home spending the time idly. In the bedroom beneath the thin mattress she had her money and she carefully counted out an amount for shopping. The rest she put away again. There was another stash, beneath a board in the kitchen floor, that she didn't touch for any reason.

She had a canvas bag that went over her shoulder, suitable for carrying almost anything provided it wasn't too bulky. Out the door again, she secured the house against break-in and set off up the hill once more. This time she would go all the way.

The forest was alive with the sound of waking birds and buzzing insects. Perquín was surrounded on all sides by pristine land, some of it under government protection. At the Cerro de Perquín a person could look down on all of it and even see into Honduras. Perquín floated in a sea of green that ran uninterrupted to the horizon in every direction.

It took fifteen minutes to walk to the market. The hour was early enough that some of the vendors were still setting up under loose awnings of canvas and along the sides of buildings. The market funneled into the gap between two sets of buildings, forming a long corridor where nearly anything could be had, even televisions and CD players.

Not far from here was the village square. In that broad space there were also preparations underway for the the Winter Festival. Marisol would be there for all five days, but first there were things to buy and planning to be done.

There was time to wait, so Marisol splurged on a bottle of Kolashanpan to drink later. It would be warm by then, but no matter. She was used to that.

When finally the market had opened in earnest, she began her shopping, going stall to stall and sometimes doubling back, looking for the best deals she could find. Sometimes she had to haggle fiercely for the right price, but that was all part of it; the vendors knew her and she knew them and both knew how much she could afford. She spent the better part of two hours collecting her ingredients and with a full satchel she headed for home.

2

She saw the *turistas* before they saw her. They were obvious in their hiking shorts and floppy hats, wearing sunglasses and carrying bottles of water on straps. A bus for tourists dropped off not far from the square, so Marisol assumed these two were with a larger group and somehow became separated. Sometimes tourists wanted to see Perquín for themselves, not guided by a professional, and though the place was small, they usually got lost.

They were a man and a woman, deeply tanned as though they had been on vacation for a long time. When Marisol drew nearer to them, the woman nudged her companion and made a "hurry up" gesture. The man stepped forward and then moved to intercept Marisol.

"*Con permiso, señorita,*" the man began. "*Donde esta—*"

Marisol smiled at the man. "I speak English, sir."

"Oh, you do? You do. Excellent. My Spanish isn't so good."

"It's all right," Marisol said. "I like to speak my English."

The woman joined the man and together the two of them looked at Marisol as if they had discovered some new species of monkey. Marisol felt her smile falter. "You need something?" she asked.

"Oh, yes. We're looking for the Museo de la Revolución. The museum of the guerillas. We made a wrong turn, I think."

Marisol pointed back up the road from where she'd come. "It's that way. You'll see signs."

"Thank you. Uh, *muchas gracias.*"

"You're welcome. Enjoy the museum."

The man and the woman made more thankful noises and then they were on their way. Marisol turned to watch them go, just to make sure they followed the road and did not deviate, until they were out of sight.

Every tourist went to the museum. It was the main attraction of Perquín. Everyone wanted to see the artifacts of the Civil War, the exhibits honoring the guerrilla fighters of the FMLN and even the big crater where a 500-pound American bomb had blasted the earth. Marisol wondered what the attraction was to seeing a hole in the ground, but she was not a tourist and didn't pretend to know what they thought.

More appealing to her was the nature preserve that abutted Perquín. The rivers and animals and just the lush, unending green were the things Marisol liked most about this land. There were places to swim there, and she knew tourists liked to camp and hike. Life was more engaging to Marisol than the relics of twelve years of war. What did she care for guns and bombs? Only the tourists and the old guerrillas that served as tour guides for the museum seemed attached to them.

She was buoyed by the unexpected use of English. When she practiced, she practiced alone from books and she was never sure if her accent was too pronounced because there was no one to ask. Maybe the old guerrillas at the museum, some of whom spoke English, but she had nothing to do with them.

"Hello, my name is Marisol Herrera," she said aloud to no one. "How are you? I am fine, thank you."

Marisol was heavy laden and it took extra time for her to make it back to the house. She saw no more tourists or any vehicles. No one among her neighbors owned a car, though one had kept a horse for a long time, before it died of old age. The only motor vehicles that passed this area were the occasional police patrol, but those kept nearly always to the village center.

Along the way she continued to speak out loud in English. She named things she saw — "tree," "rock" and "sun" — and tried out more complex phrases. "Can you please tell me where the train station is? What time does the bus come?"

When her grandmother had been alive, the old woman thought little of her efforts. "Why do you bother?" she would ask, but Marisol continued regardless. Sometimes, like now, she heard the echo of her grandmother's complaint in the back of her mind, but again she did not stop.

Back in her kitchen she spread out her purchases on a narrow shelf built into the wall. A bag of onions she put by the door. She had a dozen large tomatoes, as well, and three heads of cabbage.

These things wouldn't last, and she would have to go back to the market daily for fresh items, but she had the basic ingredients for *pupusas revueltas* assembled now. She would prepare the makings on a small counter opposite the earthen oven and bake them until they were spotted with brown. But all that would wait until two days hence, when the Winter Festival began.

Each year she brought something to the festival to sell and this year would be no exception. The *pupusas* would sell for very little, but every bit she would put toward the stash under the floorboard.

She went to the main room and found one of her English books. It was a young person's history of the United States and its cover was worn before she ever took possession of it. She turned to a random page and began to read out loud from it. When she had read twenty pages she put it away.

The English felt good, almost natural. Perhaps later she would practice more and read from a romance novel she'd found the year before, left behind by a tourist waiting for her bus. Marisol understood a great deal of English and could read more than she could speak, but the romance novel used less formal language and she found it valuable for that. Marisol's grandmother would not have approved of the content, of women consorting with men before marriage, but she did not understand that the whole world was not like Perquín and a woman in the big cities, in the *American* big cities, had different standards. Not better or worse, merely different.

Marisol's brother was in the city. He lived in San Salvador with his wife and child. She considered whether or not he and his wife, Berenice, had been together before their marriage. More than likely it was so. In Perquín everyone knew what everyone else did. There was no chance to stray outside the lines without being found out by someone. That didn't mean men and women lived apart and there was no fooling around, but the people of her grandmother's generation were there to condemn in gossip those who strayed.

For Marisol there had been Raul, but things had never gone beyond awkward groping in the dark where no one could see. He would have done more if she let him, but Marisol hadn't thought it worth the risk. She had her grandmother to think of, and besides that Raul was not the kind of man she saw herself marrying. And if they were together and an accident happened, they *would* be married; Perquín would settle for nothing less. Marisol wouldn't have that, and so Raul had moved on to Inez Alfaro. They had made a child together and they had been married. They lived on the other side of the village in a house too small for the three of them.

The heat of the day increased and Marisol opened the windows hoping for a breeze. The air was utterly still and more and more laden with humidity. The day's rain would come sooner rather than later.

She spent an hour or more in the garden, carefully weeding. By the time the first raindrops began to fall her knees were beginning to ache from crawling around and she was glad to go inside.

The rain would last a little or a long time. There was no way to know. Marisol considered the romance novel, but went instead to her bedroom. On a shelf beside a jewelry box that was virtually empty, she found a folded map. In the main room she spread it out on the little table.

Her route was traced in pencil, from Perquín to San Salvador and points beyond. The map showed Mexico, Guatemala, El Salvador and Honduras. The detail wasn't there, but she could link city to city heading north all the way to the border of the United States. The land beyond that was a blank, shaded pink. To see more she had to go to the library in Perquín and look at the world atlas they had there. This she couldn't mark up in pencil, though she traced invisible lines with her finger, sometimes east and sometimes west. She could go to New York City or Sacramento or Atlanta. Maybe she would go to Washington, DC itself.

These were exotic names, like the states they belonged to. By comparison El Salvador and all the countries around it were small enough to be swallowed whole and never heard from again. To her, Mexico seemed huge, dwarfing the nations south of it, but the United States was greater still.

"Can you please tell me where the train station is?" she asked again.

3

The next morning she stood naked in the bedroom and washed from head to foot with water from the basin. She put her best skirt and blouse and a pair of brown shoes. She applied makeup in a foggy mirror and did more with her hair than she usually bothered to do. When she was ready, she locked the house and left.

The shoes weren't comfortable for walking long distances and she felt a little sore by the time she reached the village center. Already that morning a tourist bus was disgorging a small group of white visitors. They paid no attention to Marisol and she avoided them, headed for somewhere entirely different than they.

The Cañenguez home was larger than most and had a wall around it. Marisol knew that Sr. Cañenguez owned a new car that he drove to his job with the organization called Prodetur. Marisol was only vaguely aware of what Prodetur did, though she knew it had something to do with the Rio Sapo Protected Area. Whether they administered it or merely helped maintain the preserve, she didn't know.

Marisol presented herself at the gate and rang the bell by pulling a cord. After a minute had passed, someone unfastened the bolt on the far side and the gate opened. Marisol saw the maid, Sra. Martí.

"*Buenos días,*" Marisol said. "I'm here for Lupita."

"Yes," Sra. Martí said. She was a plain woman, older but hard to tell exactly how old. Occasionally Marisol wondered if she was related to Farabundo Martí, whose name the FMLN took when they waged their war against the government, but did not have courage enough to ask. Perhaps she was some distant cousin. Did it really matter?

Sra. Martí held the gate wider for Marisol to enter, and then fixed a bar in place once Marisol was inside the walls. She went to the front door and opened that, too. Marisol followed the way she always did.

The front hall of the Cañenguez house was as large as two rooms in Marisol's home. The floor was tiled and the ceiling vaulted. A heavy cross decorated with beads and colored stone hung on one wall. A great mirror on another wall reflected the guests as they entered. Stairs led up to the next floor.

"I will tell her you're here," Sra. Martí said.

The maid went away and Marisol waited. She heard raised voices somewhere in the back of the house, a man and a woman, but she couldn't understand what was being said. Marisol studied herself in the mirror and saw how ordinary she looked in extraordinary surroundings. Suddenly she felt underdressed, though this was the same outfit she wore every time she visited the Cañenguez house. She fussed with her hair a little and cleared a tiny makeup smudge by the corner of her lip. When she looked down at her shoes, she saw they were dusty from the walk.

Sra. Martí reappeared. "Come with me," she said.

Marisol followed the woman deeper into the house. The shouting grew clearer now and Marisol thought she recognized the voice of Sra. Cañenguez. The man was louder and more insistent, and Marisol heard him call Sra. Cañenguez a word Marisol would not repeat.

They came to a sitting room with a comfortable couch and two armchairs. An abstract painting stood over a low set of shelves neatly arranged with books. This was Marisol's usual place and she knew it better than any other part of the house. She sat on the couch and waited as Sra. Martí vanished again.

The argument appeared to be over. The house fell quiet. Marisol heard a door slam. After a short while Marisol heard the sound of heels on the tiled floor and Sra. Cañenguez appeared.

As plain as Sra. Martí was, Sra. Cañenguez was lovely. She was a tall woman with light skin and beautiful eyes. No matter what the hour, she was always dressed well and carried herself in a way that bespoke refinement. Marisol had no idea what Sra. Cañenguez was doing in Perquín and only thought that she must be here because of her husband's work. She was like the woman in Marisol's romance novel: she belonged to another place.

Marisol stood up when Sra. Cañenguez came in. When the other woman was around, Marisol did not know what to do with her hands, so she kept them down in front of her. Sra. Cañenguez seemed unaffected by the argument Marisol overheard, or perhaps it was her elegance that carried through.

"*Buenos días*," Sra. Cañenguez said. "I'm sorry you have to wait for Lupita. She's being lazy this morning. I've told her three times to get up already."

"It's all right, Señora," Marisol said. "She can take her time. I'm ready when she is."

"Don't coddle her too much," Sra. Cañenguez said. "I want her to learn English, not excuses."

"She does very well," Marisol replied.

Sra. Cañenguez looked irritated for an instant, but then it passed. "My husband complains that she's learning too slowly," she said. "Do you think she's learning too slowly?"

"No. I think she's very bright."

"Good. I trust your judgment. And here she is!"

Lupita Cañenguez entered by the same hall her mother had. She was in a summer dress and buckled shoes and she was all arms and legs as girls her age were. When Marisol had first met her, Lupita had been eight. Now she was ten and growing faster all the time. "Srta. Herrera," Lupita said, and then in English: "Good morning."

"Good morning, Lupita," Marisol said in English. "How are you today?"

"I'm fine, thank you."

"Very good," Sra. Cañenguez said. "I'll leave you to it."

"Thank you, Señora," Marisol said. "Come and sit down, Lupita."

They sat on opposite ends of the couch. Marisol went to the shelves and pulled down their materials: flash cards and workbooks and paper to write on. Lupita had a small lap desk she slid out from beneath the couch. They had done all of this many times.

Marisol continued speaking in English. "What would you like to talk about today?"

"The Winter Festival," Lupita replied.

"Are you going?"

"Yes. Mother says we will. Will you go?"

"I have things to sell. I will be there."

"What will you sell?"

"*Pupusas.*"

"You'll make them yourself?"

"I will."

"What will you put in them?"

"Beans, cheese, chicharrón."

"I want to try them."

"Maybe you will. What else do you look forward to?"

"I don't understand?"

"What else do you want to do?"

"Oh. Play games. Listen to music."

"Will you dance?"

"Nobody wants to dance with me."

Marisol smiled. "Not yet, but soon you will have many partners. Let's go to our books now."

The workbooks came from a publisher in San Salvador and were filled with puzzles and wordplay. They were a challenge for Lupita, but sometimes they helped Marisol, as well. Their pattern was to do three pages, talk about them, then do flash cards for half an hour before going back to the workbooks for a few more pages. The flash cards were Lupita's least favorite thing.

Lupita did the work and Marisol graded it. "You're learning fast enough," she said.

"What?"

"Oh, nothing. You did very well today. Only two mistakes. See?"

Marisol brought out the flash cards and they suffered through them together. It was almost time to get a new set, as Lupita had mastered all but a few of them. This, too, should have pleased Sr. Cañenguez. Marisol had never known him to ask her anything about Lupita's progress.

With the second set of workbook pages done, they sat talking again. "What is it like at your house?" Lupita asked Marisol.

"It's just a simple house."

"Can I visit sometime?"

"I'm not sure if your parents would allow it."

"Mother would."

"And Father?"

"Probably not. I would like to, though!"

"And I would like it, too."

Marisol heard Sra. Cañenguez's heels again and the woman reappeared. "All done for the day?" she asked.

"Yes," Marisol said. "You can tell your husband that Lupita is very quick to learn."

"I'm sure that will make him very happy," Sra. Cañenguez said. Marisol wondered if she imagined the sourness in her tone.

"Mother, may I visit Srta. Herrera's house someday?" Lupita asked.

Sra. Cañenguez looked from Lupita to Marisol and back again. "I don't know," she said. "Srta. Herrera is very busy."

"She's going to make *pupusas* for the festival."

"How very nice."

Sra. Cañenguez had a small purse. She opened it and brought out cash, which she offered to Marisol. Marisol took it without counting it and tucked it into her pocket. It would all be there.

"I should go now," Marisol said.

"Sra. Martí will let you out."

"Good-bye, then. Good-bye, Lupita. See you in two days."

"Good-bye, Srta. Herrera."

Sra. Martí appeared to escort Marisol to the door and then out through the gate. She shut the bar firmly behind Marisol, and Marisol was alone on the street again.

4

On the morning of the first day of the festival, Marisol woke before the sun came up to make her preparations. She stoked a fire in the earthen oven until the kitchen was sweltering even with the back door open and then she made the *pupusas*.

To make the *pupusas* she used dried nixtamal, the corn meal that baked so well. She used a metal peel to put the *pupusas* in the oven and to take them out again when they were brown-dotted and hot. While they were still warm, she stuffed them with cheese and beans. The heat melted the cheese. When the *pupusas* were warmed again by the sun, the cheese would be soft and tangy, the beans hearty.

Marisol worked until after the sun was up. She made dozens of *pupusas* and gathered them up into a large, cloth-lined basket. The basket was full when she was finished.

She took a colorful sheet and folded it up and put it on top of the *pupusas* to capture their heat. She also took a few dollars from beneath her mattress and put them in the pocket of her dress. When this was done, she locked her house securely and walked uphill to the town square.

Marisol wasn't the only person setting up this early. There were booths, some elaborate, selling painted trinkets of wood and papier-mâché. Others sold food, sweets or soft drinks. There was a seller who specialized in flavored ices, and he had his generator running, chilling his crushed-ice machine for the long, hot day.

Marisol found a space and claimed it for herself. She lay out the colored sheet on the cobblestones and set the basket to one side. When it was busier, she'd put out a few of the *pupusas*, but for now she would let them settle against each other like little pouches of warmth.

A stage was set up for music at the far side of the square. Before long the performers would come and prepare their instruments. Others would come, as well, like jugglers and fire-eaters and men who did magic tricks. Everyone with a skill to amuse would come from miles around because for the next five days there would be people willing to part with money for a laugh or a moment of escape.

The first tourists made their appearance with the arrival of the buses. Traffic into the mountains would be heavier during the festival than at any other time of the year, shuttling the curious to Perquín. Of course there would be locals, but it was the tourists that had the most cash to spend.

There were also police. Most of the time their presence was inconspicuous, something easily ignored, but where there were tourists, there were men with guns. A uniformed policeman stood just thirty feet away from Marisol with a shotgun on a sling, held across his body. He paid no attention to her, instead passing his gaze across the square at large.

No one expected violence at the festival. Sometimes revelers would drink too much and make fools of themselves and occasionally there was trouble, but it was mild. The police would cart off the rowdiest ones to spend time in the village jail, to be released in the morning with headaches and regrets.

The worst thing were pickpockets and scam artists who targeted the tourists. Marisol doubted they would be dealt with by a shotgun or a rifle.

Marisol knew that in the cities it was far worse. Police were everywhere because of the gangs. Perquín did not have a gang problem, or at least it was not a problem that Marisol and her neighbors were aware of. The village was too far away from anywhere of consequence to be valuable to a gang. In Perquín the youth protested with graffiti and occasional acts of vandalism. There was public drunkenness. All of these things, too, could be dealt with without a need to resort to gunfire. Having the armed police here now reminded everyone that it could be far more troublesome in Perquín than it was.

But she was not going to think of such things now. She smoothed out the hem of her dress and sat on the stones of the square, her space claimed and her wares ready. When customers came, she would smile and offer them a *pupusa* from her basket. She only charged a dollar for them. Even a poor citizen of Perquín could afford a dollar on a special occasion.

A clutch of tourists milled around the edge of the square, conferring with one another. The festivities hadn't yet begun in earnest, so they were probably wondering when the dancing and the music would begin. They didn't realize that a little village was slow to wake, even on a festival day.

Perhaps they would like something warm and filling while they waited.

5

She sold five *pupusas* early and then the initial rush slowed. More and more people came into the square until it was bustling end to end. There was continuous music, with one band picking up for the last as if they had practiced the transition. A large space in front of the stage established itself for dancing, though soon enough Marisol could see nothing through the crowding bodies.

Whenever Marisol worried about selling another of her *pupusas*, someone came along and bought one from her. She hadn't even had to use the change she'd brought with her and she carefully rolled the bills together in a tight cylinder before putting them into her pocket.

A pair of tourists approached her. They were identically blond and dressed in white, caps pulled low over their sunglasses to shield them from the sun. Marisol smiled at them.

"What are they?" the woman asked.

"It is a *pupusa revuelta*," Marisol replied. "Very good. You should try one."

"How much?"

"One," Marisol said and held up a finger.

"We'll have two."

They made the exchange and Marisol thanked them, but they were already moving on, their hidden eyes drifting to the next seller. Marisol wasn't offended; this was what tourists had done in Perquín from the beginning. It was part of being a tourist, Marisol decided, though she had never been one.

Marisol counted her inventory. At this rate she would be nearly sold out before the sun went down. The colored lights strung around the square would come on and alcohol would flow more freely and the faces of the vendors would change as hot day transitioned to humid night. This was good enough for her, as she had to go to bed early for an early rise the next day to bake again.

"Srta. Herrera!" Marisol heard.

She looked and saw Lupita coming through the crowd with Sra. Cañenguez in tow. Both were dressed brightly for the festival, Lupita in a dress that made her bloom like a flower. Lupita had a stick of sugar candy in her fist and she waved it at Marisol.

"Look at you all dressed up!" Marisol said to Lupita when the girl drew close.

"I like *your* dress," Lupita told Marisol.

Sra. Cañenguez stood over them and Marisol had to shade her eyes to look up at the woman. "Señora," she said. "It's good to see you."

"Srta. Herrera," Sra. Cañenguez returned without much enthusiasm. There was no sign of Sr. Cañenguez, but Marisol assumed this was not the sort of thing he enjoyed. And he was probably busy the way important men always are, without time for music and dancing and candy.

"Are these the *pupusas*?" Lupita asked.

"Yes. Would you like one?"

"May I, Mother?"

"Yes."

Marisol gave Lupita a *pupusa* from the top of the basket. The sunlight kept them warm and the cheese would be melted and sticky inside, though not as sticky as the sugar candy Lupita carried.

"One dollar," Marisol said.

Sra. Cañenguez paid her from a small purse. Marisol saw what looked like a darkening spot on the woman's arm, just above the elbow, but Sra. Cañenguez pulled back before Marisol could be sure what she had seen. She looked up at the woman again, but there was no sign that Sra. Cañenguez had noticed her seeing the bruise.

"Mother and I saw a *payaso* juggling!" Lupita said.

"Did you? I saw a man with a monkey before. Have you seen him?"

"No. Where is he?"

"Somewhere. You'll find him."

Lupita bit into the *pupusa*, still clinging to her candy with her other fist. She made a pleased noise and took another bite quickly.

"Be sure to chew your food. It will last."

"It's very good."

"Thank you."

Sra. Cañenguez shifted her weight from foot to foot, anxious to be moving again. She nudged Lupita and Marisol saw the dark blotch clearly again. "Hurry up, Lupita, if you want to see everything."

"I am hurrying, Mother."

Lupita wolfed down the last of the *pupusa* and smiled. "Are you going to enjoy the festival, Srta. Herrera?"

"I'm afraid I have to stay right here."

"No dancing?"

"No, not for me. This keeps me busy."

A man approached Marisol and she was distracted a minute serving him. When she returned to Lupita, she saw that Sra. Cañenguez had the girl by the hand and was pulling her away.

"We're going to go now, Srta. Herrera," Lupita said. "I'm sorry you can't come with us!"

"I'm sorry, too. Have fun!"

Marisol waved and then Lupita and her mother were swallowed up among the moving bodies. She was alone again.

"Pretty girl," said the woman selling wooden noisemakers on a heavy blanket next to Marisol.

"Yes," Marisol said, and she felt a heaviness that pulled down the corners of her mouth. She peered into the crowd to catch another glimpse of Marisol and Sra. Cañenguez, but they were gone completely now, maybe even halfway across the square by now. Marisol hoped Lupita would find the man with the monkey.

The woman beside her wasn't finished talking. "How are you making out?"

"Not bad," Marisol said. "You?"

She hadn't paid much attention to the woman and her noisemakers before, but now she saw that they were all handmade, wooden and polished to a bright sheen. They were in creative shapes, some like animals. Paper cards with their prices were scattered here and there, but Marisol couldn't read them for the glare. They would definitely be more pricey than her *pupusas*.

"I'll get by. It's only the first day," the woman said.

"Same for me," Marisol said.

"Are you from Perquín?"

"Yes."

"I'm from Arambala. I'll be sleeping here tonight."

Marisol nodded. Many of the vendors would sleep in the square overnight, guarding over their things to save their places or simply because they had nowhere else to go. Marisol was glad she wouldn't be among them.

A cloud fell across the sun. Marisol looked up and saw that others were gathering. An afternoon shower was in the offing. This, too, the vendors would endure, though the crowd would thin and customers would be more interested in shelter than trinkets.

Marisol felt the tight bundle of dollar bills in her pocket. That was worth tolerating a little rain. Her basket wasn't empty yet, and there were hours still to go.

6

For all of the five days she rose early, cooked *pupusas* and then took up a place in the square. Twice more she was by the woman from Arambala, but on other days she was forced to take up a place somewhere else. Once she was very near the stage and the music rolled over her all day long. On that day she made her best sales as the dancers fell away from the group hungry and thirsty. Marisol wondered how much she could make if she sold drinks from a cooler the way some did.

At the end of the festival she had just over a hundred and fifty dollars. She didn't put this money under her mattress, but hid it with the rest of the cash beneath the floorboard in the kitchen. On the day following the festival she brought all her money out into the main room and sorted and counted all the bills.

She had not set upon this course lightly. Marisol knew from the beginning that it would take great effort of will and sometimes painful sacrifice, to put aside money in the amounts she needed. At first she had saved a certain percentage of what she made, but this was not enough, and soon she was putting away every last cent that she could spare.

No one knew that she saved. Even her grandmother didn't know. The old woman stepped on the loose floorboard and passed over it every day, never guessing at what was hidden away beneath it. Marisol didn't brag about her thrift, nor did she share the reasons for it. This last thing, Marisol thought, her grandmother had known, but they didn't speak of it.

When she first began saving ten years before, her ambitions had been modest. She would go to San Salvador like her brother and find work there. Over time this goal had changed and the distances she crossed in her mind grew ever greater. Soon she was beyond the borders of El Salvador, heading north and north and north until there was only one place left.

She had no illusions about what it would cost her. Marisol did whatever job she could find, sometimes two at a time, to secure the funding she needed. Work was scarce in Perquín and she was lucky to get what she did. Her longest-paying position was as a cleaning woman for the Hotel Perkin Lenca, which catered to tourists from America and Canada coming to see the mountains. For a time she lived on a coffee farm away from her grandmother, scratching out a living with barely any money left over.

Marisol would not have admitted to anyone, not even herself, that it was easier after her grandmother died. The old woman had not been able to work in the final years of her life and she depended wholly on the money Marisol's brother sent from San Salvador and what Marisol could afford. Saving money then had seemed like stealing from her own family, but by then Marisol was committed, and she could not have stopped even if she wanted to. She was leaving this place.

For a while she hoped that her brother would continue to send money even after their grandmother passed away, even just a little bit, but he had a family of his own to provide for and Marisol was on her own. Once every few months they would speak by telephone, Marisol going to a house of her neighbor's. Though the capital was only a few hours away from Perquín, it was like communicating from the surface of the moon.

Marisol put the money from the festival sales with the rest and then she counted what she had. The process took nearly an hour, with so many one-dollar bills to account for, but in the end she had a number. It was enough.

Her hands were shaking as she gathered the cash together again. *It was enough.* She had not prepared herself for when the moment came, and now that it was here, she felt overwhelmed. A sensation of lightheadedness followed her to the kitchen where she carefully replaced the money in its hiding place and put down the board. She stepped on it to be sure it was placed firmly, finding some steadiness in herself as she did so.

Though it was late, she left the house and went four houses down to the home of Adolfo Morán. Her hands threatened to tremble again when she knocked on the door and waited, but she made fists and the moment passed.

Adolfo Morán lived alone. He had been friends with Marisol's grandmother and had even courted her after a fashion, though they were much too old for such things. His home was big enough for a family of four, but all of his children were long since gone. He lived on a pension, but from whom it was not much talked about. Not in Perquín, the center of the revolution.

"Marisol," Sr. Morán said when he came to the door. "What are you doing here?"

"Were you sleeping, Sr. Morán?"

"No, no. I don't sleep. But when someone knocks on my door in the night, I fear the worst."

"I only wanted to know if I could use your telephone."

"The telephone? Of course. Who do you need to call so urgently?"

"My brother, Eduardo."

"Come in, come in."

The old man stepped aside and allowed Marisol to enter. Illumination from an electric light spilled into the short hallway from a lamp in the main room. The house was more solid than Marisol's and had more rooms.

"It's here. You remember."

"Thank you, Sr. Morán."

The telephone was wired to the far wall in the main room and rested on a narrow set of shelves crowded with books. Marisol took a straight-backed chair from beside the couch and sat on it. She dialed her brother's number and this time her fingers didn't shake.

Ringing on the other end of the line seemed distant. It rang a long time before finally someone picked up and Marisol heard her brother's voice, irritated. "Yes? Hello?"

"Eduardo," Marisol said, "it's me, your sister."

"Marisol. It's late."

"I know. I'm sorry. It's just that I have news."

"What news?"

"I'm leaving Perquín. I'll be coming to San Salvador."

"What? When?"

"As soon as I can. I will need somewhere to stay in the city. Just for a little while. I hoped I could stay with you."

"You want to live here?"

"No, just stay for a day or two. Can I do that, Eduardo?"

Her brother was quiet, thinking. Marisol held the phone in both hands.

"There's not much room at our house, Marisol."

"It's only for a day or two, I promise."

"When will you come?"

"I have to sell the house. That may take some time. Two weeks? Three? A month?"

"You're selling Grandmother's house?"

"I won't be living there anymore, Eduardo. When I leave Perquín, it will be for good."

"Selling Grandmother's house... what are you doing, Marisol?"

"I will tell you more when I get there. I will try to call you before I come."

"Don't do anything foolish, Marisol."

"I won't. Thank you, Eduardo."

They rang off. Marisol put the chair back where she'd found it. Sr. Morán was watching her from the doorway. "You're going away from Perquín?" he asked.

"Yes."

"For how long?"

"For good," Marisol said. "Just as soon as I can."

Sr. Morán shook his head. "It's no good in the cities for a young woman like yourself. You're better off here."

"I know it's not safe, but I can't stay."

"Do you drink coffee?" Sr. Morán asked. "Let me make us some coffee."

She could not think of a good reason to say no. Marisol waited in the main room while Sr. Morán went to the kitchen. She heard him moving around and the bubbling of boiling water. Eventually he returned with two small cups that steamed though the room was not cool.

"Take this," Sr. Morán said. "Drink."

They sat on the couch together. Sr. Morán had put sugar and milk in Marisol's coffee, so it wasn't strong. The old man sipped his thoughtfully, in no hurry to speak. Marisol waited.

"Your grandmother was sad when your brother left for the city," Sr. Morán said at last, "but he needed to find work, and there was little for a man to do here in Perquín besides work on a coffee plantation. Even I couldn't blame him for going. In time, I think she grew to accept it, too."

"Sr. Morán—"

"Please, let me finish. I wanted to say that it meant very much to your grandmother that you stayed. Especially at the end. And she would have been very proud of you living in that house alone, making your own way. Maybe she would have wanted you married, but maybe not. She wanted you to be happy."

"I'm doing what makes me happy."

"Running away to the city?"

"It's more than that."

"Explain it to me, then."

Marisol opened her mouth to speak, but the words didn't come. The secret had been hers for so long that it seemed impossible to share it with another person in terms they would understand. Maybe if she could show him her map, explain to him how she had taken this trip a thousand times in her mind... maybe.

"I realize I'm not your grandmother," Sr. Morán said. "You have no reason to account for yourself to me."

"Do you know what I'm thinking?" Marisol asked.

"No. It's just that I was young once, too."

"It's difficult for me to put into words."

"Then never mind. Let me tell you what I think: that the city seems like the place to be when you still have more years ahead of you than behind. But the city is full of crime and heartbreak. I fled it just as soon as I could. I found peace in Perquín when there was no peace to be had anywhere else in this country."

"Things are different now."

"Different, but no better. There is no civil war, but there is no harmony."

Marisol swallowed. Her mouth was dry, so she watered it with coffee. "And what if... what if I went farther than the city?"

Sr. Morán looked at her for a long time. "So that's it," he said.

It was easier to say it now that he knew. "I'm going to go all the way," she said. "To the United States."

"You know how long that will take?"

"Yes."

"You know how dangerous it will be?"

"Yes."

"And yet you still want to go?"

"I can't stay in Perquín. Not forever."

Sr. Morán sighed deeply. He drained his coffee cup and put it aside. "You'll lose everything on that journey. Your history will be lost."

"But I can do so much else."

"The land of opportunity?"

"Yes."

"You know, the United States helped turn our country into a killing field during the war. Their bombs. Their guns. They trained Salvadorans to kill other Salvadorans. We were lucky to survive such a thing. Now everyone looks to them for salvation."

"The war is over."

"It is over," Sr. Morán said sadly. "And the Americans won."

Marisol put her cup down unfinished. "I have to go," she said.

Sr. Morán rose from the couch and offered Marisol a hand. She took it, felt the calluses there. Once again she wondered what he had done to earn his pension, what he had done during the civil war. It was hard to imagine him as anything other than what he was: an old man living in Perquín, alone, waiting to die. She would not be like him.

"Thank you for your phone," Marisol said.

"My phone is always yours to use."

They went to the door. Sr. Morán let her out. Marisol paused on the doorstep. "I'm sorry I can't stay here."

"At least sell your grandmother's house to good people. So her spirit won't be in bad company."

"I will."

"Good night, Marisol. And if I don't see you again, good-bye."

"Good-bye, Sr. Morán."

She left the house and Sr. Morán closed the door, shutting off the golden light of the electric bulb. For a time she stood in the street just listening to the night sounds of the forest. She wanted to feel as Sr. Morán felt, that this place had a hold on her that could not be released, but she did not feel it. There was only the steep road and the woodland and a village falling steadily into sleep.

Marisol walked back to her house and went inside. When she slept, she dreamed of her grandmother sweeping the floors endlessly, and when she woke, it was day again.

7

The family's name was Ramirez and they had two small children. They showed up in the late morning before the rains, dressed as well as they were able, though their shoes were worn and dirty. Marisol invited them in and offered them water to drink, which they took.

It was crowded in the main room with all five of them gathered together and Marisol suggested that the children go out in back to play in the little space it provided them. "Be careful of the garden," she told them and let them out the back way.

When she returned to the Ramirezes, they were still standing uncomfortably in the center of the main room, as if afraid to touch anything. Marisol smiled and tried to make them feel more at home. If they purchased her grandmother's house, then it would be.

"As you can see, it's not a large house," Marisol said. "Would you like to see the bedroom?"

The couple mumbled yes and Marisol escorted them to the next room. It was even tighter here with the bed and the dresser and the little table that held her pitcher and basin. Light came through the window and landed harshly on the

bed. The temperature was very warm. Marisol opened the
window. Not a breath of air came in.

"I will leave the furniture," Marisol said. "The bed is solid.
The sofa can be slept on. There's room enough to lay out
pallets for the children in the main room. When my grandmother and brother and I lived here together, it was close, but
we managed."

"It's good," Sr. Ramirez said without looking at her.

The two of them radiated nerves despite Marisol's best
efforts. Perhaps it was because they would have to talk about
money, and money talk was always awkward when there was
very little to go around. Sr. Ramirez and his wife probably
both worked, dividing childcare between themselves and
some other relative. Every dollar they saved would go into
this place. Marisol wished she could give them a palace.

"Would you like to sit down on the couch? You can see
for yourself how comfortable it is."

They returned to the main room and the Ramirezes sat
close together on the small couch. Sr. Ramirez drained his
glass. He offered it to Marisol, who collected it from him.
Sra. Ramirez had not yet sipped from hers.

"We are not rich people," Sr. Ramirez said.

So it was the money. Marisol was suddenly struck with
the idea that she had asked too much for the place, that she
would be seen in a bad light as someone trying to take advantage. She didn't want to be perceived that way; she wanted
only what was fair for her little house and its little plot of land.

"If it is too much...," Marisol began.

"No, no, it is not too much. But my wife and I must
discuss it."

"I'll leave you alone."

Marisol went to the kitchen. The back door was open and she could see the children playing in the dirt. They were young enough that they did not need an organized game. All they required was the earth and their pudgy little fingers and toes. Marisol saw that they had both discarded their shoes. Doubtless their parents would be upset at the stains they were garnering on their clothes.

She watched them and paid no attention to the murmuring coming from the next room. One child, a little girl, was forming a thick patty of mud. When she was done with that, she mashed it into the ground, squishing it between her fingers. It made her laugh and Marisol smiled at the sound.

Marisol was twenty-eight. Girls much younger than her had been married and had children. Sra. Ramirez could not be older than twenty-four. Only in that moment was Marisol truly aware of how much she had sacrificed over the last ten years. It was more than just the money; she had given up on everything else, too. Knowing it was transitory, knowing that it would all be abandoned when the time came.

If she had children of her own there would be no America for her. She would be forever attached to Perquín, orbiting her grandmother's house in perpetuity as her children filled the tiny space and her husband went off to work and came back with dirt under his fingernails.

It wasn't that she rejected the idea of marriage, of children. She wanted these things. But she was not willing to surrender the ultimate prize for the chance at something more ordinary. Marisol supposed that made her selfish. Her grandmother would have thought so. Maybe her brother would think the same thing. Sr. Morán might have had the identical idea, though he expressed it differently.

The Ramirez's little boy hopped like a frog in the mud, dangerously close to where Marisol's tomatoes were. She felt herself tense, then let it go. Soon this would not belong to her — not the garden or the bed or the walls themselves — and she would be away from it forever. If the Ramirezes did not buy, someone would. A house, any house at all, was better than a shanty, and Perquín had plenty of those.

"Señorita," Sr. Ramirez called from the next room.

Marisol left the children. She came back to Señor and Sra. Ramirez, who were still so closely paired on the couch that they appeared conjoined. Sra. Ramirez had at last drunk her water and held the glass carefully in both hands as if fearful that she would drop it.

"We will pay," Sr. Ramirez said.

"I'm glad," Marisol replied. Her heart quickened.

"When... when will we be able to move in?"

"Once I have the money I will be out within the week. It will be all yours."

"Okay," Sr. Ramirez said. "Okay. I will have the money in three days."

"Three days will be fine," Marisol said. "You can find me here."

For now you can find me here, she thought. *For now and for now only.*

"*Sí. Muy bueno.*"

It was good. Marisol felt like she could swell up and burst the confines of the house. Her feet felt light. The sensation did not pass when the Ramirezes gathered up their children or when they paused at the door to say good-bye or even when they walked out of sight up the steeply inclined road. Marisol was moored to the earth by the most delicate of strings.

She prepared a meal for herself in the kitchen with the door open and the marks of the children's play still on the ground. *Their* ground. It was almost as if the house itself already belonged to the Ramirez family and she was only a ghost in it waiting for passage to the next realm. She ate her food without tasting it and napped through the afternoon rains without dreams.

8

Marisol presented herself at the Cañenguez home the next day. She was dressed as she always did for such visits, only now she felt the echoes of the Ramirez family and the way they had prettied up their simple clothing to appear more respectable than they really were. Did Marisol seem cheap to Sra. Cañenguez? She found the thought disheartening, but it was far too late to do anything about it.

Sra. Martí let her in and escorted her to the sitting room as was their usual routine. Marisol pulled down the flash cards and workbooks with a deepening sense of melancholy because this would be the last time for all of that.

"Srta. Herrera!" Lupita said when she entered the room. Marisol found herself putting out her arms to hug the small girl, though she had always been careful not to do such a thing before. She thought she caught a look of dismay on Sra. Martí's face, but the maid was gone before Marisol could look again.

"It's good to see you," Marisol said. The edge of her voice trembled and already she knew that she would not be able to go through with today's lesson without shedding a tear. It seemed cruel to prolong it, even if Lupita had no idea what came next. Marisol took a deep breath and held it before exhaling slowly. Serenity.

"Are you in a hurry today?" Lupita asked.

"What? Why?"

"You already have the things out. That's my job."

"I'm sorry, you're right. Forgive me. I was just so excited for our lesson today."

"Are we doing something different?"

Marisol reflected that perhaps she should have planned something different for today, but she hadn't. It hadn't seemed real, the going away, until she had someone to say good-bye to. She was not prepared.

"Maybe we can skip the workbook?" Lupita suggested.

"All right, we'll leave the workbook alone," Marisol agreed. "Today we'll just talk. Practice our English. What do you think?"

"Okay."

"How are your mother and father?"

"They are well, thank you."

"Does your father still think you are learning too slowly?"

Lupita's eyes darkened for a moment, but then she blinked it away. "He doesn't talk to me about it."

"Then I guess you are doing all right," Marisol said.

"I asked Mother if you could come to our house more. More than twice a week."

Marisol felt another stab of guilt and hoped not to show it in her face. Instead she tried a smile, though it felt false. "What did she say to that?"

"She said no."

"I'm sorry, but she's right. You don't need to see me so often. In fact, you don't need me at all anymore. Your English is so good, you can practice on your own!"

"I like to practice with you."

"And I like to practice with you," Marisol said, "but nothing lasts forever."

"What does that mean?"

"It means...," Marisol said and she faltered. "It means that if I went away, it wouldn't be the end for you. You could still learn and grow better all by yourself."

"But I don't want to."

Marisol took another deep breath, let it out evenly. "I know you don't. But... I have something to tell you. I warn you: you will not like it."

Lupita's eyes widened and the girl sat absolutely still.

"I'm going away from Perquín."

Lupita was quiet for a while, but Marisol could see the wheels turning. Finally she said, "When will you go?"

"Very soon. Within the week."

"Why?"

"Why am I leaving?"

"Yes."

"Because I have somewhere to go. Somewhere far away from here. I've been planning to leave for a long, long time and now I have my chance."

Lupita was still motionless, as if transfixed. "Where will you go?"

"Far north. To the United States."

"The United States?!?" Lupita exclaimed, and she threw up her arms suddenly. "That is so far! Why do you want to go so far away?"

"It's hard for me to explain," Marisol said. "It's been my dream to go there for many years. I've saved my money, worked very hard. Now it's time."

"But what about me?"

"I wish I could take you with me," Marisol said.

Lupita cast her eyes down at her hands, which she held in her lap. All at once the life seemed to drain from her and she was limp. Marisol saw the girl's chin quiver and immediately felt another pang of conscience. She should have done this better. It should not have been so sudden.

"Lupita...," Marisol said. She put her hand on Lupita's shoulder, and the girl flinched with an indrawn breath.

She saw the bruise peek out from beneath the strap of Lupita's dress. It was round and dark and fresh and just touching it had caused Lupita pain. The bottom dropped out of Marisol's stomach, stirring up more than just self-condemnation.

"How did this happen?" Marisol asked.

"What?"

"This bruise. How did you get it?"

Lupita's eyes were wet and a tear crossed her cheek. She threw herself into Marisol's arms and buried her face in the material of Marisol's blouse. She sobbed openly. Marisol was careful when she put her arms around the girl, conscious of the bruise and fearing more. She felt anger now.

"Don't go away, Marisol!" Lupita said. "Please don't go away!"

It was impossible to hold back tears of her own, and Marisol clung to Lupita as the girl clung to her. They cried together on the couch, heedless of the surroundings or of whoever might come upon them.

"I have to go," Marisol said after her crying slowed. "It's all arranged. But I'll write to you. I'll write to you every week. It will be as if I was here!"

Lupita's eyes were bloodshot and puffy. She dragged her forearm across them and parted from Marisol reluctantly. "It won't be the same."

"It will. I'll send pictures."

"It won't be the same!"

Marisol did not hear the approaching click of Sra. Cañenguez's heels and when the woman appeared, it was by surprise. Marisol saw Sra. Cañenguez look from Lupita to Marisol and then back to Lupita again. Her jaw worked and then she said, "What's going on here?"

Lupita fled the couch and went to her mother. With her back to Marisol, the bruise was plainly visible, angry and black on her flesh. "Srta. Herrera is leaving, Mother! She's going away from Perquín!"

"Is this true?"

"Yes, it is true," Marisol said. "This is my last lesson to Lupita. I'm sorry."

"Where will you go? The city?"

"At first."

"This is all so sudden."

"I wish it wasn't. I wish I could stay. For Lupita."

"I expected you to at least last through the summer."

"I am sorry."

Lupita sobbed freely again, and Marisol wanted to gather the girl up in her arms and squeeze the tears from her. If she held on tightly enough, there would be no pain, no reason to cry.

"It's clear this lesson is over," Sra. Cañenguez said. "I have your money."

"I did no teaching today. You can keep the money."

Marisol rose from the couch. Her gaze kept coming back to the bruise. She wanted to say something about it, but the words wouldn't come. Every time she looked at it, she felt sick inside, as if nothing was right. If she could just bring Lupita with her....

"If that is all, then I think you should go," Sra. Cañenguez said.

"All right. Lupita? I'm going to leave now."

"Just go! I don't want to see you anymore!"

More tears rolled down Marisol's cheeks and she wiped at them angrily. Sra. Cañenguez's eyes were on her and hot. Marisol could not bring herself to look directly into the woman's face.

"You know where the front door is," Sra. Cañenguez said.

"Yes. I'll go. Good-bye, Lupita."

"Good-*bye*, Srta. Herrera," Sra. Cañenguez said.

Marisol saw herself to the door and was out the gate before Sra. Martí could appear to escort her out. The maid glared at Marisol once as she stepped out onto the street and then slammed the gate shut. Only then could Marisol no longer hear Lupita crying.

Her legs weakened and she sat down on the side of the road and wept, for how long she didn't know. No one passed. Marisol was glad of that, because she didn't want to be seen this way. She felt bereft and considered ringing the bell and asking to see Lupita one last time. She wouldn't be allowed, of course. Lupita was gone now, the way Perquín would soon be gone and everything in the village that she knew.

After a while, Marisol made it back to her feet and she walked away. By the time she reached the town square she felt steadier, could breathe without the air hitching in her chest. She lingered in the square, alone except for a lone man selling slices of fruit from a cart. In time her eyes no longer burned and her nose stopped running. She didn't feel like running back to Lupita and begging for forgiveness.

It occurred to her that this was one of the last times she would stand in this square. As soon as she handed over her grandmother's house, she would return here to take the bus south out of the mountains, but there would be no more Winter Festivals, no more fresh *pupusas* for sale.

She turned away to market row and when she walked, she walked unfalteringly. There would be no more tears today.

9

At the market Marisol bought a hard-sided suitcase big enough for three changes of clothes and the few things of value that she wanted to take with her. Among her treasures was the history of the United States that she had read and reread so many times. She had a ring her grandmother wore that was too large for her finger. She had a piece of lace from her mother's wedding dress. Her passport. Photographs of Eduardo, his little girl Sofia and some of herself and her grandmother. She had so little.

Sr. Ramirez turned up early on the morning and they said their greetings and good-byes. Marisol took his money and put it in the suitcase for the time being. The rest of her funds she wore underneath her dress in paper packets held together with tape. She had already decided to spend only from the dollars she got for the house and not a cent of anything else. Not until she got to Mexico.

Marisol had only the key to the padlock on the door to turn over to Sr. Ramirez. There was no official title to the house or the land; it had simply belonged to Marisol's grandmother, and this was the accepted thing. Now it belonged to a new family, and the neighbors would accept this, too.

Sr. Ramirez wished her luck. Marisol said thank you. She left the house without looking back.

A fog lay in heavily over the village that morning and the square seemed ghostly when she reached it. Marisol expected others to be there, waiting at the bus stop, but there was no one. She was alone and the fog muted the sounds of the world so that she could have been the last woman on Earth.

After an hour she heard the bus's engine. The old vehicle pulled up through the fog, headlights carving out the way ahead, and came to an unsteady stop before her. Its air brakes wheezed. The driver opened the doors. "San Miguel?" he asked Marisol. She could not find the voice to say yes.

She started to board the bus, but the driver held up his hand. "Your case goes on the top. There's not room enough for it in here."

Marisol stepped back and looked at the bus. There was a rusty ladder at the tail end leading up to the roof. The driver showed no inclination to help her. She went to the ladder and put a foot to it, testing it. The rungs were firm.

Getting to the top was clumsy work. On the roof were a variety of packages and boxes and cases much like hers, all held down with bungee cords and rope. Marisol clambered onto the roof and found a place to wedge her suitcase. She pulled a bungee cord over it, lashing it to a box marked FRÁGILES. Then she made her way down to the ground again.

The driver was out of his seat, stretching by the nose of the bus. The engine was still on, turning over roughly from cycle to cycle. He was a short man with stooped shoulders. He wore a money pouch on his waist, zippered across the front, with the name of a bank half rubbed off. "San Miguel?" he asked again.

"That's right," Marisol managed this time.

"Twenty dollars."

"It's so much?"

"Twenty dollars," the driver repeated, and Marisol knew that it was *not* so much, but the man was asking for it anyway. She had some money in her skirt pocket and she paid. The driver put the bill into his money pouch and produced a white ticket which he punched with a device from his own pocket.

Marisol climbed aboard. The bus smelled like close bodies and mildew. She saw rows of faces looking back at her, strangers from nearby villages that she did not know and had never visited. Marisol felt overdressed in her blouse and skirt. She made her way back.

There was a place to sit near the rear of the bus with room enough for two. Marisol sat beside the window and looked out at the fog-laden square. The place was almost unrecognizable in its mantle of haze.

The driver did not board the bus again right away. He stayed outside, wandering around aimlessly, as if waiting for passengers that were late but sure to come. The bus' engine began to idle more and more harshly until finally it made a coughing sound and stalled out. No one on the bus moved or spoke.

Only then did the driver climb reluctantly up the stairs onto the bus. He pulled the doors shut and turned over the engine. It ground and ground and then caught, rumbling back into life. "Arambala!" he called. "Next stop Arambala! After that, Joateca."

Finally the driver put the bus in gear and the vehicle lurched forward. They drove the perimeter of the square until they turned onto the paved road that led out of the village. It seemed to Marisol that they drove very slowly.

They quickly left the buildings of Perquín behind, plunging into dense forest on a road that picked up a steeper angle with every mile they passed. It was not a straight path, but meandering down the side of a greened mountain, the driver riding the brakes as they made the turns and surging ahead when the road cleared for a little while.

Marisol watched out the window as the sun began to bake away the fog. The trees were unwound and the sky cleared and it was a hot, bright morning. When she turned around to look out the back of the bus, she saw no sign of where they'd come; Perquín was swallowed up.

The other passengers didn't look back at Marisol. Some of them began to talk to each other in close tones, while others remained stolidly silent. From time to time Marisol saw the driver glance up into a mirror above his head to see the passengers. She couldn't tell if he was looking at her. After a while she decided he was not.

They drove and Marisol waited.

10

They traveled in a southerly direction through villages and towns Marisol was familiar with only by points on a map. Sunsulaca. Lolotiquillo. Gotera. San Carlos. Their white buildings sprang up out of the forest cover like sudden mushrooms. In some places the road was paved, but more often than not it was just a muddy track, slithering back and forth through uneven terrain, making a long trip longer. Occasionally, a truck or a car would pass going the opposite direction and the bus would have to pull well over to the side to allow them room. Sometimes Marisol worried they would be stuck miles from anywhere.

She got off the bus when she could just to breathe open air and feel the circulation return to her legs. As they moved closer to San Miguel, the bus grew more crowded, and soon Marisol was forced to share her seat with not one but two other women. The three of them bunched in tightly together, the third nearly off the seat and in the aisle, but they didn't talk to one another. Marisol kept her attention on the passing greenery, which never seemed to change, no matter how many miles they came.

This was farther than she had ever gone from Perquín in all of her life. Her brother had departed for San Salvador years ago, but she had never visited him. Marisol was unsure if her grandmother ever set foot outside Perquín once. All of Marisol's memories were tied up in a village she would never see again.

The other villages they passed were much the same as Perquín, which led Marisol to believe she hadn't missed much in her time. Some were even more threadbare than Perquín, without even an organized square at the center of things. In those places the bus pulled up to what seemed like a random building, wheels grinding in the mud, and waited until someone appeared or didn't. Those villages were like ghost towns, with hardly a person in sight.

The towns were different. The roads into them were often paved and there was a clear berth for the bus when it arrived. Men and women waited nearby with refreshments to sell — fresh fruit, juice or soft drinks — and once or twice Marisol treated herself to something. The glimpses she caught of the towns as they moved on were of close-built buildings marching away into the green, because even here the forest was an implacable, irresistible presence.

Eventually, the roads stayed paved and grew wider, as well. More cars passed them on the road, only there was no need to go through the same pains to let them go by. The first buildings of San Miguel cropped up shortly after that, little houses and shops at the very outskirts of the city.

The driver guided them into the heart of San Miguel. Street after street of low buildings interconnected and for the first time they were caught in actual traffic that slowed them down. They were three hours out of Perquín, but the world was different. For one, they had come down from the mountains, and though she saw great hills here and there along their way, it was not the same.

When at last the bus pulled into the station, the passengers jostled one another to get off. Marisol was one of the last. She passed the driver, waiting at the door outside, and said, "*Gracias.*"

People scrambled all over the roof of the bus gathering their things. Some of the passengers tossed their bags down to waiting companions. Marisol's suitcase was not one of the ones thrown down. Finally, she had the chance to climb the metal ladder to the top, where she found her suitcase flung haphazardly to one side. She checked it for damage, but it was all right.

Marisol had never been inside a bus terminal before and she was surprised at the number of people gathered there. Long wooden benches were crowded with people reading, sleeping upright or simply staring off into space. A big clock over the ticket counters didn't match Marisol's watch and she hurried to adjust the time.

She stood in the back of a seemingly endless line, creeping forward every minute or two, until finally she faced a ticket agent through a metal screen. "One to San Salvador," she told the man.

"One way?"

"Yes."

The cost of the ticket was less than Marisol had paid the driver to come from Perquín to San Miguel. The thought made her angry. She hadn't expected the greedy to come calling so soon. The ticket agent gave her a long, blue ticket with the time of her departure printed on it in red ink.

The restrooms in the bus terminal were kept cleaner than she expected. She saw women putting on makeup in the mirrors above the sinks and briefly felt self-conscious because she wore none. Again she had to wait, this time for a stall, while the conflicting smells of perfume and urine battled for her attention.

When she was done, she looked for a place to keep herself until it was time for her bus to depart. The benches were all full and there were plenty of people simply standing around. She found a neglected corner near a bank of pay telephones, put her suitcase down as a small seat and perched herself on it.

Everywhere there were people and the electric fans placed here and there and on the ceiling did little to disperse their heat. Marisol perspired, whether from nerves or the mugginess or both she didn't know. To distract herself she tried people-watching.

She knew that many of these people had to come from the villages and towns outside of San Miguel just as she did, but they did not behave as the people of Perquín would: besides those who'd planted themselves on the benches unmoving, the rest were constantly in motion. The babble of voices carried up to the high ceiling and echoed around. Marisol couldn't pry one conversation apart from another.

Occasionally she saw men looking her way and on those occasions she tried to make herself as unassuming as possible. She was aware she was a woman traveling alone and that this presented challenges unique to her position. The less notice men paid to her, the better, and now Marisol was glad she hadn't chosen to wear makeup. Let her appear plain and she might be left alone all the way to San Salvador and beyond.

She waited, and the hours crawled by until finally it was time.

11

The next bus was nicer and had clean seats. Marisol's suitcase went into a compartment in the bottom of the vehicle, along with everyone else's luggage.

Their trip to San Salvador proceeded along a major highway, so there was no need to slog through pitted mud roads from place to place. The towns and villages along the highway seemed healthier than the ones she'd seen on the road from Perquín. Some were still very small, barely registering on the edge of the highway before crawling back into the forest. For the most part they served only as stops along the way, where travelers were picked up and deposited with regularity, each on their own, hidden journeys Marisol would never know.

She knew when they were close to San Salvador because the character of the land changed. There was still the close press of the forest, but there were large, vacant lots that had been cleared for construction and more and more buildings. It started to rain heavily and Marisol watched out the window as cars sped past, kicking up white spray in their wake. The bus continued on, heedless of the weather.

The structures around them grew taller as they wound their way into the city. Traffic was as bad here as it had been in San Miguel, perhaps worse. Out of the suburbs there was very little green, except what was packed into little squares here and there. Over the streets hung ribbons of electrical wire, lacing buildings together in a rubber and copper webbing. Everywhere there were stores with light-up signs and windows filled with displays, though most were meshed with metal to protect against vandals and thieves.

The bus passed through a busy intersection slowly and Marisol saw two policemen watching a third directing traffic. All three were armed with automatic rifles. A black police van was parked to one side, its lights darkened. The rain drummed on the roof of the bus.

Eventually they moved into an enormous bus terminal, four lanes of buses sheltered by a concrete roof. The driver turned on the bus's interior lights. The passengers rose from their seats and bustled to the front with Marisol close behind.

The noise and smell of buses were thick at the terminal. Marisol waited while the driver opened the belly of the bus and got her suitcase after most everyone else had gotten theirs already. She crossed the bus lanes carefully and entered the building itself.

This place was larger by far than its sibling in San Miguel, but no less busy. People were in motion everywhere and on the benches and opening and closing for-pay lockers. Marisol saw more police here, their weapons held casually, watching the barely contained chaos with disinterested eyes.

She went to ticket sellers, a dozen employees behind glass and brass fittings. A large board was marked with buses coming and going. A man with a long stick changed plastic letters and numbers while she watched. She looked for a bus bound for Guatemala City. It left once a day and had already gone today. The next would be tomorrow afternoon.

Marisol looked back to the policemen. She approached one of them.

"Excuse me, sir. Do you know where the public telephones are?"

The policeman looked her up and down, then pointed. "That way," he said.

"Thank you very much."

She followed in the direction the policeman pointed and rounded a corner. There she found a bank of battered, old telephones, most of which were in use. Marisol went to one and warily put her suitcase down between her feet where she could hold onto it with her ankles. She searched her pockets for coins. When she had enough, she fed them to the phone and called her brother's number.

The phone rang ten times with no answer. Marisol hung up reluctantly and collected her money. She checked the time. Eduardo was probably still at work. She could wait here, but she did not like how busy and crowded it was.

She considered calling again, but it would be no use. She brought her suitcase back to the great hall where all the benches were and found the pay lockers again. Marisol found one big enough to take her suitcase and paid for the key. Afterward she found the way out through the front of the building to the street where the rain still fell.

In retrospect, it had been foolish to leave Perquín without an umbrella, but she had been focused on bringing only the essentials for her trip. Standing beneath the sheltering edge of the bus terminal, watching the rain sheet down, she wished she had been more extravagant.

The weather couldn't last forever and finally it slowed to a drizzle before it stopped altogether. The streets steamed. Marisol ventured out of the bus terminal and down the block, not knowing exactly where she would go or what she would do once she got there.

She was hungry for something more substantial than she'd had all day, and after a half-hour of walking she found a little place with a neon sign in the window advertising *sándwiches*, *sopa* and *café*. Just inside the door a fan blew strongly into Marisol's face. The diner was hot otherwise and the air smelled heavily of cooking meat. There was a counter and a couple of booths. Marisol chose the counter.

A woman in a waitress' uniform brought her a menu. Just a few feet away was the flat-topped grill and a deep fryer. A thin man in a t-shirt worked with a wedge of metal scraping the grill clean. "How are you?" the waitress asked.

"I'm fine, thank you. May I have a glass of water, please?"

The waitress went away for the water and Marisol looked at the menu. There were many choices, some of which she didn't recognize. The only restaurant in Perquín to serve the locals had simpler fare. She could expect the city to be different.

The water came. Marisol drank some. "Thank you," she said.

"Do you know what you want?"

"I'm not sure. What is good?"

"The cook makes good *panes con pavo*."

"I'll have that."

"There's plenty of it. You'll have some to take with you."

The cook went to work. Marisol watched him, her glass held tightly between her hands. She was aware of the waitress watching her from the end of the counter, but she didn't dare turn her head and look back. She wished someone else would come in and distract the woman.

When the sandwich was ready, the waitress returned. She refilled Marisol's water. "Where are you from?" she asked.

"How do you know I'm not from the city?"

"I can tell. You have it all over you."

Marisol blushed. She looked down at her sandwich. "I'm from Perquín."

"Up in the mountains, huh?"

"Yes."

"What's it like up there?"

"Different."

"I'll bet. Eat your food and call me if you need anything."

The sandwich was good, the spiced and roasted turkey playing games with her mouth. Like the waitress said, there was too much to eat in one sitting and Marisol left half. The waitress approached with a paper bag.

"Like it?" the waitress asked.

"Yes, thank you."

"More water?"

"No, I'm fine."

The sandwich was wrapped up in wax paper and put away in the bag. Marisol brought out her money and paid for it. The waitress made change, then went back to looking at Marisol with a cocked head. "Are you visiting the city?" she asked.

"Yes. Just visiting."

"You have people to look after you?"

"Yes."

"Good. I don't know if you heard, but San Salvador is no place for country folk," the waitress said. "I don't mean that to be insulting. It's just a fact. Stay close to your people. Don't go out at night."

"I won't," Marisol said, and she meant it. By nightfall she hoped to be with her brother and his family. She could not imagine navigating the city streets in the dark with no destination in mind. She wasn't sure she knew exactly how to get back to the bus terminal, but she would manage. There were police everywhere. If she needed to, she would ask one of them.

"Enjoy the city," the waitress said. "It really is something."

Marisol nodded but didn't say anything. She collected her bag of food and headed out the front door where the rain had picked up again. Retreat was not an option, so she ventured out into the drizzle, steering her way back along the streets, dodging water splashed by passing cars. Within minutes she was soaked. She feared someone would be able to make out the makeshift money belt under her clothes.

Just when she thought she had made a wrong turn, she spotted the bus terminal. She made it to a side entrance as thunder rumbled and the sky threatened to split open. Standing dripping in the hallway, clutching her sandwich bag, she searched the faces of the strangers around her, but they suspected nothing.

She went back to the phones and tried her brother's house again, and this time there was an answer. Marisol identified herself. "Is this Sara?" she asked.

"Yes. This is Marisol, Eduardo's sister?"

"That's right. I called ahead to say I would be coming soon. I'm in the city now. At the bus terminal downtown."

"Eduardo is still at work. He has the car."

"When will he be home? I only need a ride from here."

"He will be late. I don't think you'll want to wait so long."

Marisol looked at herself, dripping on the dirty tile floor. The air was so humid, it would be hours before she was completely dry. "I don't have a choice," she said. "I wanted to see him before I leave the city. The bus departs tomorrow."

"I'm sorry, but I don't have a car to pick you up. You should have told Eduardo exactly when you were coming. We aren't ready for visitors."

Sara was right, of course. She should have called ahead, but she hadn't wanted to face Sr. Morán a second time. Marisol was working too fast, getting ahead of herself, rushing into things. She forced herself to slow down.

"I can take a taxi to you," Marisol said at last.

"I told you—"

"I don't have to stay. I can find somewhere in the city. I only want to see my brother before I go. *Por favor*, Sara?"

The woman paused on the line. Marisol heard the burbling of an infant in the background and the white noise of a television set. Sara sighed. "All right. I'll give you the address. And don't think I'm being cruel. I'm sure Eduardo will want to see you, too. I'll call him right away and tell him you're coming."

"Thank you, Sara. It means a great deal to me."

Sara gave Marisol the address and Marisol memorized it. Then the women said their good-byes. Marisol went to the lockers, retrieved her bag, and carried it with her to the front entrance where she waved down a taxicab.

"The traffic is bad," the taxi driver told her. "It could take a while."

"It's all right," Marisol said. "I can wait."

They pulled away from the curb and left the terminal behind in the rain.

12

Eduardo Herrera's home was not as small as the place he'd once shared with his sister and grandmother, but it was not large. He lived on the north side of the city, down a winding street closed in on both sides by houses built right to the very limits of their lots. Graffiti were everywhere, gang signs and symbols Marisol could not decipher. Children played on the road and scattered when the taxi came through.

The ride was more expensive than she liked, but she paid with a tip. The rain had stopped and she stood before her brother's house almost dry after the long drive. She still smelled the odor of the driver's cigarettes on her.

The house had a small porch where there were a couple of balls and a plastic tricycle, along with a pair of cheap metal chairs. The front door was behind a second door made of black-painted iron and double-locked. Marisol knocked.

Marisol had met Sara only once, at the wedding of her brother in Perquín. She was surprised how much older the woman looked when she answered the door, a child balanced on her hip. Always slight, she seemed underweight, though the child was healthily fat, wearing only a diaper.

"Marisol," Sara said. "Good to see you."

"The same. May I come in?"

Sara unlocked the iron door and allowed Marisol inside. It was cooler there with all the windows opened, but barred, and an oscillating fan in the middle of front room. Children's toys were strewn around. The television was on, showing some kind of talk show. Marisol did not watch television at home.

"May I put this somewhere?" Marisol asked and showed her suitcase.

"Anywhere will do."

Marisol put the suitcase by the couch. Sara made a gesture that she should sit and she did. Sara sat on the far end, shifting the child in her arms around so the little one could sit on her knee.

"Is this my nephew?" Marisol asked.

"Yes. His name is Eduardo also."

"Where is Sofia?"

"With my mother today. She's giving me a break. Would you like to hold him?"

"Yes, please."

Sara passed little Eduardo to Marisol. Her nephew was about eighteen months old with a full head of curly hair like his father. He still smelled like a baby.

"Hello, Eduardo. I am your Auntie Marisol," Marisol said. "You are a very handsome little boy."

Little Eduardo smiled at her and squirmed, but not to get away.

Marisol held little Eduardo a while longer. She counted fingers and toes and played "got your nose," and then allowed him to go back to his mother. Sara watched all of this without expression. When she held little Eduardo again, she offered the boy a pacifier, which he took greedily.

"He's beautiful," Marisol said. "I look forward to seeing Sofia. I've only seen her picture."

"She's grown a lot," Sara said. "You'll hardly recognize her."

Marisol looked around the room. There were photographs on the wall in frames, and she recognized one of her grandmother. The floor was plain concrete, the ceiling plastered with cracks. Eduardo and Sara had little furniture and where the back of the room opened onto a kitchen, Marisol saw a small table and chairs, including a high chair. "Your house is nice," she said.

"It keeps us dry," Sara remarked. "We haven't been broken into since we had the bars installed. Before that we were burglarized a dozen times. Twice when we were all at home."

"Is it so bad?"

"We live between two gang cliques, Mara Salvatrucha and 18th Street. They both rob through here. Just the other day, a young boy was shot two doors down. I don't go outside without someone with me."

"That's terrible."

"It's San Salvador."

"Don't the police help?"

"When they can. They have the whole city to protect. We're only a small part of it."

Marisol shook her head. In Perquín they talked about the violence, but it did not touch them. She tried to imagine living here, behind bars, and could not.

The idea had occurred to her that she might travel as far as San Salvador and wait a while. Find a job. Save more money. That idea dissolved now. San Salvador was not the place for her. Instead, her lot lay far to the north of here, on the other side of a great river, where her old map showed only featureless pink. She was doing the right thing and now she knew it more than ever.

"What time will Eduardo come home?" Marisol asked.

"Eight o'clock. He works a long shift three days a week."

"Does he know I'm here?"

"Yes, I called him, but he can't come home early. It's his job, you know."

"I understand. My bus doesn't leave until tomorrow afternoon. There's time."

Sara nodded, but said nothing. There was no offer to stay.

"I'm sorry, but is there somewhere I can lie down? I've been traveling since very early and suddenly I'm tired."

"You can use the bedroom."

Sara led Marisol down a hallway to a pair of doors. Through one was the children's room, the white walls painted with balloons and animal shapes, the floor scattered with still more toys. Through another was Eduardo and Sara's room, where a large mattress stood on a cheap frame with wheels on the legs. There was no headboard and little decoration. Laundry waited in baskets. A dark chest of drawers barely fit into the space it had. The window was barred.

"You can sleep here," Sara said. "If you don't wake up in a couple of hours, I'll come to get you."

"Thank you again, Sara."

"You're family. Sleep well."

When Sara was gone, Marisol unbuttoned her blouse and checked the money belt. The damp and the tape had begun to irritate her skin, but she could deal with that. Lying down was awkward, the packets of bills pressed against her flesh, but she was tired and sleep came quickly. She dreamed of the bus ride and the endless forest and the steady beat of the rain.

13

Marisol woke when Sara rapped lightly on the door frame a couple of hours later. She stretched and felt the money packets peel away from her skin. Her clothes were finally dry.

They spent a few hours playing with little Eduardo and talking about nothing. Every once in a while a vehicle would pass in the street outside and Sara would freeze up, as if she expected something terrible to come crashing through the front wall of the house. Once Marisol heard something that might have been a gunshot, but she had never heard a gunshot before.

When the shadows grew long, Sara put on the lights in the front room. Insects buzzed around the glass globe on the ceiling as she went to the kitchen to cook dinner. Soon there were rich smells of spice and meat. Marisol remembered the rest of her sandwich but decided to save it for tomorrow. It was unspoken that Sara would feed Marisol tonight.

Sara's mother returned to the house with Sofia in tow. The little girl romped into the room and was shy when Sara introduced her to Marisol. Sofia would not talk to Marisol after that, but played quietly in front of the television set with her brother. Marisol didn't blame her; children at her age were never comfortable around strangers, and Marisol was a stranger. The realization made her sad.

Eight o'clock came and went, and Eduardo was not home. The clock crept toward eight-thirty until finally they heard the clang of the driveway gate. Headlights flashed briefly through the front window. Eduardo came in a minute later.

Sara gave her husband a hug and a kiss. Marisol stood waiting.

"Your sister is here," Sara said.

Eduardo looked much older than Marisol remembered him. His hair was still black and his mustache full, but he had new lines around his eyes and his mouth. Like his wife, he looked underweight, though they seemed prosperous enough to Marisol. Eduardo owned a car and a house big enough for his whole family. In Perquín this signaled great success.

"Marisol," Eduardo said. He put his hands out to her.

Marisol hugged her brother and kissed him on the cheek. "It's good to see you," she said.

"It's been a while. Sara, is dinner ready? Come sit with us."

The family assembled around the table. Sofia sat next to Marisol, though she still had nothing to say. They all linked hands to say a prayer before eating. Sara's creation was a zesty beef stew with root vegetables. They dipped tortillas into it to sop up the gravy.

"You got here sooner than I expected," Eduardo told Marisol.

"Things happened quickly."

"The house is sold?"

"Yes. To a nice family."

"It's strange to think of people I don't know living in Grandmother's house."

"It's strange to me, too. I think they'll take good care of it."

"And now you can't go home," Eduardo said.

Marisol said nothing to that. She ate her food and wiped her plate with a tortilla, carefully avoiding her brother's gaze.

"Where do you go next?"

"Guatemala City."

"But you won't stay there, either."

"No."

Eduardo put down his fork. "Why do you have to go to the United States?"

They hadn't discussed it before, but now it was in the open. Eduardo knew without being told. Marisol felt suddenly embarrassed, as if a great secret had just come out. Her hands shook a little and she put them in her lap to still them. "It's something I have to do. I've known it for a long time."

"It's thousands of miles away and you're a woman traveling alone. You've never been away from Perquín. What makes you think you can go all the way?"

"Eduardo—" Sara began.

"No, Sara, I want to know the answer," Eduardo said. Marisol saw his eyes light up, and she knew he was angry. "You couldn't wait to leave, could you? You only stayed because Grandmother was alive."

"I stayed until I had enough money to make the trip. It had nothing to do with Grandmother."

"What would she think of this idea? They'll stop you at the Guatemalan border. Or the border into Mexico. And that's long before you make it to America. How will you live? Who will look after you?"

"I will look after myself."

"You'll be taken advantage of. Just another country girl."

"That's not how it is!"

"Don't tell me how it is. I've been living in the city long enough to know that it's a hard world out there, and people won't make allowances for you the way they did in Perquín. You have a lot to learn."

Marisol's hands were fisted in her lap now. She felt her palms perspire. "I can do it," she said.

"What makes you think that? Because you speak a little English?"

"Because I *can*."

"You're as foolish as Mother was."

"Don't bring her into this."

Eduardo made a disgusted noise and rose from the table. Both Sara and Sofia were looking at their plates while little Eduardo chewed a plastic spoon unaware. "She left us with Grandmother to chase her own, foolish dream. And look what happened to her. Do you want the same thing to happen to you?"

"No. It won't."

"We'll see. If we ever see you again."

Eduardo went away, and after a while Marisol heard him slam his bedroom door. Silence reigned in the kitchen, interrupted only by the soft sounds of the television in the next room. Marisol wiped a tear from her cheek. "I'm sorry," she said to Sara.

"He doesn't mean what he says," Sara said.

"I think he does."

"No, he doesn't. He's been worried ever since you called. He's scared for you."

"Doesn't he know that I'm scared, too? I've been waiting for this since I was a girl and now it's here. I don't know if I will succeed or fail. I just wanted him to know that I can try."

Sara stood up and began to clear the table. "You can talk to him again tomorrow. Tonight you can sleep on the couch. Take a shower, change your clothes. He'll be better in the morning. You'll see."

14

Marisol did what she was told: she showered in the house's little bathroom and changed into fresh clothes the next morning. She was up earlier than everyone and sat quietly on the couch until Eduardo reappeared.

"Good morning," Marisol said to him.

"Good morning," Eduardo said. "Do you want breakfast?"

"Only if that's all right."

"Of course it's all right."

He prepared them oatmeal and they sat at the table together. Sara hadn't yet emerged from the bedroom, though Marisol heard the children. She was giving brother and sister time to themselves.

"I'm sorry about last night," Eduardo said. "I lost my temper. I shouldn't have done that."

"Sara told me you were just worried."

"I am worried. Worried that you don't know what you're doing. I meant what I said last night: no one will stop to lend you a hand along the way. You'll be on your own."

"I've been on my own since Grandmother died. I'm not a china doll, Eduardo."

Eduardo nodded slowly. He scraped his bowl with his spoon. "I'll drive you to the bus terminal today. It will have to be early; I have work."

"Thank you."

"You know...," he started and then his voice trailed away.

"What?"

"You could stay in San Salvador for a while. Find work, an apartment. I could help you out if you needed it."

Marisol shook her head. "San Salvador is not for me."

"And the United States is?"

"I believe it is."

"How many people make the journey, Marisol? How many reach America? You have to realize that the odds are against you. All along the way there will be police trying to arrest you, to send you right back where you started from. And now you don't even have Grandmother's house to go to."

"I have to try."

"That's what you said."

"It can't be more dangerous than staying here. Sara told me about the gangs and the crime. I don't belong in a place like this."

"You belong in America."

"Yes."

"Where everything will come to you on a silver platter," Eduardo said bitterly.

"No, I don't believe that. But in America I will have a chance for something better than selling *pupusas* at the Winter Festival, walking to a well for water every day and tending to a garden because it's too expensive to buy food from the market. You couldn't stand to be in Perquín any more than I could. You left as soon as you were able."

"And here I sit. Should I have gone to America?"

"You have a family now. You have roots. I don't anymore."

"So you're free and I am not."

"Don't look at it that way."

When Eduardo looked at her, Marisol saw that his eyes were wet. The corner of his mouth quivered. "How else can I look at it? You're my only sister and you're going away to God knows what. You could die on the way. And either way I would never see you again."

Marisol put her hand across the table and took Eduardo's. "I may be able to come back. I don't know. But first I have to get there. To do it. The rest will follow."

Eduardo pulled his hand from her grasp. "I still say you shouldn't go."

"And I'm still going to go."

"I've never understood your fascination with the United States. Even when you were a little girl, with all your questions. Learning your English from Sr. Quiñones. You were never going to stay."

"Now you know that's true."

"I have to get ready to go," Eduardo said abruptly. "Will you be ready in half an hour?"

"Yes."

"Good," Eduardo said and he left the table.

When he was gone, Sara emerged with the children. She let Marisol hold little Eduardo while she prepared breakfast. Sofia sat beside Marisol again, watching her with dark eyes. "Would you like to talk today?" Marisol asked her.

"No," Sofia said.

"But you just did."

The slightest of smiles passed Sofia's face. "You are my *tía*?"

"Yes."

"How come I've never seen you before?"

"I don't know," Marisol confessed. "I never came to visit. I'm sorry now that I didn't."

"And now you're going away again?"

"I am. Far away."

"Is it because you don't want to see us?"

Marisol was conscious of Sara watching them, but she kept her attention on Sofia. "No, no," she said. "It's nothing like that. If I could stay, I would, but I have a long journey to take and it won't wait for me."

Sofia nodded sagely. "Will you write?"

"Yes. And I will send pictures. Will you do the same for me?"

"I will if Mother and Father say it's all right."

"It's all right," Sara said.

Marisol touched Sofia's hair and smiled. She felt a sadness welling up in her and she knew it would get the best of her if she didn't wrestle it down again. "I'm sorry I can't stay longer. One day I hope you will understand. And your mother and father, too."

"Time for breakfast," Sara interjected. She took little Eduardo and put him in his high chair. Marisol strayed into the next room while they ate and repacked her suitcase. Before long it was time to go.

15

E duardo drove Marisol to the bus terminal in silence and
when they reached her destination, they embraced one
last time. "Be careful," were Eduardo's last words to her, and
then he let her go.

She spent the morning and the first part of the afternoon waiting on a heavy wooden bench for her bus to leave
and when it was time, she was the first on board. The bus
was packed with people and she found herself sitting next
to a man a few years younger than her. He wore a t-shirt,
a cap and a denim jacket, and when he sat, he jiggled his
knee a lot.

They were a half-hour out of San Salvador when he turned
to her. "I'm Heriberto," he said.

"Marisol."

"*Mucho gusto.* Are you from San Salvador?"

"No, I come from Perquín."

"Oh, so you came a long way. Why are you going to
Guatemala City?"

Marisol considered telling him the truth, but she hesitated. Eduardo's words were still in the back of her mind.
"I'm on a pleasure trip," she said finally.

"You'll like the city. Bigger than San Salvador. I work there. I come to visit my family in San Salvador twice a year."

Marisol nodded politely.

"Your family lives in Perquín?"

"No, my brother lives in San Salvador. I just saw him."

"It must be very different, seeing the city. Perquín is such a flyspeck."

"It is small."

This seemed to satisfy Heriberto and he was quiet after that. Marisol directed her attention out the window, though there was nothing to see but green. She thought she felt Heriberto watching her, but she didn't turn to look.

The bus seemed to go slower and slower the closer it came to the border with Guatemala, until finally they were there. Soldiers in uniforms carrying weapons openly awaited them at a metal gateway three lanes wide. The passengers were told to disembark and bring their luggage. They stood outside a small building where they filed through one by one.

When it came to be Marisol's turn, she entered the building. Three men and a woman staffed a broad counter that stood at waist height. Marisol saw the man in front of her stuffing his clothing back into his bag before venturing out on the Guatemalan side. She was very aware of the money underneath her blouse.

"Put your suitcase on the counter, please," said one of the men. "Open it up."

Marisol did as she was told. The man sorted through her things, then shoved the open suitcase down the line where another man did the same thing, only this time testing the inner lining of the case with his fingers.

"Do you have anything to declare?"

Marisol swallowed. Her mouth was dry. "No," she said.

The man looked at her hard and for a moment she thought he was going to have her searched. She tried to suppress a shiver, but it passed through her anyway. He noticed. "Why are you coming to Guatemala?"

"I'm traveling," Marisol said. Her voice was tight and she cleared her throat. "I'm traveling to Mexico."

"Mexico? What for?"

"Work."

"There's no work in El Salvador?"

"Better work."

"Better, huh? I think you'll be disappointed. Move along."

She came to the woman. A variety of stamps and an ink pad were arranged in front of her. "Passport," the woman said and Marisol presented it. The woman stamped it. "This tourist visa is good for thirty days."

"Yes. Thank you."

"Next."

Marisol emerged onto the Guatemalan side of the building shaking all over. The bus was already waiting for them. Marisol's knees felt weak and she made her way to the bus unsteadily. She made herself breathe more slowly.

The passengers reassembled on the bus one by one. Heriberto sat down beside her again. "Red tape," he remarked. Marisol could only nod.

A few minutes later they were on their way, driving through a little town whose name Marisol didn't know. She was out of El Salvador, the first hurdle cleared.

She felt drained and she leaned her head against the window and let herself doze. She wasn't sure how much time passed, but she was stirred from sleep by a touch. It took a moment for wakefulness to come, but then she felt the hand

on her thigh, her skirt pulled up past her knee. She sat up
sharply. "What the hell are you doing?"

Heriberto snatched his hand away from her. "Hey, it was
nothing," he said.

"Don't put your hands on me! Get away from me!"

"Hey, lady, I don't know what you're talking about!"

Marisol rose from her seat as much as she could, but she
was trapped between Heriberto and the window. The overhead luggage rack forced her to bend over. "You're touching
me!"

The other passengers were looking and Marisol saw the
driver peering into his mirror. Heriberto tried to grab her
hands and sit her down again. "Hey, calm down!"

"Stop it! Stop touching me!"

A man left his seat and approached down the narrow aisle.
"What's happening here?"

"This man touched me on my leg while I was sleeping!"

"I didn't do anything!"

"You touched me under my skirt! Help me get away from
him!"

The man put his hands on Heriberto. "Come on, let the
lady out."

Heriberto struggled. "I didn't do anything," he repeated.
"She's crazy!"

"Just get up!"

Heriberto lunged at the man and then they were strug-
gling in the aisle. The whole bus lurched as the driver hit the
brakes. People raised their voices and the inside of the bus was
pandemonium.

The man grabbed Heriberto by the jacket and pulled it up
over his head. Heriberto was throwing punches blindly, hit-

ting seats and people around him, but not the man he wanted to strike. Marisol's heart was pounding.

The driver intervened and it was a three-way grapple between them. Heriberto was dragged to the front of the bus and kicked out the door. People pressed up against the windows to see, but Marisol did not.

The door was closed. The man came back to Marisol. "Are you all right?" he asked.

"I think so, yes. Thank you."

"Perverts. They're everywhere."

"Everyone sit down!" the driver called. "Everyone relax! The fight is over!"

Marisol sank back into her seat and straightened the hem of her skirt. Her thoughts whirled. The man returned to his place. The bus started up again. They were in the middle of nowhere, naked forest all around. The driver had left Heriberto with nothing but what he carried. She couldn't see Heriberto from where she sat.

It took a long time for her relax into her seat. She kept looking at the empty place where Heriberto sat, felt his hand on her thigh. She shivered as hard as she had when she faced the gantlet at the border. When people turned her way, she thought they were staring at her.

The bus kept on.

16

Guatemala City was as large as Heriberto promised. It was broad streets and high buildings and concrete everywhere. Nature didn't intrude into her at all. It seemed cleaner than San Salvador and there weren't armed policemen at every intersection. At the bus terminal in the city she found an air-conditioned place with high, painted ceilings and a snack bar.

Her bus did not leave until the next morning. She walked two blocks and found a little hotel that didn't cost very much. She checked herself in. There were women lingering in the lobby and Marisol wondered if they were prostitutes. They didn't dress provocatively, but perhaps they couldn't without a visit from the police.

The room was small, but it had a bed and a bathroom with a working shower. The door had three locks. Marisol heard a television blaring through the wall. She washed and changed her clothes again. Soon she would have to find somewhere to launder her clothing. She didn't want to travel dirty and disheveled. That would give her away as a migrant, and she did not want that.

Sleep was restless and she woke more than once thinking she felt a hand on her. She tried watching television but it didn't interest her. She finally ate the rest of her sandwich. It was the first thing she'd eaten all day.

Marisol was back at the bus terminal in the morning. She ate an egg and bacon at the snack bar and then boarded a bus headed west. This time she sat alone and she was glad of it. She kept her suitcase with her and put it in the seat next to her to discourage anyone from coming near.

The bus traveled along the spine of a mountain range, the Sierra Madre. The greenery was different here than it was in El Salvador. Where the forests were deep and wet around Perquín, these were drier, and unfamiliar trees grew. Marisol was surprised at the number of towns they passed through, quite unlike the strings of little villages that dotted the mountains of her home country.

Eventually they began their descent, and Marisol knew before long they would reach the river separating Guatemala from Mexico. A few hours later they were there.

Marisol disembarked with the other passengers. She saw the broad expanse of a river to the west and a highway passing into a bridge. There were people dotting the riverside, some with rafts made of inner tubes. She saw more crossing on them, swimming against the current, with their things tied down to keep them from the water.

She had to walk a long way to reach the bridge. A foot-bridge adjoined the larger lanes intended for vehicles. Traffic was stacked up for a mile along the highway, vehicles steaming in the sun. She went onto the footbridge, where ahead there lay another building marked with the flags of Guatemala and Mexico.

This time she had no fear. She waited in a line behind a half-dozen others and when it was her time, she presented her suitcase and passport to the Mexican officer behind the counter.

The man looked over her passport. He didn't touch her suitcase. He glanced up at her twice, checked her passport photo, then examined the stamp she'd gotten from the Guatemalan border agents. "You haven't been that long in Guatemala," he said finally.

"I'm traveling," Marisol said, and her voice was strong.

"Where are you traveling to?"

"North. Mexico City."

"Who do you know there?"

"I have a cousin who lives there," Marisol lied. It was so easy.

"What is your cousin's name?"

"Eduardo Herrera."

The man opened her suitcase. He rummaged around in it for a moment, then closed it up. He gave her passport back. "At this time I cannot provide you with a visa."

"Why not?"

"I don't believe you have a cousin in Mexico City. If you plan to come into Mexico to work, you must apply for a work visa."

"I don't want to work in Mexico."

"I'm sorry, but you can't have a visa."

"What if I come back tomorrow and you're not here?"

"You want to do that?" the man asked. "We'll put up your picture. You won't get through."

"I just want to travel to Mexico City."

"You won't be traveling today. Please make way for the next person."

Marisol opened her mouth to speak and then shut it. She hefted her suitcase and exited the way she came in. The person following her presented their bag and passport. Marisol caught the fading edge of their conversation as she walked away.

She felt tears coming, but she tamped them down. Her chest was tight, threatening to smother her. She breathed deeply. At the foot of the bridge she stopped and could not contain herself any longer. She wept.

Marisol did not hear the policeman approach her, and it was only when his shadow fell over her that she looked up. She straightened and wiped her eyes and tried an impassive expression that would not hold.

"They won't let you through?" the policeman asked. He wore a pistol on his hip and a short-sleeved uniform shirt that he had sweated through. His eyes were hidden behind sunglasses.

"No," Marisol said.

"Don't worry. They're suspicious. They hardly let anyone through."

"But I have to go to Mexico."

"Doesn't everyone?"

Marisol looked at the policeman. She couldn't read his face.

"Talk to one of those boys down by the river," the policeman said. "For a thousand quetzales they'll get you across."

"I only have American dollars."

"They'll take those, too. Go and see them."

Marisol turned back toward the river. She saw two young men, stripped to the waist, dragging a raft made of six inner tubes onto the bank. One of them lit up a cigarette. They seemed to be going nowhere.

"I'm telling you, it's the best way to get across," the policeman said.

"*Gracias,*" Marisol said.

"Don't cry. Everywhere there is a way," the policeman said, and he smiled. Marisol tried to smile back.

The policeman walked away.

Marisol picked her way down the rock-strewn riverbank to where the men stood smoking by their raft. They saw her coming and they flicked away their butts. One of them waved her closer. "*Hola*," he called. "Right here."

She approached them and the men put on smiles. Once again her heart was beating fast. She felt exposed, even though they were the ones without shirts on. They were deeply tanned.

"Going across?" asked the man who'd spoken.

"I want to."

"You came to the right place. I'm Adolfo. This is Felipe. We can take you across."

Marisol looked up at the sky. The sun was almost directly overhead. "Now?" she asked.

"When else?"

"Won't they see?"

"Sure," Adolfo said.

"I don't understand."

"Where are you from?"

"El Salvador."

"Let me tell you how it works in Guatemala: you pay, we take you across and on the other side you pay again."

"Pay you?"

"No, you pay *them*. Look across the river."

Adolfo pointed and Marisol followed his finger. She saw another raft of inner tubes dragging up on the far bank and approaching the crossers were two figures. One of them seemed to be carrying a rifle.

"The police are waiting on the other side?" Marisol asked.

"Of course. It costs to get past them, but it's not so bad. One hundred and fifty quetzales, or something like that. Not much after you pay us 1,000."

"I don't know how much that is."

"You are from El Salvador. You have US money?"

"Yes."

"We'll take one hundred dollars. Guaranteed crossing. We'll do it right now."

Marisol hesitated. It was not the money. She had the money. It was the sun and the open river and the people crossing without fear of what lay on the other side. *This is what you are,* Marisol thought. *This you can do.*

"Here. Take the money," Marisol said and she gave them five twenties from her roll of bills. She was aware of Adolfo and Felipe watching her money and she put it away quickly. "Take me across."

"First we wait for a few more. Then we go. Just sit down over there."

Marisol sat on the edge of the inner-tube raft. People approached the river in twos and threes, coming down from the road with their little bags and meeting with other men like Adolfo and Felipe. She looked back where the bus had dropped her off and there was another bus disgorging a new load of passengers. Half of them came down to the river directly.

It took an hour for them to round up three more passengers for the crossing. A man and his girlfriend held hands tightly. Another man traveled alone. When the money had been collected from everyone, Felipe and Adolfo wrestled the raft into the water. Marisol took off her shoes and waded in. Her skirt began to soak.

They helped her tie down her suitcase and Felipe lifted her onto the raft. She was still going to get wet, but she would not be soaked the way they would be. Adolfo and Felipe swam alongside the raft, kicking powerfully, guiding the inner tubes along the swiftly flowing river.

The sun reflected off the water and dazzled Marisol's eyes. The far side of the river seemed a long way off, but it came quicker than she expected. Before long they were splashing through the shallows onto the pebbly riverbank on the Mexican side. "*Buena suerte*," Adolfo told Marisol, and then he and Felipe were pushing off once more, headed back.

Marisol saw a pair of Mexican policemen come down toward them. One carried a shotgun, the other a rifle. For an instant she saw them shot down at the water's edge, crossing illegally, but the policemen didn't raise their weapons.

They went to the couple first and demanded money, which the couple paid. Then the lone man paid his passage before they came to Marisol.

"Time to pay the toll," said the policeman with the shotgun.

"How much do you want?"

"How much do you have?" asked the policeman with the rifle.

"Will you take American money?"

"Sure," the first policeman said.

Marisol turned away from them so they could not see how much she carried. She peeled off a pair of twenties and offered them to the policemen. "Is this enough?"

"It's good enough," the first policeman said. "Where are you headed?"

"The United States."

"You have a long way to go. It's illegal for you to be here. You get caught, they'll send you back to Guatemala."

"I just need to take a bus."

"Bus? No bus from here. People like you, they take the train."

"People like me?"

"Illegals. You're on the wrong side of the law now. Someone gives you aid or shelter, they can go to jail for six years. Nobody will want to help you."

"But how can I make it north?"

"Like I said: take the train. If you hurry, you might catch one before nightfall."

"Thank you."

"Don't thank us," the second policeman said. "We just want the money. The next cops you find might not be so friendly."

Marisol took up her suitcase and marched up the bank until she reached a paved road. She put on her shoes, looked back at the river once, and went on.

17

There were many other migrants headed to the trains and Marisol followed them. She expected a terminal where there were seats and tickets to be purchased, but the flow of people carried her to a large and crowded train yard. A long section of hurricane fencing had been trodden down and she crossed it.

"Where is the train station?" she asked a man headed in the same direction.

"No station," he replied.

"How do we take the trains?"

"On top," the man said and illustrated with his hands.

She saw that there were many people clambering aboard train cars not meant for passengers. At least a dozen were in a car heaped with coal and others clung to the top of a tanker. Everywhere there were border crossers being helped up or climbing on their own, mounting the trains.

Not far away, a train whistle blew. The cars nearest to Marisol jerked and began to roll forward. The people atop a cargo container began yelling to her. "Come on! Climb up! Hurry!"

The cargo container had a ladder on the side, but Marisol had to hurry to catch up to it as the train picked up speed.

She got one hand on the lowest rung and struggled to hang onto her suitcase and get a hold with her other hand.

A woman above her stretched out an arm, but she was too far away; Marisol would have to climb.

The ground tripped past beneath her feet, and she knew she would fall if she waited too long. She hauled herself up by her free hand, making the next rung. Her other hand burned with the effort of gripping both rung and suitcase handle.

"Drop the case!" the woman above her yelled.

The train moved still faster.

"I can't!" Marisol shouted back.

It took monumental effort to make the next rung, and then she was free of the ground, scrabbling with her feet to find some purchase. She found the lower edge of the flatbed car that held the container, just a tiny ridge her toes barely fit, but it was enough. She clawed her way up to the next rung and then the next, so that her feet could make the ladder.

"Give me the suitcase!" the woman said. Marisol handed it up.

The last few feet were easier, though her hand cramped. When Marisol made it to the top of the ladder, she flopped onto the roof of the cargo container, her body trembling and sweaty. A breeze played across her and grew stronger as the train sped along the tracks.

There were three women and six men on the roof. A few had little backpacks for their things, the rest were empty-handed, though they had close to them gallon jugs of water or three-liter bottles of soft drink. The woman who held Marisol's suitcase gave it back. "You should have left it," she said. "You might have fallen."

"Then I would have nothing," Marisol replied.

"It's the wrong kind of bag, anyway. How are you supposed to carry it when your hands get tired?"

Marisol shook her head. She looked backward and forward and saw border crossers on cars in both directions. Some looked back at her, while others kept their eyes on the front of the train, many cars ahead.

"I am Alicia," the woman said to Marisol. She didn't offer her hand.

"Marisol. Where is this train going?"

"North," said one of the men.

"North," repeated Alicia. "No one knows how far. The train is long, though; that usually means it has a great distance to go."

"We ride all the way?"

"And then we get a new train."

Marisol turned her head toward the side of the container and had to snap her gaze away. The sway and motion of the car made her feel dizzy, as if she was teetering on the edge. Looking ahead was better.

Alicia had a bottle of water. She drank some of it and offered it to Marisol. "Here. You don't have anything?"

"I didn't know I would need it."

"You're going to want to buy something when we stop, if you can. The sun and the heat... they'll dry you up."

Marisol was careful not to drink too much of Alicia's water. Already she felt foolish. Bus stations? Cafés? Cheap hotels to sleep in? These were the things she expected when she crossed the border into Mexico, not this. In Guatemala they hadn't cared to know her reasons for heading north, but the policeman said she was little more than a fugitive now. "Do the police arrest people on the trains?" Marisol asked.

Alicia nodded. "Sometimes."

"You've done this before?"

"Four times."

"You're going all the way? To the United States?"

"If I can. The trains will take me most of the way. Then I'll walk. The farther north you go, the safer it is to ride the bus or hitch a ride. I have enough for a bus to the border. And to pay the *coyote*."

"Where are you coming from?" Marisol asked.

"Honduras."

"Have they ever caught you?"

"Why do you think I've done this four times?" Alicia asked and she laughed. "Where are you from?"

"El Salvador."

Alicia turned to the others on the roof. "Anyone here from El Salvador?"

A man raised his hand. "I am. César."

"She's also from El Salvador," Alicia said. "You should travel together."

Marisol looked at César. He was younger than her and very thin, so that his t-shirt hung loosely on his torso. He had both a pack and a gallon of water. His shoes looked new. He was clearly more prepared than her for what must be done. César returned her gaze briefly, nodded and then turned away.

"It's always good to travel with your own people," Alicia said. She indicated three others on the roof. "We're all from the same place. We'll go all the way together."

Then Alicia fell silent, and Marisol found herself with nothing to do but watch the country go by. The train moved quickly, fast enough that if she fell she would be left behind instantly, or ground beneath the wheels faster than anyone could save her. She moved carefully away from the edges, unconsciously closer to César, but not far from Alicia. After a while she let her head hang and dozed, lulled by the sound of steel on steel.

They spent all of that day riding north and into the night.

18

She woke with the moon high in the sky overhead, looking dingy and yellowish. All of the others were asleep,
sprawled out on the roof of the cargo container. None of
them rolled over in their sleep, somehow knowing that they
would plummet if they did so and be caught under the wheels
to be chopped to pieces. They were like corpses, utterly still.

The train had passed through villages and towns without slowing or stopping. Some of the villages were like those
Marisol knew from home: just a line of shanties abutting the
railroad tracks, without power or water. Children and dogs
sometimes ran alongside. The children waved. Marisol waved
back.

Marisol was thirsty, but she didn't want to ask anyone for
a mouthful of their water. César was nearby and his jug of
water was unattended. The temptation to steal it from him,
just for a drop, was stronger than she anticipated.

She sat up and surveyed the other cars. Everyone was
asleep. She was the only one awake. With the moon sentinel
above her, she watched the light-frosted land pass by.

A plan had begun to form in her mind and now she took
the time to examine it. She would take this train as far north

as it would carry her, of course, and then she would take another. Maybe César would accompany her, or maybe not. They would travel until it was safer to go where Mexicans went and catch a bus. Also, she needed a place to wash her clothes and a real bed to sleep in, and maybe she would find such a thing along the way. She realized it was not much of a plan.

She wasn't sure about César yet. Twice she had tried to make conversation with him, if only to find out where in El Salvador he had come from, but he was close-mouthed. She did not even know if this was his first time taking the journey, though from his preparations she suspected it was not.

The memory of Heriberto was still fresh. César did not seem to be that type, but how would she know? She wished that she had a woman to travel with. It would make things so much easier.

Marisol stayed awake as long as she was able, but the monotony of the scenery made her eyelids heavy again and she slept.

When she woke, it was daylight and César and the others were eating snacks like granola bars and chips. Marisol's stomach was tight and she wasn't sure she would be able to eat even if she had something. Her mouth watered, though, and that at least made the thirst easier to take.

César noticed her watching him and offered her a half-finished bag of corn chips. "Go ahead," he said, and that was almost as much as he had said to her all along.

Marisol ate sparingly and was sure to give the bag back with chips remaining. César folded the bag shut and put it away. He drank some water and extended the jug to her when he was done.

"Thank you," Marisol said.

"*De nada.*"

César capped the jug and went back to staring off into space. Marisol thought to talk with Alicia some more, but she was deep in conference with her Honduran companions, sharing food amongst themselves.

"They say we should travel together," Marisol said to César. "Because we're Salvadoran."

César might have nodded. It was difficult to tell.

"Do you know where you're headed?"

Marisol thought he wasn't going to say anything, but finally he adjusted his cap so that he could look at her directly and said, "Ojinaga."

"Is that a place?"

"It's a town. On the border."

"You'll cross there?"

This time when César nodded, Marisol could tell. "Where will you cross?" he asked.

"I don't know."

"You didn't think this through at all, did you?"

Marisol felt her cheeks flush. She looked at her hands. "I thought one place was as good as another. As long as you have a guide and can pay."

"It's not the same. Some places it's too dangerous to cross. Too many cops. You have to go where they aren't."

"Ojinaga?" Marisol asked.

"Ojinaga."

"Will you show me the way?"

César looked at her sharply. "Why do you want me to show you?"

"Because you know what you're doing."

"I think it's better if I go alone."

Wheels turned in Marisol's head and she said quickly, "I can pay my way."

Again César looked at her. "What do you mean?"

"I have a little money. I can share it with you."

"You don't know me, lady."

"I don't know anyone."

"I'm not a *coyote*."

"You just have to show me where to go and I'll find one myself."

César didn't say anything. He turned away from her and Marisol thought that was the end of it, but finally he examined her out of the corner of his eye and said, "How much money do you have?"

"Enough for us to buy food. Stay in a hotel. Ride the bus."

"Let me see."

Marisol hesitated, and then brought out the roll of bills. César did not snatch them from her hand; he merely looked and nodded again.

"Okay, we'll go together. But we need to get north of Mexico City before we start going to hotels and catching buses. Farther to the south they're always looking for migrants. It's trains for now."

"All right," Marisol agreed.

"And you pay for any bribes we have to make."

"I'll do that."

César seemed satisfied and resumed his vigil over the passing countryside. Marisol wanted to talk to him more, but he was uninterested. She pulled her suitcase to her and ran her fingers over the rough texture of its outer shell. On the one hand she felt better having made a deal to carry her the rest of the way, while on the other the sensation of being a fool hadn't left her. César was maybe twenty years old and he knew the way of things better than she did. All of her carefully penciled routes across maps were just dreams. The reality rode aboard a freight train in the back country of Mexico.

19

S he had no idea where they were when the train finally
stopped. They were in another rail-yard, this one as large
or larger than the one where they began. There were trains everywhere, a labyrinth of rolling stock that the migrants aboard
Marisol's train began to navigate, rat-like and quick-footed.

Marisol looked to César for her cues. She was slow getting
down off the cargo container, and he was already on his way,
nearly lost in the press of bodies pouring down from other
cars. Everyone was silent, or conversed in whispers, so Marisol did not shout for him to slow down.

They made their way past seemingly identical sets of tracks
and trains. César was looking for something Marisol couldn't
see. Once he stopped to confer with another small band, and
then he motioned for her to hurry up to his side.

"There are police here," he said when she was close.

"Where?"

"Out there," César said and he waved his arm vaguely.

"What do we do?"

"We find a train and hope they don't find us first. If they
catch us, we'll have to pay them."

"How do you know which train to take?"

"I'll know it when I see it."

He led her on and from time to time Marisol caught sight of other groups of migrants doing the same thing. Finally César stopped near the open bay of a freight car and climbed up.

"Here?" Marisol asked. She could not tell this train from any other.

"Here."

Marisol lifted her suitcase into the car and then scrambled up. The freight car was empty, the floor dusty and strewn with what looked like hay. It smelled of rust and oil. "I think—" she started.

"Shh!"

César shrank back from the open door of the freight car until he was hidden in shadow. Before he vanished, Marisol saw him waving her into cover. She gathered up her suitcase and mimicked him, conscious of the sound of her shoes on the wooden floor and the leaden silence outside.

They didn't move for long minutes, until Marisol was certain César had been mistaken, but then she heard the crunch of gravel and the sound of two men walking.

A pair of shadows fell across the open door. Someone lifted a shotgun and rested it on his shoulder. "Anybody in there?" a man called.

Marisol put her hand over her mouth and tried not to breathe. She couldn't see César, but she imagined him doing the same.

The shadows didn't move away. "If there's anyone in there, show yourselves. It's the police. Don't make us come in and get you."

"If we come in and get you," a second man said, "it'll be bad for you."

Marisol froze. She heard the scrape of a sneaker on wood and César stepped out into the light. "Don't shoot," he said.

"Is it just you?"

"No."

Now Marisol moved. She still clutched her suitcase, found she couldn't let go of it, and when the sun fell onto her, it seemed suddenly very hot and bright.

The policemen were thin men in ill-fitting brown uniform shirts with badges. Both were armed, but the smaller of the two carried the shotgun. They both smiled, but Marisol and César did not smile back.

"Just two?" asked the policeman with the shotgun.

"It's only us," César said.

"There's room enough in there for plenty more."

"No, it's just the two of us."

"Get on down here."

César climbed down. The second policeman, the one without the shotgun, helped Marisol with her suitcase and offered a hand to steady her as she hopped off.

"Where are you two from?"

"Guatemala," César lied. Marisol did not try to contradict him.

"Are you two married?"

"No, señor. She's my cousin."

"Well, you both go back together."

"Please," Marisol said abruptly.

The policemen both looked at her. The one with the shotgun said, "What do you mean?"

"Please don't send us back." Marisol's vision blurred and she realized she was tearing. She held her hands up in supplication. "We don't want to stay here, we just want to get to America. Please. Let us go on."

"It's the law. You're illegals."

"We'll pay," Marisol said. "We have money. We'll pay if you just let us go on."

"How much will you pay?"

The question stopped her. If she gave them all her traveling money, it would leave only the cash she had strapped to her body and then everyone, including César, would know how much she carried. That was her final secret.

"How much will you pay?" the policeman with the shotgun asked again.

"How much do you want?"

The policeman considered. "Two hundred dollars. Each."

Marisol flinched. That was nearly everything in the roll. "Will you take American money?"

"You have American money? What are you doing with that?"

"Please, will you take it?"

The policemen looked at each other. They nodded.

Marisol paid them. She still wasn't sure if it was enough, but the policemen seemed satisfied, and a part of her unclenched. The money quickly disappeared.

"You'll need a lot more to cross the border," the policeman with the shotgun said.

"Lots more," said the other policeman.

"We'll be all right," César said.

"Is that backtalk?"

"No, señor."

"Get on your train, then. This one's going to Zacatecas, I think."

Marisol hurried to get back into the freight car, conscious of the policemen's eyes on her. César helped her up, the first time he had done such a thing, but she couldn't read his face.

The policemen lingered. "It's not going to get any easier for you when you get to the States," the one with the shotgun said. "The Americans, they don't take bribes."

With that they turned away. Marisol watched them go. When she couldn't hear their footsteps anymore, she let her breath out. César sat down beside her. "Thank you, God," he said. "I was scared."

Marisol looked at him. Still she could not see through his expression. He was blank, except for a tightness around his eyes and mouth. She did not understand him. "You were scared?" she asked.

"Of course. You never know if they'll take the money."

She wondered how old César was that he would know these things and still be so young. She felt like the younger one, blundering around, while he was steady. Her heart was still beating fast.

"Zacatecas," César said. "That's good. You want to wash and sleep and catch a bus? We can do it there."

20

The trip took three days, and during that time César's food ran out and so did his water. They did their best to ration them both, but it was not enough. The weather was hot and being in the shade of the freight car hardly seemed to help. Sometimes Marisol saw spots in front of her eyes.

On the third day clouds rolled in and a great thunderstorm crashed down upon them. They came into the train yard at Zacatecas with the weather still punishing them, and they escaped the yard only by dashing across a field of sticking mud.

They walked for miles in the rain until finally they reached a motel. The clerk at the desk did not remark at their state and gladly took Marisol's dollars. Their room was on the second of two floors and the rain drummed on the roof.

The room had two small beds, a television and a telephone. Out of the rain, Marisol saw how César's shirt clung to his body. He was whippet-thin when their journey started and the deprivation hadn't helped.

Marisol put her suitcase on one of the beds. She wrung the water out of her skirt. Her shoes were caked in mud. She would try to clean them, but she didn't know if she could.

César went into the bathroom and she heard him drinking water from the tap. When it was her turn, she drank greedily, until her stomach felt heavy. Maybe it would make her sick, but she was almost two days without anything to put in her stomach, and this would do.

"Let me have some money," César asked her when she returned. "For food."

Marisol gave him some. He left then, and she was alone in the small room.

She went into the bathroom and stripped out of her wet clothes. Though she had not had an opportunity to wash them, her other clothes were at least dry, and she changed into them. The others she hung up in the bathtub from the curtain rod.

César returned with bread and meat and soft drinks. Heedless of the water dripping from him, he tore into the food on his bed while Marisol ate her share. The first bite made her feel ravenous. They emptied the bag he'd brought.

"I saw a *lavandería* on the way to the store," César said. "And a place where you can buy new shoes. Those are no good anymore. You need something you can walk a long way in. We'll buy more food."

"How much farther do we have to go?"

"By bus? Two days maybe. We have to look clean and neat so no one suspects."

"We can do that."

César nodded, and for the first time he smiled, though only a little. "We can do that."

They stayed at the motel for two days, eating and resting. Marisol took their dirty clothes to the *lavandería*. She found a place where she could buy sneakers like César's.

When they left the motel, they made sure to shower and make themselves presentable. César put some gel in his hair and Marisol put on makeup. As before, the clerk at the desk paid them no mind and called a taxi when they asked for one. The taxi took them to the main bus terminal. There they mingled, Marisol feeling as though at any moment the police would come for them and snatch them right out of their shoes. César was relaxed and bought their tickets for them. He came back to her and even held her hand. "Okay?" he asked.

"Okay," Marisol replied. "It's done?"

"Yes. From here to Torreón, then on to Chihuahua. That's where we get the bus to Ojinaga. We'll be in Chihuahua by tomorrow."

So close, Marisol thought.

"What do we do now?" Marisol asked.

"Nothing. It's in the hands of God."

God. Marisol realized she had no idea what day it was, not even the date. If it had been Sunday, would she have gone to the church and said a prayer for their safe passage? In her way she had been saying that prayer every day. She was glad to have César here, glad to have come so far and glad that before long it would all be decided at the Río Bravo.

21

The bus in Zacatecas was not like the buses she had taken before. This one had air conditioning and the seats were high and plush. Marisol boarded with César beside her, very conscious of herself, watching the eyes of those around her for the telltale sign that they knew her for a fraud. The driver had a radio; he could call the police to take them away by the side of the road.

Someone had left a magazine behind. It was a celebrity weekly, full of glossy pictures of men and women she didn't recognize and advertisements for products she had never heard of before. She read every word carefully and then read the magazine again and again as they traveled. When she could not stand to read it any more, she finally put it aside and tried to nap.

She dreamed of the river. In none of the books or maps had she ever seen a photograph of the place, so it was entirely of her imagination. She envisioned a broad, deep river bounded on both sides by slippery rocks. Frogs lived between the rocks, and she came down to the river barefoot as she listened to them chirp. There were reeds on the far side, so deep that she couldn't see the bank, and winged insects flew there.

When she put her hand in the water, it flowed quickly through her fingers, away and away to the Gulf of Mexico. She did not know what the sea looked like, either, and could not conceive of its sights and smells. Maybe she would see an ocean once she was in the United States. Maybe she would live on one of its great shores. She was carried away by the dream.

Perquín came to her, distant and tiny, as if viewed through the wrong end of a telescope. Everything was small — the streets, the buildings, her grandmother's house — and was swallowed up by the deep green forest around it. She felt as distant from the village as someone who had never been there; it was strange and otherworldly. Perquín was so tiny that Lupita was barely a speck.

And now she rolled down a remote highway, big wheels turning beneath her. She was afloat on cushions that skimmed the water. Water turned by wheels. And the beautiful, smiling faces of strangers came to her.

She woke. It was dark. Across the aisle from her, César was asleep, his head canted at an angle, his mouth open. She heard him snore.

They were in the dry, wrinkled land that spread out blackly beyond the window of the bus. Lights glided into view as they entered the outskirts of a city that must be Chihuahua. They were almost there.

Marisol watched the city form up out of the dust by signs and streetlights and passing cars. She didn't know what time it was, but the city was still awake. Marisol stretched and thought of waking César. He looked much younger sleeping, lacking the guardedness of his waking expression.

Around her the other passengers were stirring. She wondered how many of them were stopping here and how many were going on. Where were they headed? To the border? Would they see some of these same faces on the way to Oji-naga? Were those people also going to the border?

César woke, and Marisol looked away so that he would not see that she'd been watching. When she looked again, his mask was back in place. He nodded to her.

Because of the late hour, the bus terminal was nearly deserted and all the ticket counters were closed. A lone policeman walked through the main hall, not seeming to care if there were people sprawled on the benches and across chairs sleeping. Marisol was careful not to look the policeman in the eyes.

César left to check the posted schedules. Marisol waited at a bench, her suitcase across her knees, hoping she looked like any other Mexican traveler. She had money if they had to pay another bribe, but what if this time it was not enough? They were too close to Ojinaga to be turned away now.

"We have to wait until morning," César told her.

"I don't want to stay here," Marisol said.

"Why not?"

"The policeman," Marisol replied quietly.

"Okay."

They left by the front doors and found a taxi lingering under the lights, the driver reading a book and smoking. Marisol told the driver to take them somewhere inexpensive where they could stay the night and got into the back seat with César beside her.

The taxi took them a few miles away to a small hotel. An old woman checked them in and offered them clean towels. The room had only one bed.

"You sleep there," César said. "I'll take the floor."

"You don't have to. I can sleep on the floor just as easily."

"No, it's all right."

Neither Marisol nor César had anything to discuss, no plans to mull over, no dreams they wanted to share. Marisol knew he was like her: focused on the border. She lay awake a long while imagining what it would look like, the images from her dream feeding into her waking mind. It would not be that way, of course. It would look like nothing she envisioned.

After a while Marisol heard César lightly snoring from his place on the floor alongside the bed. She wasn't sure if she would be able to sleep at all. The room was too small for her to stand up and pace. Eventually she sat against the headboard staring at the dark walls.

What was happening in her grandmother's house at this hour? All of Perquín would be sleeping. And what about on the street where her brother lived in San Salvador? Did they dream of her? Did they see her from a distance in their mind's eye?

A truck with a rumbling engine drove by outside and, for an instant, the room was bright with its headlights. Marisol lay down again, and this time she could sleep.

22

The taxi company they called was slow to dispatch a driver, and so they very nearly missed their bus. It was not as nice as their last bus, but was still worlds away from the one that took Marisol from Perquín. The morning was still cool and Marisol put her window down to let the breeze in.

The highway stretched along a desolate sweep of land that was sparsely populated by cactus, dry grass and twisted trees. Marisol could not remember the last time she had seen the kind of verdant green that had been all around Perquín. She must have left it somewhere in Guatemala. That was forever ago.

They rode three hours until Ojinaga drew into view. It was a flat town in a flat pan, its buildings scattered around until they formed loosely around a center. Marisol saw many signs advertising dentists. People were out on foot. There were few cars parked along the main road and traffic was light.

Ojinaga did not even have a proper bus terminal. The station was just a small building with a ticket office inside and a pair of concrete islands separating two bus lanes. Marisol and César were under the eye of the sun as they disembarked. The glare was intense.

Marisol was hungry and the smell of cooking food led them across the street to a small café. There they had eggs and chorizo and fresh orange juice. The staff treated them the same as the other customers in the little place, and Marisol wondered if they had completely shed their foreign-ness and become like all the other Mexicans. They were clean and neat and spoke good Spanish. They were not aliens from another world.

"What do we do now?" Marisol asked as they cleaned their plates and waited for the check. "A *coyote*?"

"Yes," César said. "But it's too early. We'll have to wait until night to find them."

When they were done in the café, they walked north because they had nowhere else to go and nothing to do. Before long they saw the river and bridge crossing it.

Marisol had been right: it was nothing like she imagined. She did not anticipate how dusty and forbidding the ground would be that the river flowed through, or the ugly functionality of the bridge. A line of vehicles, cars and trucks, stood waiting for their turn across the span. At a distance Marisol could see the dark figures of Americans at work, checking every one.

There would be no marching across the footbridge into the United States. She had no visa to be in Mexico, no identification except what the state issued her in El Salvador. It was not a question of bribes any longer; the Americans would not stand for that.

She looked to her right and saw César staring across the river, too. What went through his mind she had no way to tell. Unless she asked. "What are you thinking?"

"I think this is the last time I want to do this."

"How many times have you been?"

"Three."

"You couldn't have been very old."

"I wasn't. Every time I went with my mother. Every time *la migra* caught us and sent us back. She couldn't do it again, but she wanted me to go. So here I am."

"Do you think you'll make it this time?"

César turned his distant eyes on her. "Yes. This time I will make it."

They went away from the border then and walked the streets of Ojinaga. Marisol felt her suitcase drawing stares and wished she had somewhere to store it, but there was none. Eventually they discovered a kind of public park with a full-sized shade tree and a little *fútbol* pitch. There were monkey bars for the children, though no children were out to play. Marisol sat down on a bench and after a while César sat, too.

"Thank you," César said after a long time.

"For what?"

"You've been generous to me. You didn't know me, but you shared your money."

"You shared with me," Marisol countered.

"It was nothing. I have a sister. You remind me of her a little."

"She didn't come north?"

"No, she's happy where she is. Three kids and a husband. He has a good job. They do all right. I'll write to them when I make it to America."

Across the park Marisol saw a woman carrying a baby and leading a small child along. They entered over the *fútbol* pitch, closing in on the monkey bars. Marisol felt suddenly uncomfortable. They were sitting here with bags packed for travel and with nowhere else to go. Marisol did not know what the woman would make of them.

"I'll write to my mother, too," César continued. "When I find work, I will send her money. She's not well. She can't keep a job."

"Where is your father?" Marisol asked. The woman was closer.

"Gone. I don't know where."

"Then you are the man of the family."

"I guess so. I don't think about it."

The child reached the monkey bars and immediately began clambering up to the top. His mother trailed behind with the baby, angling toward the bench. Marisol's breath hitched in her chest.

"*Buenos días*," the mother said when she was close.

"Hello," Marisol said. "Would you like to sit?"

She vacated her spot and the mother sat down. She was young, like Marisol, and she sighed audibly. "Thank you. This little one is heavy."

"She's very pretty. A girl, yes?"

"Yes. Luz. I'm Manuela."

César turned his body away from Manuela, putting his pack between himself and the woman. Marisol could not do the same. "I am Marisol. How old is Luz?"

"Eight months."

Marisol nodded. She did not know what else to say.

Manuela broke the silence: "You are traveling?"

"Yes."

"Going across the river?"

Again the Marisol's breath caught. She saw César stiffen, but she nodded. "Yes, we are. We don't want any trouble."

Manuela smiled and waved the thought away. "You don't look like trouble to me. We see crossers all the time here. How far have you come?"

"A long way."

"I hear your accent. It must have been a very long way."

"You have no idea," Marisol said, and the tension flooded out of her. The little boy on the monkey bars squealed with delight, and suddenly the bright sunlight and the heat seemed less oppressive. There was only the four of them at the bench and there was no fear.

"Have you found a *coyote* yet?"

"No."

"Go to El Vaquero. It's a bar on the west side. Anyone can tell you where it is. You'll find *coyotes* there."

"Thank you," Marisol said.

"Just be careful," Manuela replied. "You seem like a nice woman. I wouldn't want anything to happen to you."

23

A s Manuela said, it was easy to find El Vaquero. They came to the bar after nightfall, when the crowd was thickest, many trucks in its gravel parking lot. César insisted that they hide their bags in a clump of prickly bushes. "We don't want to look like yokels," he said.

Immediately upon entering Marisol was assaulted by cigarette smoke and alcohol fumes. Music blasted from a speaker directly above the door. She saw a naked woman on the stage and averted her eyes.

Marisol gave César cash before they entered, and he used some now to buy drinks at the long bar. As long as he was beside her, Marisol did not feel so exposed, but when he disappeared among the throng of men to get their drinks, she felt as if every eye was on her.

César pushed a cold glass into her hand. Marisol leaned close to him and said, "I don't drink."

"It's only soda water," he told her.

There was nowhere to sit and even less room to stand. Eventually they were forced into a corner of the bar near an ancient cigarette machine, directly facing the stage and the parade of nude girls. Whenever a fresh one came out, a new song blasted out of the speakers, pummeling Marisol's ears. She looked at anything else she could to avoid seeing the women, even if she had to stare directly at the ceiling or the floor.

"I have to go," César said at last.

"Go? Go where?"

"I have to find a *coyote*."

"Wait," Marisol said, and she caught his sleeve. "Take me with you."

"We can't move around together all the time. Just stay here and wait for me."

Before she could say anything else, César moved away from her into the gathering of men. On stage a new girl came out in a bikini and the crowd hollered.

She watched him as long as she could, until finally César disappeared. She swallowed her heart and felt her pulse beat painfully. Her glass was empty and she clutched at it fiercely. If anyone touched her, she would grind it in their face.

It was a a handful of songs later when César reappeared. He motioned for her to join him, and she shuffled past a group of men, careful not to touch them. She put out her hand and César caught it, pulling her the last of the way into a little island of calm.

"Did you find a *coyote*?" Marisol asked him. She had to lean close and shout into his ear; the music was louder than ever.

"*Sí*. Come with me."

They left the bar. Marisol realized she was still carrying her glass.

They met a thin young man, younger even than César, in the parking lot by a dirty white pick-up. The young man had a thin mustache, barely a wisp. "This her?" he asked when they came near.

"My cousin," César said.

"You explain to her how much?"

"Not yet."

The young man sighed. He turned to Marisol. "It's five thousand to cross. You come with me now, you pay. No discounts, no haggling."

"We'll cross now?" Marisol asked.

"No. We put you up. In a day or two, we cross. You have the money?"

"Yes."

"Then get in the back of the truck."

"My things," Marisol said.

The young man sighed again. "Hurry up!"

César retrieved their bags from where they were hidden and climbed into the bed of the truck. He helped Marisol in, and the young man got behind the wheel and turned the engine over.

It was dark and the temperatures were cooling rapidly. Marisol wished for a sweater. They drove twenty minutes.

The truck stopped at an apartment building. The young man waved them out of the bed, herding them toward a door on the first floor. He produced a key. "You'll stay here. Someone will be by to collect the money. Have it ready."

The door was opened and the smell of humanity rolled out. A desk lamp stood on the floor in the corner of a front room littered with mattresses. There were people waiting inside and they looked hopeful as the young man pushed them inside.

"Don't go outside," the young man said. "Don't open the windows. Keep quiet."

"I'm ready to pay," Marisol said.

"I told you: when someone else comes."

"You'll be our *coyote*?"

"Stop asking so many questions! Just get in there!"

Once they were through the door, the young man closed and locked it. Marisol saw there was no way of unlocking it from the inside. It was stuffy in the room and very dark despite the lamp. Marisol thought she smelled urine and other things.

No one spoke a word. Marisol and César went from room to room. There were three bedrooms and all of them were the same: laden with mattresses and occupied by people. They found some space in the smallest room and sat down with their things. There was a man with a little girl. He nodded when Marisol looked at him.

"Is this what happens?" Marisol asked César. Her voice seemed unnaturally loud in the quiet.

"Yes," César said. He put his backpack at the end of one mattress like a pillow and lay down. Across the room, the little girl was staring.

24

O n the first day no one came. Marisol went into the bathroom and discovered the toilet was clogged. The stink of the bowl was powerful. The shower worked, and she cleaned herself. When she emerged, she didn't hide her money anymore. On her mattress in the little bedroom she counted out five thousand dollars. She had a little over one thousand left and she put it in her suitcase.

There was nothing to eat and only water from the tap to drink. One of the people in the front room filled the ice trays in the freezer and shared the cubes around. It was not as good as food, but it was something to chew if only for a short while.

Marisol learned the names of the man and the little girl. His name was Rudolfo and hers was Inez. She was his niece and she was almost eight years old. They did not talk much because silence seemed better in the close confines of the apartment with the heat ticking up by degrees. Talking was tiring.

On the second day there were keys in the door and a man appeared that Marisol hadn't seen before. He was thick through the waist and big and carried a gun openly. People approached him with questions, but he brushed them all off. "Where are the new ones? Two new ones, where are you?"

Marisol presented herself with César. "Here," she said. "You owe me money."

"Are you our *coyote*?"

"Just give me the money. Five thousand dollars."

Marisol had the money in a thick stack and handing it over was painful. She felt the reluctance as it left her hand and she knew loss as the man counted it. All of the time spent getting it was nothing compared to the instant when it was gone.

César paid, and after the man checked the amount, he shoved all of the money into his pockets. "Good," he said. "You're lucky: we're going tomorrow, so you don't have long to wait. And your *coyote*, he's the best. You'll get what you paid for."

After that the man locked them in again, and the apartment went back to the way it had been before. Every few hours there was a new ice cube to chew; it was how Marisol marked the time.

She slept fitfully in the hot room overnight and woke early. Inez was already awake, leaning against her uncle as he slept. She smiled a little smile at Marisol, but she had nothing to say.

The third day was the longest, knowing that they would soon be gone. Marisol didn't know how long the others had been held here, but she could see the space behind their eyes where a kind of desperation had begun to set in. If she was forced to stay in that apartment a week, she might have felt the same way.

When the sun went down, she was glad of it and waited at the door of her room for the click of the lock and the return of the man with the gun. She shared ice cubes with the others one last time before the sound of a truck engine rumbled through the thin walls and she heard raised voices talking, the jingle of keys.

It was the man with the gun, and this time he brought a new man, one wearing a blue windbreaker. The man with the gun introduced them all as if they were old friends, then retreated outside for more discussion. Marisol heard them disagreeing.

The man with the gun came in a pickup and before long a second pickup arrived, the same dirty white truck that brought Marisol and César here. The man with the gun called the young man *Ignacio* and the man in the windbreaker *Luis*. Marisol listened carefully and caught the name of the man with the gun: Ángel.

"Let's get moving," Ángel said. "Get them all out here."

All the people from the apartment assembled in the parking lot between the two trucks. Seven women and four men. Marisol held the handle of her suitcase tightly in both hands.

"You bunch, into the white truck," Ángel ordered. "The rest of you, get in mine. Hurry up now!"

They did as they were told. Marisol saw the man called Luis standing to one side with an expression like dismay. He was not like the other two and he said nothing to them. There was only the look of him, and that said enough.

Before long the trucks were on the move in under the night sky, driving down deserted streets. At first it seemed like they were headed to the bridge, but then they turned off the main roads and proceeded down narrow lanes that transformed into bumpy dirt strips. Headlights picked out the occasional jackrabbit sprinting from cover. Marisol tried to keep track of where they were headed, but she lost all sense of direction after just a few minutes.

The dirt road became open ground and the trucks proceeded more slowly. There were no landmarks at all that

Marisol could see, just the stars and the trees that leapt out of the darkness.

After a long while they slowed and stopped. The trucks killed their engines, and all was silent save for the ticking of metal. Ángel and Luis spilled out of their truck with Ignacio just behind. They conferred for a little while and then Luis came to them. "Get down now," he said. "The crossing isn't far."

The group gathered together in the dark. Marisol was conscious of César at her elbow. Starlight cast silvery illumination down on their heads, so Marisol could see when Luis began to lead the way.

25

S he couldn't see it or smell it, but Marisol knew the river was near. They kept a quick pace heading north until the dark bulk of another truck materialized out of the shadows. Two more men joined Luis and the others, but no one said their names.

"Listen up!" Ángel announced, though he did not raise his voice. "Here is where you earn your way across. That money was just a down payment. From here on out you carry for me."

The tailgate of the truck was down and in the back were square bundles. The two men unloaded the bundles onto the ground among the crossers. Up close Marisol could see they were bound with duct tape. She didn't recognize the odor rising from them.

César stepped forward to take one of the bundles. It had straps made of tape and rope and could be worn like a backpack. He rearranged his burden and came to Marisol. "Here," he said. "Let me help you."

The bundle was heavier than it looked and the cheap straps cut into Marisol's shoulders. All around her the other crossers were taking the weight without complaining, and she did not want to be the first. All the men, Luis and Ángel and the others, watched silently. Only little Inez did not get a bundle.

The two men who unloaded the bundles brought out large packages of yellow plastic. "Are you finished?" Luis asked and Marisol thought she heard strain in his voice. "Then let's go."

They walked a hundred yards or maybe more before the ground beneath their feet began to smooth out. Suddenly Marisol could see the river clearly, reflecting the light of the stars. She wanted to run for it, to feel the water splash up around her, but instead she walked steadily with the rest though her heart was surging.

The two men and their plastic packages were still with them. They dropped them on the ground and unlimbered something short and black. Marisol realized it was a pump and the yellow packages were deflated rafts.

It took an eternity for the rafts to be inflated even with the pump. Marisol and the others sat or crouched in the dirt waiting. Marisol watched Luis, who paced incessantly but didn't give his agitation any voice.

When at last the rafts were ready, they were put into the shallow water at the river's edge. The two nameless men assembled folding oars and climbed aboard. Ángel urged the crossers forward. "Two at a time in each boat! Move it!"

Marisol was not first and she wasn't last. The nameless men ferried the crossers over the river slowly. Marisol was separated from César, who went with Ignacio. She went with Luis. He did not look at her the whole way across.

She did not feel different on the other side. In truth, she hadn't known what to expect, but a part of her expected some great sensation to pass through her once she set foot on American soil. There was nothing. The bank was flat and sandy like the bank on the far side, and it was still chill the way a desert night is chill. She was still led by strangers among strangers, and there was nowhere in sight for her to go if she left them.

Again Luis guided them away. They left the nameless men and their rafts and proceeded onto rough ground once more. From time to time he stopped and looked up, and Marisol realized he was navigating by the stars.

They marched a mile or more. Marisol had no way to tell. She saw a lone tree standing a spur of dry earth up ahead. They made for it and when they came closer, Ángel called a halt.

"What are you doing?" Luis asked. "We have a long way to go."

"I want to get something out of the way," Ángel replied.

"No! No more surprises!"

"You shut the fuck up!"

Ángel and Ignacio turned to face the group of crossers. Ángel drew his gun. "I want you to split up. Women over here. Men over there. Do it now."

"What are you doing, Ángel?"

"I said shut up!"

The crossers obeyed. Marisol's heartbeat began to rush. She could see César among the men, recognizable from his cap but with his face a shadow. Would she have seen anything there anyway?

Rudolfo stayed with Inez. "Señor. What about—?"

"I *said* men over there, women over here!"

The man gave in and let Inez go. He shuffled to be with the other men.

Ángel pointed his gun at one of the women. "You. Get over here."

When the woman came close, Ignacio grabbed her sharply by the arm and twisted it. The woman made a pained sound, but didn't shout.

Ángel spoke again: "Get your pants off."

"Ángel, no!"

"You interrupt me one more time, Luis, and I'll shoot you right here and go on myself."

"There's a child here!"

"Looks like a little woman to me," Ángel said, and he and Ignacio laughed.

Marisol was stone. When she breathed, it was shallow, strangled. She could not move from her spot as the two men, Ángel and Ignacio, stripped the woman and bore her to the ground. There was the sound of buckles and zippers. It happened.

When Ignacio was finished with the woman, he took her underpants and draped them from the branches of the lonely tree. Ángel swapped his gun with his companion. "I get the next one," he said.

Marisol did not understand. The women lined up, and when the gun was pointed at them, they did as they were told. One after another. The men took turns. Standing above them, Luis was a black shadow as immobile as she. César and the others made not a sound.

Something touched her hand and Marisol looked down. Inez stood beside her and she wound her fingers between Marisol's.

Blood flowed into Marisol's body again and this time she took a full breath. Ángel and Ignacio were busy violating another of the crossers and the gun was not pointed in her direction. She took a tentative step, pulling Inez along with her, closer to Luis.

Another step and a third. Marisol shouldered her way out of the straps of her bundle and let it fall to the ground. It made almost no noise when it struck the ground, as if the earth caught it in its arms. She picked up her suitcase again.

"Ángel...," Luis said. He put his hands to his head.

They were finished with another. The tree was festooned with underpants. There was no one between Marisol and the gun. Ángel pointed it at her. "Now you," he said.

She swung the suitcase sharply across her body, putting her full weight behind the blow. Marisol felt it connect with Ángel's arm and the gun did not explode in her face. Then she turned and fled, grinding stones beneath her feet with Inez in tow behind her.

Luis was there. "Run!" he said. "Run! Run!"

The three of them ran. Marisol felt Luis at her back, heard the scrabbling of his shoes in the dirt. Nothing was as urgent as her breath, her heartbeat, the sudden crying of Inez.

"Goddamn you, Luis!"

The gun thundered once and then again and again. Marisol felt, or imagined she felt, a bullet pass just by her. She heard Luis gasp and looked back.

He stumbled forward, awkwardly, his arms splayed, and then he collapsed face-forward into the dirt. Marisol did not have to touch him to know that he was already dead.

The gun went off again, but the shot did not come close to her. Marisol ran with Inez, tripping on rocks and in folds of the earth, scrambling onto her feet again after she fell and cut her hands.

They ran until they could no longer hear the shouting and no more gunshots came. The trees were thicker here and Marisol took cover underneath one, clasping Inez close. The girl shivered all over and her heart tripped against Marisol's chest.

She expected the men to find them again, but time passed and Marisol heard and saw nothing. When she was certain they were completely alone, she eased out from beneath the prickly tree and started walking, though she did not know to where.

They walked until sunrise, when Marisol found a shallow draw they could crouch down in and survey the countryside. All they saw were more trees and more dirt and nothing of the men or the crossers. She kept Inez there until the sun was well off the horizon and the day was growing hot before she dared move again.

"Where is my uncle?" Inez asked.

"I don't know," Marisol answered.

"Will we find him?"

"I don't know."

Marisol oriented herself by the sun and struck off in what she thought was a northerly direction. Everything looked the same and she couldn't tell if they walked straight or not.

The barbed-wire fence seemed to spring out of nowhere and marched off through the scrub land in two directions, as far as Marisol could see. Instead of crossing, she followed the line for what seemed like hours, until she found a two-rut roadway in the dust.

The road led to a gate and beyond the gate to more open land. Marisol was thirsty and knew Inez had to be also, but there was no water in Marisol's suitcase and Inez carried nothing at all.

They walked and kept walking and then finally the road met pavement. Two lanes of blacktop bisected by a broken yellow line. Marisol saw no sign indicating where they were, and wouldn't have recognized it anyway. The sun had passed overhead and now she wasn't sure which way was east and west.

She sat down by the side of the road and let Inez sit on her suitcase. The girl's dress was dirty. Marisol wet her thumb with her tongue and wiped a patch of grime from Inez's cheek.

"Will my uncle come now?"

Again Marisol said, "I don't know.'

Together they baked in the slow heat as the sun moved. In time it had sunk enough that she knew which way the road went, though this knowledge was useless. Which direction was the nearest town and how far? What could she tell the people she met? She was no longer in Mexico.

She had just decided to head west when she spotted a dash on the horizon from that direction. She watched it grow into a truck, blowing up dust behind it as it sped down the highway. It seemed to go slower the closer it came and then it was upon them, roaring by.

Marisol turned to watch it go and saw its brake lights brighten. The truck slowed to a stop two hundred yards down the road and then started backing up along the shoulder.

Up close she saw the truck was not new, and it had a wooden frame built into the bed and no tailgate. The license plate was wired in place. The truck kept coming, and Marisol ushered Inez out of the way so it could stop in front of them.

The man behind the wheel was sun-blasted and wrinkled. He had a Latino face. "*¿Estás perdido?*" he asked.

"We are lost," Marisol said in English.

"How long have you been out here?"

"Too long. The little one, she needs water."

"Get in my truck. We'll get some water."

He let them in, and Inez sat between them. Marisol put her suitcase on the floorboard. The man looked them over again and then nodded to himself.

"How far can you take us?" Marisol asked.

"As far as you need to go."

ABOUT THE AUTHOR

Sam Hawken's first novel, *The Dead Women of Juarez* was published in the UK, France and Germany and short-listed for the CWA "New Blood" Dagger Award 2011. He is also the author of *Tequila Sunset* nominated for the Gold Dagger 2013.

Sam Hawken's fiction embraces a broad spectrum of genres, from southwestern *noir* to historical fiction and literary horror. All of his work involves extensive research, authentic flavor and a devotion to illuminating issues both historical and contemporary.

A native of South Texas, he currently resides near Washington, DC with his wife and son.

To learn more about Sam, visit *www.samhawken.com* and *www.betimesbooks.com*

Printed in Great Britain
by Amazon.co.uk, Ltd.,
Marston Gate.